A GOOD CHANCE

Praise for Ali Vali

One More Chance

"This was an amazing book by Vali...complex and multi-layered (both characters and plot)."—*Danielle Kimerer, Librarian (Nevins Memorial Library, Massachusetts)*

Face the Music

"This is a typical Ali Vali romance with strong characters, a beautiful setting (Nashville, Tennessee), and an enemies-to-lovers style tale. The two main characters are beautiful, strong-willed, and easy to fall in love with. The romance between them is steamy, and so are the sex scenes."—*Rainbow Reflections*

The Inheritance

"I love a good story that makes me laugh and cry, and this one did that a lot for me. I would step back into this world any time."—*Kat Adams, Bookseller (QBD Books, Australia)*

Double-Crossed

"[T]here aren't too many lesfic books like *Double-Crossed* and it is refreshing to see an author like Vali continue to churn out books like these. Excellent crime thriller."—*Colleen Corgel, Librarian, Queens Borough Public Library*

"For all of us die-hard Ali Vali/Cain Casey fans, this is the beginning of a great new series...There is violence in this book, and lots of killing, but there is also romance, love, and the beginning of a great new reading adventure. I can't wait to read more of this intriguing story."
—*Rainbow Reflections*

Stormy Seas

Stormy Seas "is one book that adventure lovers must read."—*Rainbow Reflections*

Answering the Call

Answering the Call "is a brilliant cop-and-killer story...The crime story is tight and the love story is fantastic."—*Best Lesbian Erotica*

Lammy Finalist *Calling the Dead*

"So many writers set stories in New Orleans, but Ali Vali's mystery novels have the authenticity that only a real Big Easy resident could bring. Set six months after Hurricane Katrina has devastated the city, a lesbian detective is still battling demons when a body turns up behind one of the city's famous eateries. What follows makes for a classic lesbian murder yarn."—*Curve Magazine*

Beauty and the Boss

"The story gripped me from the first page...Vali's writing style is lovely—it's clean, sharp, no wasted words, and it flows beautifully as a result. Highly recommended!"—*Rainbow Book Reviews*

Balance of Forces: Toujours Ici

"A stunning addition to the vampire legend, *Balance of Forces: Toujours Ici* is one that stands apart from the rest."—*Bibliophilic Book Blog*

Beneath the Waves

"The premise...was brilliantly constructed...skillfully written and the imagination that went into it was fantastic...A wonderful passionate love story with a great mystery."—*Inked Rainbow Reads*

Second Season

"The issues are realistic and center around the universal factors of love, jealousy, betrayal, and doing the right thing and are constantly woven into the fabric of the story. We rated this well written social commentary through the use of fiction our max five hearts."—*Heartland Reviews*

Carly's Sound

"*Carly's Sound* is a great romance, with some wonderfully hot sex, but it is more than that. It is also the tale of a woman rising from the ashes of grief and finding new love and a new life. Vali has surrounded Julia and Poppy with a cast of great supporting characters, making this an extremely satisfying read."—*Just About Write*

Praise for the Cain Casey Saga

The Devil's Due

"A Night Owl Reviews Top Pick: Cain Casey is the kind of person you aspire to be even though some consider her a criminal. She's loyal, very protective of those she loves, honorable, big on preserving her family legacy and loves her family greatly. *The Devil's Due* is a book I highly recommend and well worth the wait we all suffered through. I cannot wait for the next book in the series to come out." —*Night Owl Reviews*

The Devil Be Damned

"Ali Vali excels at creating strong, romantic characters along with her fast-paced, sophisticated plots. Her setting, New Orleans, provides just the right blend of immigrants from Mexico, South America, and Cuba, along with a city steeped in traditions."—*Just About Write*

Deal with the Devil

"Ali Vali has given her fans another thick, rich thriller...*Deal With the Devil* has wonderful love stories, great sex, and an ample supply of humor. It is an exciting, page-turning read that leaves her readers eagerly awaiting the next book in the series."—*Just About Write*

The Devil Unleashed

"Fast-paced action scenes, intriguing character revelations, and a refreshing approach to the romance thriller genre all make for an enjoyable reading experience in the Big Easy...*The Devil Unleashed* is an engrossing reading experience."—*Midwest Book Review*

The Devil Inside

"*The Devil Inside* is the first of what promises to be a very exciting series... While telling an exciting story that grips the reader, Vali has also fully fleshed out her heroes and villains. *The Devil Inside* is that rarity: a fascinating crime novel which includes a tender love story and leaves the reader with a cliffhanger ending."—*MegaScene*

By the Author

Carly's Sound

Second Season

Love Match

The Dragon Tree Legacy

The Romance Vote

Hell Fire Club in Girls with Guns

Beauty and the Boss

Blue Skies

Stormy Seas

The Inheritance

Face the Music

On the Rocks in Still Not Over You

A Woman to Treasure

Calumet

Writer's Block

One More Chance

A Good Chance

The Cain Casey Saga

The Devil Inside

The Devil Unleashed

Deal with the Devil

The Devil Be Damned

The Devil's Orchard

The Devil's Due

Heart of the Devil

The Devil Incarnate

Call Series

Calling the Dead

Answering the Call

Waves Series

Beneath the Waves

Turbulent Waves

Forces Series

Balance of Forces: Toujours Ici

Battle of Forces: Sera Toujours

Force of Fire: Toujours a Vous

Vegas Nights

Double-Crossed

Visit us at www.boldstrokesbooks.com

A GOOD CHANCE

by
Ali Vali

2022

CREDITS
EDITORS: VICTORIA VILLASEÑOR AND RUTH STERNGLANTZ
PRODUCTION DESIGN: STACIA SEAMAN
COVER DESIGN BY TAMMY SEIDICK

Acknowledgments

Thank you, Radclyffe, for your friendship and support—I treasure both. Thank you, Sandy, for all you did to get me back on track and for all the extra time. You're the best, and I value your friendship as well. As for my BSB family, there are no words I can think of to let you know how much I care for every single one of you. The storm piled months of recovery and hard work on my community, but all the calls, the help, and care packages were the bright spots in the last year. It's a gift to have such rock-solid support. Thank you all for your care and support in tough times.

Thank you to my awesome editors, Victoria Villaseñor and Ruth Sternglantz. Vic, thank you for all your gentle lessons. It's been an honor to work with you. You get me. You and Ruth have been an awesome team. Ruth, thank you so much for the time and attention you give every manuscript. I appreciate both of you. I'd also like to thank Tammy Seidick for the great cover.

A huge thank you to every reader who reached out after the storm. You guys send the best emails, and I appreciate your encouragement to get back to writing, and to keep smiling through the tough times. As always, every word is written with you in mind.

This one was difficult to write. After spending the last eight months in the offices of our local domestic violence program, I have a hard time with how many cases they deal with on a weekly basis. I'll be making another donation for every book purchased on behalf of my readers. If you can, think of supporting your local domestic violence program in your community.

It's been a tough time, but it's nice to be getting back to writing the stories in my head. Now I'll raise an old-fashioned and count the days until we see each other in person. I'm ready for new adventures with my navigator in all things, C. Verdad!

For C
&
The Brave Survivors of Domestic Violence

Chapter One

O nly you can decide when enough is enough," Desi Basantes said to the women sitting around her. "Being trapped in a violent relationship can only be understood by someone who's experienced it, so don't let anyone make you feel less than for your choices. Leaving takes courage, more than you ever thought you possessed, and you should celebrate yourself for taking that first step to a new life."

Almost a year had passed from the day Desi had not only gained her freedom from her abusive ex, Byron Simoneaux, but had also gotten back the life stolen from her by her equally abusive father, Clyde Thompson. Opening her eyes and finding Harry Basantes in scrubs next to her hospital bed had been a gift that had saved her from an abyss of pain and misery. That was the last day Byron put his hands on her.

"I'm terrified he's going to find me and kill me," a young woman in the group said.

The soft voice was something she remembered using. It helped you be small, invisible, and unimportant. Sometimes it was all that let you go one day without pain, and others in the group nodded as if understanding. Being trapped in an abusive relationship wasn't exactly a unique story. Domestic violence was like a cancer that destroyed you slowly and painfully, and it knew no boundary of color, social standing, or financial means. It was an insidiousness that touched every part of society.

Abject fear was hard to explain to someone who'd never truly lived with it. That sense in your guts that began the moment you opened your eyes in the morning, paralyzing you with the knowledge that it could be your *last* day. She'd tried her best to do everything right so Byron wouldn't hit her, but at times the slights were contrived. All he'd wanted was the excuse to hit her no matter what she did because it made him feel strong, important, in control.

Her fear had kept her from running and finding Harry, and it'd come close to costing her everything. The moment Byron had stood over her with a bat, though, she would've gladly accepted the oblivion of death. Anything would've been worth stopping the pain that dominated her life. She'd reached the very end of her will to live another moment if living meant facing him and his anger.

"The last day with my ex-husband almost came to that. He was going to kill me," Desi said softly. Talking about all this wasn't her favorite thing, but it helped purge all those fears and horrible memories. Safe Haven was the shelter her sister Rachel had tried talking her into going to for years. Now she was a volunteer and donor since she and Harry had added them to the organizations they supported. "I was ready to give up, but it wasn't my time."

"Did he saddle you with that?" One of the other women pointed to her belly. "Running alone is hard enough, but a baby will make them relentless. That's my husband's biggest threat. He keeps telling me he's going to take my kids and I'll never see them again."

"Oh no." She smiled, placing her hands over her midsection. "I'm not going to lie to you by saying starting over is easy, but finding someone who truly loves you can help make it possible. Take the time here to find a place you and your children can find peace. You deserve better than someone who lives to hurt you. That's what I found, and Harry taught me that while she loves me, it's important I love myself. The only one to blame for everything that happened is Byron—not me."

She glanced at her watch and saw that their hour was up. There was still time to work in her studio before her very first event that night. The women thanked her, and she hugged Rachel when she came in to ride back to the house with her. Finding Harry had been the best thing that could've happened to her, but her sister had also been set free of the past with Harry's help. The tension Rachel seemed to carry from the moment Byron had come into their lives had unraveled in the house they shared with Harry.

"I could've driven myself, you know." She kissed Rachel's cheek. "I need to practice." Byron hadn't allowed her to drive much, but Harry had gotten her a new Yukon, saying it'd be safer for the baby. They'd spent plenty of time in empty parking lots on the weekends until she passed her driver's test and got her license.

"I'm off the rest of the day and needed a ride home. Harry dropped me off this morning, and it's not a long walk from the salon to here." Rachel linked arms with her and guided her out. "Do you like doing this? I think you've paid a lifetime of hell by now. There's no reason to keep raking yourself over the blistering coals that asshole lit for you."

"The group meetings help a lot, and I don't think of them as reliving bad times. If anything, they make me realize how lucky I am and that the life I have with Harry is magical. Some of the other women who come back to the meetings tell me it's been years, but they're still afraid of their abusers. I don't want to go day-to-day, thinking about Byron and his family."

"Harry *is* a catch."

She buckled into the passenger side, content to let Rachel drive. "I totally agree, but that's not what I meant."

Rachel backed out carefully, stopping to stare at her. "What's on your mind then?"

There were things in her life that made her wonder why she was deserving of such devotion, love, and loyalty. That was true of what Rachel gave her—had always given her. They were three years apart, yet Rachel, the younger, had been the nurturing one. Her sister had tended to her wounds, given her something to live for, and had been her champion when she'd been forced into a life with Byron she didn't have the ability to fight off.

"A lot of families get so fed up with someone's inability to leave, and eventually they give up on the woman who refuses to separate from her abuser. You never did, so that makes me lucky." She squeezed Rachel's hand when she offered it, glad that Rachel hadn't abandoned her. She would've never survived Byron on her own. "I love that you're my sister."

"Thank you, but we're both lucky, so let's leave it at that. You think I don't realize what you did to keep Clyde away from me. I do, and it makes me love you as much as I hate him. He's dead, and I still hate him. I'll never think of him as our father." Rachel stopped at the smoothie place she liked and picked up some for them and one for Mona. Harry's longtime housekeeper had adopted them, and it was nice having someone who gladly stepped into that maternal role.

When they reached the house, she changed, and Rachel followed her out to the studio at the back of the property. Months of reacquainting herself with the pottery wheel had also been cathartic in releasing her pain and bringing back the part of her that loved to dream about the future. And the reacquaintance had resulted in enough pieces for her first exhibit. Well, with Tony's help.

Tony Reynolds and his husband Kenneth had graduated high school with her and Harry, and while Kenneth was a pediatrician, Tony spent most of his days with her in this studio. He painted and she made pottery, and together they planned to have a gallery of their own. She loved his over-the-top personality, and that he listened without judgement. Tony had been an important part of where she was now. His nurturing nature along with Harry's love had made it easy to step into the light.

"How are you and Serena doing?"

Serena Ladding was an old girlfriend of Harry's who'd stayed in Harry's life because of her young son, Butch. Any jealousy Desi had in the beginning because of the beautiful, put-together assistant district attorney passed when Serena assured her all she wanted was to help get Byron out of her life.

"Hot and cold, mostly cold lately." Rachel sat in the recliner Harry liked to nap in. "I think the novelty of the rebel hairdresser is over."

"There's no way that's true." Desi put the finishing touches on what she was working on and prepared it for the kiln. She was experimenting with different color clays and was finding more and more satisfaction in the end products, like the jade-colored vase with the intricate lines she'd carved into the side. Each piece she finished gave her a sense of accomplishment she hadn't experienced in years. "You two really spark."

"I'm not disagreeing, but she's been working late all week, and Butch's been staying with her parents. That's *after* I told her I didn't mind keeping him. Her refusal is a big hint, I think."

Rachel tried to play it cool, but Desi knew better.

"Sometimes working late just means working late, babe." She stretched her back and glanced at the clock. "Let's sit outside. That won't be ready until tomorrow, and I don't want to start anything else." Harry had bought some comfortable lawn chairs and placed them in the garden, and they made their way out to enjoy the late afternoon sunshine. "If you want my input, Serena cares about you."

"I'm sure she does, but she's also a perpetual dater. It's something we have in common, so I don't fault her. That she doesn't want me taking care of Butch means she doesn't want me around too much, which could give him the wrong idea." Rachel laughed, but it didn't ring of happiness. "I'm no relationship guru, sis, but that doesn't have the makings of what you and Harry have. The other part is that I'm not exactly the woman who's going to fit into her life like a puzzle piece."

"I think you need to give her more of a chance to prove herself, sweetie. Harry hasn't heard from her either, so I believe she really *is* working. As for Butch, she might think it's too much of an imposition on you. She hasn't asked us to babysit, either." After the life Rachel had endured because of her, she wanted her sister to be happy and in love. Rachel deserved nothing less, and it hurt her heart to know Rachel hadn't found love yet.

"Don't worry, I'm not writing her off. Enough about that—are you ready for tonight?"

The one thing Rachel was good at was deflection, and Desi let it go for now. "I'm not sure. All this seems so surreal." It really did. The last eleven months had been like waking from a nightmare, and there were still moments she expected things to go wrong.

"All you need to do is remember to smile and have fun. What you two have? You deserve all of it. Don't let anyone tell you different." Rachel kissed her cheek and hugged her tightly. "Let go of all those doubts and concentrate on Harry, what you're starting tonight, and what's coming soon." Rachel pointed to her belly. "Baby Basantes came along way fast, and I can't wait to be an aunt."

"We've wanted and planned this baby since high school, so it wasn't a rash decision even if it seems like it. The timing is so that we can hopefully fit in another one before we're too old to chase after them." She glanced at her watch. It was time to start getting ready.

"If I haven't mentioned it, I'm proud of you." Rachel hugged her again and took her hand. "Go ahead, I forgot something in the car."

"Thank you." She didn't know if it was the hormones or the day, but she'd never been this happy. The worry that something could go wrong evaporated. There was nothing left that could hurt her. Nothing.

She found Harry outside on their balcony after her shower with a chilled bottle and two glasses, and it made her warm. Harry wasn't just who she loved, but the woman she craved in the most primal of ways. "Hey, you look good." She ran her hand along the lapel of Harry's jacket before kissing her.

"Thank you," Harry said as she zipped her up. "I thought it was time to give you the rest of your gifts." It was her birthday, and Harry had already given her plenty, but seeing the swing at the edge of the space started the tears in earnest.

"I can't believe you found it."

Harry had placed a towel down so they could sit and enjoy the sparkling cider and toast her birthday. "I'll give it a makeover, but tonight I thought we could relive some old memories. I want you to know how much I love you."

"Me and Baby Basantes love you, honey." She smiled when Harry wiped away her tears. "You always think of what will make me happy, and this is the best birthday since your family took us to the beach that year."

Harry smiled and tucked her hair behind her ear. "You're worth everything to me. And if there's something you need, all you need to do is ask." The swing they'd fallen in love on was Harry's way of reminding Desi how wonderful it'd been to fall in love.

"I have you, our baby, and all these people who love me. My life is a miracle now. That's something I was telling Rachel today." She leaned against Harry when she put her arm around her. "This swing reminds me that not all the things in my past were horrible."

"This thing holds a lot of good memories, and I'll be glad to tell the baby about it when they're older. There's also the chance to make some new good memories out here, now that it's so close."

"Let's not corrupt them right off," she said and smiled. "But thank you for this."

"Don't get upset, but there's one more thing," Harry said, turning and facing her. "My mother will be there tonight, so it's important."

"Honey, it's too much. I don't need anything else."

Harry kissed her to stop her from talking. "There can never be too much when it comes to you. And I was kidding about my mother." Harry dropped to a knee. "I've wanted to give you this for a while, but today seemed like a special day to do it."

"Are you okay? You seem nervous." Desi's heart raced at the sight of Harry kneeling in front of her.

"This reminds me of the night I worked up my nerve to kiss you, but I figure that worked out really well." Harry took her hands, and Desi leaned down and kissed her.

"It worked out pretty good for me too."

"I've known you almost all my life, Desi. We've lived through pain and forgiveness, and we've found love. I want to enjoy the life we have, loving you, raising children with you, and showing you how much I cherish you." Harry took a box from her pocket and opened it. "Will you marry me?"

Desi's eyes were so full of tears she barely saw the ring. "Yes," she whispered, holding out her left hand.

Harry hesitated and read her the inscription on the inside before putting it on her finger. "Thank you, my love," Harry read, then showed her, before slipping it on her finger and kissing her hand.

"Thank you?" She turned her hand this way and that, watching the light reflect on the stone.

"For so long I wished and prayed for one more chance with you," Harry said. "I tried moving on, but my heart wouldn't forget you. So thank you. You came back, and I get that chance to love you forever." Harry kissed her again, and she twisted the ring to prove to herself it was real.

"I love you so much," she said, pressing herself to Harry. Her body felt too small to contain the joy that filled her soul. Now she truly had everything she'd ever wanted, and it had been all the things she'd chosen. That was one of the best things Harry had taught her since they'd been together. She was free to live the life she wanted, Harry said all the time, and what she wanted was Harry.

❖

Harry Basantes stood to the side in the gallery on Magazine Street and watched her fiancée interact with the crowd. She'd proposed a couple of hours earlier before they'd left the house, not wanting to wait another moment to let Desi know what she wanted. The expression on Desi's face when she dropped to her knees and opened the ring box would forever be one of her favorites. They still had a month before the baby's birth to plan a small, intimate wedding. If Desi wanted something more, they could do it after the birth. But she wanted more than anything to have Desi as her wife before their baby was born. It was old-fashioned, maybe, but that didn't matter.

So much had changed in a year, and it proved to her that all that pain when Desi left had been worth it to have Desi back. She was still angry at what had happened, and that she couldn't change the past, but Desi's sense of honor and compassion didn't surprise her. She'd tolerated the life her sadistic father had chosen for her to keep herself and Rachel safe. Sixteen long years of abuse, bruises, pain, and fear inflicted by Byron Simoneaux were hard to forget, much less forgive.

All she could do going forward was to listen when Desi needed to talk about things, and while she'd asked a few questions, she didn't try to push too much. Her reasoning for not asking questions had nothing to do with not wanting to know, but she was trying to give Desi the space to open up at her own pace. Desi's life had been an eternity of suffering. That she'd volunteered for it to protect the people she truly loved was something Harry would never be able to repay.

Seeing Desi now, though, made it hard to imagine the broken, despondent woman she'd found in the emergency room. Desi had left that life behind to become an artist who'd flourished into a strong woman who still had the gentle soul Harry had known all her life. The nightmare of misery now belonged to Desi's ex-husband Byron, his father, and his brother Mike. It'd be years before they walked out of Angola, the Louisiana State Penitentiary, and she hoped every day of being locked in that hellhole brought as much pain as Desi had lived through.

"What's this one called?" Abe, one of her residents, held one of Desi's pieces in one hand and a boiled shrimp in the other.

"Exactly how much have you had to drink?" She handed him a napkin before he smeared rémoulade on Desi's work. "It's a bowl." She glanced around—the only residents on her rotation missing were the ones on call, and given the busy nature of the emergency room, there was no way they were coming.

"It *is* a bowl and it's called Blue Sapphire." Desi slipped her hand into Harry's and smiled at Abe. He blushed so deeply that Harry thought about jabbing an EpiPen in his thigh. "Thanks for coming, Abe." Abe wasn't the only one of her residents, male and female, who turned into socially awkward people around Desi. "Don't let her give you a hard time."

"Sorry, I had no idea the bowls had names." She stood still as Desi leaned heavily into her. "If you don't want to end up on the news for all the wrong reasons, don't let Tony name anything." The way Desi stared up at her before grabbing the lapels of her jacket made Harry's eyebrows rise. She brought her head down when Desi pulled and embarrassed herself by moaning when Desi bit her bottom lip before kissing her. Abe was still standing there when the kiss ended. "She's not doing that with every purchase, so move along, Abe. There's still plenty to see."

"Harry." Desi lengthened her name in mock warning. "Take a look around, Abe, and let me know if you have any questions."

"This is a great turnout," Harry said. The gallery was large by Magazine Street standards, and Harry was happy about the number of people milling around. She'd done all she could to encourage Desi's budding career, from building shelves in her studio to laying out all the supplies Desi needed every morning. Desi was now a few days shy of eight months pregnant, and she didn't want her lifting anything that weighed more than a coffee cup. "Your work is as beautiful and unique as you are."

Desi's pieces had a complicated glaze on them, and the *New Orleans Magazine* had taken notice and done an extensive article on the newcomer. Once the show was announced, people had flocked to the space, and it was clear to see they loved Desi's work. "Thank you, but you might be a little prejudiced on the subject."

"Don't be modest." She held Desi as she leaned against her again. "Are you doing okay?"

"My back's starting to ache." Desi put her arms round Harry's waist and pressed the side of her face to Harry's chest. "I need someone to volunteer to rub where it hurts."

It was such a blessing to get Desi back, and having her relaxed enough to tease and flirt was miraculous. That broken woman afraid of everything and everyone had faded once Desi knew Harry had no intention of ever letting go of her again. The volunteering Desi was doing at the women's shelter, as well as the time she spent in her studio, had built her confidence. Harry was at peace, knowing that, with or without her, Desi realized and believed she deserved respect and was willing to stand up for herself to get it. That Desi wanted a life with her was like getting all her wishes at once.

"I know everyone in here, including Abe, would love nothing better than to sign up for that job, but I'll be happy to rub wherever you like." She kneaded Desi's lower back gently and kissed the top of her head. "I also know everyone wants to meet the genius behind all these designs, but let's go home. If you're tired, there's no reason to take any unnecessary chances. We're in the home stretch, and Mona will hire a hitman to kill me slowly if I let anything happen to you."

"Just a little while longer." Desi gazed up at her and it was hard not to give in to what she wanted.

Harry noticed her mother talking and laughing with a group of women twenty feet away, but her eyes were on her and Desi. Her parents had flown in for Desi's show, along with her brother Miguel and his family. Any apprehension her mother had at Desi's return had disappeared when they shared the news of their baby. Hurricane Rosa Basantes had been full of advice since then, and all her ire had been aimed at Harry for skipping big, important steps before Desi got pregnant.

The truth was she hadn't asked Desi to marry her before now because she was unsure of the future she planned. She wanted to give Desi the freedom to choose the life she truly desired. Harry had sworn to herself that she'd help her no matter what, but she wasn't going to pressure Desi into something more out of a sense of obligation. Her mother had informed her that was ludicrous since Desi loved her, and Harry'd been adamant about showing Desi how much she loved her in return.

"How's my grandbaby?" Rosa placed her hand on Desi's abdomen and smiled. She kissed Desi's cheek and ignored Harry.

"We're doing great, Mami. Are you having fun?" Harry asked. Her mother nodded, finally glancing her way. "Instead of giving me a hard time, you should be out there convincing all your old buddies to buy whatever's left." Harry jutted her jaw toward the women her mother had been talking to. "If not, I see rent in your future, considering you want to stay until the baby's born."

"Don't worry, Desi will be busy after the baby comes, trying to fill all the orders from everyone who missed the chance to get something tonight. Right now, I'd like to see Desi's left hand." Her mom held her hand out, waiting for Desi to take it.

"She asked and I said yes." Desi's smile made Harry happy. The ring and the promises she'd made seemed to infuse Desi with joy, and it was contagious. "Isn't it beautiful?"

Her mother nodded as she held Desi's hand. There'd been plenty of offers to take her shopping for the perfect ring since her mom's arrival. The offers were to make sure she got it right since Desi would be wearing it for the rest of her life, but Harry figured she'd done okay on her own. "It is—congratulations, Desi. I'm happy to know Harry has *finally* remembered to give you the kind of commitment that goes with raising a child together. That it's taken this long makes me want to put you over my knee, Harriet."

The very un-Hispanic name came from her mother's best friends growing up in Cuba. Harriet Brown's father ran the sugar refinery in their hometown for an American company before the revolution. Unfortunately for Harry, her mom's friend had a very uncool name. "I didn't want to rush her, and I hope Desi knows how much I love her, ring or no."

"That's the excuse you're going with? Harry, you have loved

only this girl from the moment you stepped out of the car the day you met in elementary school. It makes me happy that you found someone who loves you as much in return." Her mom spoke from the heart, and Desi's smile widened as her eyes got glassy with tears. "All that's true, so just admit you were wrong for waiting so long." Her mother crossed her arms and narrowed her eyes at her.

"I was wrong," she said to keep the peace.

"Good, so we'll plan something for the next couple of weeks. Does small and intimate sound all right with you two?" They nodded at the suggestion. "We'll have a big reception after Baby Basantes is born. Speaking of which, how do you feel about the name Basantes, Desi?"

"Rosa, I've dreamed of being Mrs. Harry Basantes since my fourteenth birthday. When my divorce became final, our lawyer took care of the name change. I'm already a Basantes." Desi moved away from Harry and hugged her mother. "I'll show you my driver's license when we get home, but not to worry. Everyone will have the same family name when we welcome our baby."

"We were going to surprise you, but you're the most impatient woman I know. Like I said, Desi knows how I feel, and my love and commitment are for the rest of my life."

"Remember those exact words when I get you to an altar." Desi's comeback made her mother laugh. "Thank you, Rosa, for being so kind to Rachel and me. I know I'm not your first choice—"

"You're wrong, mi hija. I was never blind to what you share, so that means you're my only choice. Just remember she's a lot like her father. They're as brilliant as they are hardheaded, so having a lot of patience is the key. That'll be really important when you have this baby and find that they'll act just like her. They are good looking, don't you think?"

"Don't worry, I'm rather fond of her hard head." Desi glanced back at her and blew her a kiss. "And you're right, they are incredibly handsome."

Tony pushed his way to Desi's side and kissed both her cheeks. "You're a success, sweetie. People are wild for your stuff, and I even managed to sell a few of my pieces." As always Tony was hyped up and dramatic. "We should've gone with my gut and charged more."

"This is the first money I've made since we worked in the yard pulling weeds at Harry's when we were in high school. I'm thrilled with what we made." Desi placed her hand on Tony's chest, and the sparkle seemed to capture his attention.

"Good God, my friend, you *are* good." He wiggled his eyebrows at her, and it made Desi blush, which made Harry's mother laugh.

"Stop teasing me and lead me to a chair." Desi followed Harry to the nice leather chairs at the front of the gallery, and Abe jumped up so she could have his seat. "Honey, could you get me some water?"

The bar wasn't far away, and her mom followed her to it. "I'm proud of you, mi amor. The last time I saw that big a smile on your face was the day you graduated from high school. Until recently, I'd been cursing Desi ever since, and that makes me ashamed."

"I feel the same way," Harry said, "and I lose sleep sometimes when I think about all the times I felt sorry for myself instead of looking out for her. I could've stopped what she went through so much sooner." She tried hard not to dwell on the past, but her heart wouldn't let her completely forget. She'd failed Desi in spectacular fashion.

"When I think of what she went through to keep you and Rachel safe, I want to go back in time and take them away from that bastard." She'd had a private talk with her mother before she'd brought Desi to visit them in Florida. Desi's story wasn't hers to tell, but she'd warned her mother about giving Desi a hard time. "I know, Mami, I know."

"Why did he do that? Those girls were a delight to have around."

"I wish I could give you an answer that makes sense, but he took those secrets to the grave. She deserves to be happy and cherished, and that's what I'm going to do." They walked back, and Mona was glaring at her.

"It's time to go, Harry." Mona gave orders, and when it came to protecting Desi, everyone was expected to follow them. Her housekeeper and friend had been with the Basantes family for years, and not even Harry's mother stood up to Mona when it came to Desi's welfare. "She's got to put her feet up, and you're just standing there like you're glued to the floor, so maybe you didn't hear me."

"I'll be right back." She handed Desi her water and went looking for Rachel, realizing then she hadn't seen much of her since their arrival.

That Serena hadn't made it for Desi's big night hadn't escaped Harry's attention. Rachel and Serena dating hadn't been a good idea, but she'd kept that opinion to herself. She loved them both, but Serena's one disastrous foray into the land of men had ended badly, tainting all relationships going forward, no matter the gender of her partner.

Serena's ex-husband was another abusive prick who'd left her with a broken jaw and an unplanned pregnancy. Butch was now the center of his mother's world, but after escaping her marriage, Serena had become a perpetual dater. It was a strategy to protect her heart, which was why Harry wanted someone different for Rachel. She wanted someone ready to give Rachel all the things she needed because when it came down to it, Rachel and Desi weren't all that different. The sisters saw the world through the prism of family and commitment.

"Hey," Rachel said. She was talking to a woman at the back of the room. "This is my friend, Wynter Pellegrin." Rachel introduced them and shook her head at Harry's offer of a ride when she said she and Desi were leaving. "You guys go ahead. We might grab another drink somewhere quieter. Wynter won't leave me stranded."

"Okay, be careful and call me if you need me to pick you up later." Harry kissed Rachel's forehead and nodded in Wynter's direction. Wynter was tall, attractive, and from the way she was looking at Rachel, she was interested in more than pottery and art. Rachel's love life wasn't her business, but the only way to avoid drama was to end one relationship before starting on a new one.

Desi didn't appear thrilled when Rachel didn't go home with them, but she stayed quiet. They thanked the gallery owner, and Desi put her arms around Harry as they stood outside.

"Congratulations, love. I'm so proud of you." She kissed Desi and pressed her hand to the side of her neck. "You're extraordinary."

"Thank you, and I mean for everything. None of this would've happened without you. I love you and this life you've given me. Some days I can't believe I wake up next to you. You've been the one constant in my life, my person, and having nothing to be afraid of is an added bonus." Desi cocked her head into her touch, and it melted Harry's heart.

"You never have to worry about any of that again." She meant that. The best thing for the Simoneaux family was they were locked up and out of her reach. "All you need to concentrate on now is us and our family. Anything else, and Mona will lock me out of the house."

"You got that right." Mona made Desi laugh, a sound she loved. "Harry, go get the car. It's cold out here, and it's not good for Desi and the baby."

"Yes, ma'am." Harry saluted with her free hand, but Desi didn't let her go.

"Come on, Mona. It's not that far, so let's walk," Desi said. Harry threaded their fingers together, liking having Desi so close.

This life they were building together was more than she'd ever thought possible, and she wanted to concentrate on just that. A little more than a month and they'd welcome a baby, and it was something to be celebrated. Even with all that, she had a feeling she needed to be vigilant. It wasn't something she could pinpoint, but it wasn't something to be ignored. No matter what, this time nothing was going to take Desi away from her. Not without a fight.

Chapter Two

Y ou're begging me for the hole, Simoneaux." The prison guard on horseback didn't raise his voice as he threatened Byron.

When the state of Louisiana sentenced him to hard labor, they meant it. Spending the rest of his life in the fields of Angola made him consider hanging himself or taking a chance and running, consequences be damned. The hope of running was a good motivator to stay alert, especially when he thought of Desi and the bitch who'd put him here. Twenty-five years was a fucking eternity.

"Yeah, boss." He stepped away from the canteen of cold water and took to hoeing again. Angola had no machinery of any kind. The warden had declared years before that they didn't need mechanical help, considering he had close to sixty-five hundred men with nothing to do. Fieldwork wasn't optional, no matter who you were. The farm, as it was called, was fairly self-sufficient—they grew all their own food, raised their own livestock, and planted crops like cotton to sell for what they couldn't make.

It was the same fucking thing every fucking day. They ate a shitty breakfast, then walked out with a white bread bologna sandwich to a ten-hour day of this shit with two guards sitting on their horses ready to kill them if they stepped out of line. The only normal part of his day was having his brother Mike and his father working alongside him. It was probably the guard's attempt at humor to keep them together. There were another nine guys in their section, and the guard ordering them around loved to say on a daily basis that they were his special group of fuck-ups.

"Come in, Tim."

The radio came to life, and Byron slowed down. The day was

almost over anyway, and they would finally get out of the sun. It was cold, but hoeing all day worked up a sweat.

"Go ahead."

The guard had a twang that Byron hadn't been able to pinpoint. All he knew was it aggravated the hell out of him.

"Sue needs to see Paul before she leaves for the day. Want me to send someone to relieve him?"

Tim rubbed his chest and laughed, though his eyes were tight. "I got enough bullets to keep these guys in line. Besides, we only have three hours left. If it don't take that long, Paul can come back. Get going, Paul."

The other guard turned his horse toward the administration building and rode off, and Tim turned his attention back to the prisoners. "Simoneaux, God dammit. My granny can work faster than you. Put your back into it, or I'm going to make you pay."

Byron turned to the guy, wanting to punch him off the horse and teach him a few things. A deep sense of joy came over him when Tim suddenly clutched his chest, grunted, and fell lifeless to the ground. He seemed to still be breathing, but his eyes were closed, and he was unconscious. It was like a gift from God, and he couldn't have cared less what happened to the asshole.

The field they were working was at the farthest point to the south, and there was no need for a fence. Angola had one road in and out—the rest was surrounded by miles of swamp. No one could run fast enough through the water and muck to escape the guards. It was something they'd pounded into his head from his first day. Run, and the hell you'd face would make you wish the gators had gotten you first.

The big African American guy, Tyrell, threw his hoe down and headed for the levee. Freedom was worth facing whatever was waiting in the swamp, and Byron wasn't letting him go alone. He dragged his father and a reluctant Mike along and ran. Only two guys stayed behind to help Tim. The rest of the prisoners followed Tyrell as well.

"Come on, move it." He pushed Mike into the water and then his father. "We got to get some miles behind us before they start looking for us."

"This is a mistake," Mike said. They were already waist deep in the water, and Mike kept looking over his shoulder.

"What, you got some boyfriend I don't know about? This can't be the rest of my life."

The water was starting to get deeper and darker as the large cypress trees growing out of the swamp blocked the sun. There was no land in sight, from what he could tell, but Tyrell seemed to know where he was going. The big man didn't talk often, but Byron had heard he'd already served six years of a forty-year stretch.

"I've got two years left, and I don't want to fuck that up." Mike had gotten a lighter sentence for pleading guilty and had been a model prisoner. He'd gotten that sweet deal by testifying against him, and that was something Byron would never get over.

"Guess what, asshole, being soaking wet is going to be hard to explain, so move it." He tried his best to ignore whatever was bumping his legs and caught up to Tyrell. "What's the plan?"

"What are you talking about?" Tyrell barely looked at him. "There's about fifteen miles of this shit before we hit land again. If we're lucky enough to do that, you and your crazy family are on your own. If you're following me right now, you best shut the fuck up and walk, all of you."

They moved two abreast as fast as they could manage. Ahead of him he and Tyrell spotted a black snake swimming on the surface, but thankfully it was headed away from them. Once they lost the little light they had, this would become a nightmare. He had no choice, though. Desi, that little piece of shit, had to pay for what she'd done to him. Once she was dead, he'd disappear and start over. He deserved that. Right now they'd have to kill him to make him go back.

"Don't forget the pickled okra on the side," Desi called as Harry went downstairs. It was one in the morning, and Desi was about to get out of bed when Harry woke up. These late-night snack cravings didn't happen often, but there was no way she'd let Desi go down for them. "And only toast one side of the bread."

"I won't forget." They'd known each other for most of their lives, and for all those years Desi had detested pickled anything. It was funny to watch her now eat pickled okra, shivering the entire time as she blamed Harry and the baby. The other thing Desi couldn't get enough of was Mona's pecan chicken salad with red grapes. They'd gone through buckets of the stuff, since it was the only thing that didn't make Desi nauseous. Morning sickness had gone on way longer than it normally should have, and that was also her fault.

Her mother and Mona had both warned her about arguing and told her to do everything Desi asked.

"Add tomato juice with a little orange juice in it, and I'll be set." Desi's voice followed Harry downstairs.

That combination made *her* shiver. If there was one thing she didn't care for in any form it was tomatoes.

She made it to the kitchen without any other shouted requests and was taking the bread out when the doorbell rang. "What the hell?" No good news came from someone ringing the bell this late, and there was no way Rachel had lost her key. The possible bad news made her forget her dilemma of how to toast bread only on one side.

"Sorry, Harry," Serena said as she stepped inside. Her old friend's hair was falling out of her ponytail, and she was pale.

"What's wrong? Is it Butch or your parents?" She walked Serena to the kitchen so she could sit down. The back door opened, and Rachel stared at both of them with an expression Harry found unreadable. This was not the time for her to get caught in the middle of someone else's drama.

"What's going on?" Rachel sounded aggravated. "Now you show up? You're six hours late." That she was aggravated at the sight of Serena wasn't hard to figure out.

"Rach, let's give her a minute." She started making Desi's sandwich, glad when Rachel stuck two pieces of bread in the same slot in the toaster, then got the tomato juice ready. They all silently watched the toaster until the bread popped up. "To give you a hint," Harry said to Serena, "your minute is up." She cut the sandwich into four equal-size triangles, having been schooled on that as well. "In case you missed it, like Desi's show, that's your cue to talk."

"Sorry, it's been a long night." Serena combed her hair back and took a breath and held it longer than Harry thought safe. "I want to talk to all of you if that's okay. Is Desi awake?"

"This is for her. She woke up hungry." She held the plate with everything Desi had asked for while Rachel held the glass. "I'm sure whatever you have to say is important, but remember she's pregnant. Don't upset her."

"Trust me, if I could skip this I would, and I wouldn't have missed her show if it wasn't important." Serena followed them upstairs where Desi was sitting up with a mound of pillows behind her. "Hey, sorry about this."

Desi nodded as she took the plate from her, then took a bite without saying anything. The way Desi closed her eyes in pure enjoyment as she chewed made Harry smile. "Hopefully you still love me as much as you do that sandwich."

"Harry, sit and stop talking," Desi said, obviously not in the mood for teasing. "What can we do for you, Serena?" The question was clipped.

"I'm sorry I missed your show." Obviously Serena was trying to placate both sisters.

"Come on, you didn't come over here at one in the morning to tell me that. What is it?" Desi sounded impatient and angry, nothing like her usual self, but Harry knew fear and worry could change anyone. And everything from Serena's tone to her posture screamed there was something wrong. But she was glad Desi's reaction wasn't to cower in fear but to stand up for herself.

"I was with Detective Roger Landry this afternoon. I'm sorry, Desi, but at around two, Byron, Mike, and their father escaped with some other inmates. Roger and I were sure they'd have found them before we had this conversation, but with their almost four-hour head start, they're still out there. The warden assures me it's only a matter of time, but I wanted you to hear it from me and not on the news."

"How could that even be possible? What happened?" The small piece of sandwich in Desi's hand fell to her lap and her eyes were wide. "I didn't think I had anything to worry about when it came to them. Not for years, anyway. This *cannot* be happening again. Harry?" Desi said, looking at her as if she wanted a definitive answer.

Serena explained how it had happened and about the swamp they'd disappeared into. Desperation was the only reason to chance an alligator- and snake-infested landscape. In Byron's case, though, she had to add the need for revenge as his motivating factor. "There are plenty of people searching, so hopefully I'll have some good news for you soon," Serena said. "Roger or someone on the case will be by as soon as they can, and he said not to worry."

"Thanks for coming and telling us, and I'm sorry for before." Desi sounded better, but she had a strong grip on Harry's bicep. "It's not something I ever expected to hear, so please let us know what's happening. Honey?" Desi said, gazing up at her again.

Harry heard Desi over the blood rushing through her ears. These assholes were unbelievable, and if they were lucky enough to make it to New Orleans, they wouldn't live to regret it if they came within a thousand yards of Desi. The only thing *she* regretted now was letting

Byron off with so few injuries. Rabid animals gave you no choice but to put them down.

"Are you all right, Harry?" Serena asked.

"No, I'm not fucking all right." She hated cursing, especially in front of Desi, figuring she'd had enough of crude behavior for a lifetime. "That asshole and his family have done enough, and Desi deserves peace. You can go ahead and tell the police I'm going to kill him if he comes anywhere near Desi or Rachel." She tried to calm down, but the guilt over the life she'd left Desi to haunted her. Thinking about it had become a compulsion.

"Harry, please stop talking," Serena said. "I'm an officer of the court, and you can't make threats like that."

"Threats? It's a promise."

"Honey, please calm down." Desi placed her hand on Harry's back and rubbed small circles. "Could you two please excuse us a moment? Don't leave, Serena."

"I should've—" Harry started when they were alone.

Desi placed her fingers over her mouth and shook her head. "Listen to me, okay? My truth is that the life I had without you was horrible, but in my mind, and more importantly in my heart, all that's over. You and our baby are where my future lies. Promise me you won't do anything that'll mess that up." Desi fisted Harry's T-shirt and peered into her eyes. "You doing something like that isn't you."

"You can't ask me to sit back and let something happen to you. Don't make me promise that." Sixteen years was a long time for anyone to exist in the life Desi had survived, and Harry's wish that she'd checked on Desi never went away. Having Desi's father condemn his daughters to that level of abuse had been her fault, and there was no forgiving herself for that.

"Love, I have no doubt you'll protect me, Rachel, and the baby, but you don't have to go looking for trouble. We haven't gone through all this for me to lose you to a place I can't touch you—where the baby won't get to know you." Desi pulled her closer and kissed her cheek. "You promised me a long life, and that's what I want."

"I love you, and I'm sorry this crap never ends."

"You have nothing to be sorry for, and stop cursing in front of the baby. No matter what happens I have you—we'll be okay." Desi kissed her, then took the plate back. "Let them back in, and remember, Serena didn't help them escape. Make nice so she keeps us informed."

Harry opened the door to Serena and Rachel, and Mona was

there in her fuzzy slippers as well. Harry's parents were there too, not appearing very happy. "All of you didn't have to get up."

"I need to make sure all this racket isn't you trying to pester my girl." Mona walked in and went to Desi's side, followed by her mother.

"Is there anything else, Serena?" Her mom's question sounded like a dismissal as she took Desi's hand and held it while her father put his arm around Rachel.

"I know it'll be hard," Serena said, "but try to get some sleep. I'll come back with Roger to give you an update as soon as I can. If they're apprehended tonight, I'll call." Serena glanced at Rachel, but Rachel didn't move away from Harry's father.

"Okay, thank you." Desi smiled, but it seemed forced. "Again, thank you for telling us."

"It's late, so everyone get some sleep." Mona shooed everyone out as she walked to the door. "Desi needs her rest."

The room grew quiet, and Harry held her breath as a way of centering herself. Being unable to control what was happening was enraging. Not that she was a freak about needing to dictate her surroundings, but having a man loose in the world who wanted to shatter everything that made her happy brought on a helplessness she couldn't shake.

"Honey," Desi said, placing her hand on her back, "I'm so sorry."

"What do you have to be sorry about?"

"Your life shouldn't have all this drama in it. Byron wouldn't have even remembered who you were if I hadn't come back here." Desi's tears and expression were pure misery.

"Listen to me." She moved the tray out of the way and held Desi. "We're meant to be together. You coming back to me was everything I ever wished for, and what you endured while we were apart fills me with shame because my anger paralyzed me. What that animal did to you is on him—you didn't ask for that." The image of Desi's leg injury was tattooed on the back of her eyelids, making it impossible to forget. Byron Simoneaux was an animal who thought what he'd done was his right because Desi had been his wife.

"I love you," Desi said, pulling her closer.

"I love you too, and it's time to leave the past in the grave it deserves." She closed her eyes for a moment and shook her head, trying to clear it. "I'm sure they'll catch them before they get anywhere near us, but there's no way I'm going to let anything happen to you or the baby." She placed her hands under Desi's nightgown and rubbed small circles over her abdomen as she kissed her temple. "Only a few more weeks to go, and we'll have everything we ever wanted."

"*Almost* everything we ever wanted." Desi moved and slowly straddled her lap. "You promised me at least one more, so we're not done just yet. And I've tried to leave it all in the past, but Byron and his family make it impossible. This time, though, he's not going to steal my joy. This time, he's not going to win."

"The thing about wanting things that don't belong to you is it's frustrating as hell. You belong to me, and soon the whole world is going to know it." She didn't stop Desi when she took her nightgown off. Sometimes loving and touching Desi were the best ways to keep both their minds from skittering off into dark places.

"I do belong to you, always have. The thought of you is how I survived. That you still want me is my miracle." Desi kissed her as she struggled to get her T-shirt off. "I have never stopped wanting you."

Those words had given Harry chills from the first time she heard Desi say them. Desire and pleasing someone had been lessons she'd learned with Desi, and if she got her wish, it would be a lifetime commitment of lessons. She wanted to rush, but she'd never been rough with Desi, and she was extra careful now. Desi leaned in and kissed her as if she was desperate.

"No more holding back." Desi sounded commanding and sure. "You could never hurt me, so no more holding back."

The press of Desi against her was a reminder of all she had, and all she could lose. It wasn't the time to think about it, so she tried to erase it from her mind. There was no place for Byron when Desi was this close to her. "Tell me what you want."

"You—you're all I've ever wanted, and I need you to touch me."

Desi tipped her hips forward and lifted up enough so she could come down on her fingers hard and fast. She stopped as if wanting to enjoy the fullness, and Harry shivered at Desi's groan. The way Desi looked at her made her realize how much she was loved and how damn lucky she was. With Desi this was more than about release. It was all those things that she didn't have to say because she knew her that well, and it was always good because she loved Desi more than anything in her life.

"Please, honey." Desi gripped her shoulders and moved her hips.

She was so wet, and Harry wanted it to last. This had become Desi's favorite position since lying on her back had become uncomfortable.

"Harder. I need to feel you." Desi's hips sped up, meaning she wasn't interested in the scenic route, so Harry gave her what she wanted.

"I love you." She closed her eyes when Desi bit her shoulder as if to keep quiet.

"God, baby, don't stop. I'm almost…almost—" Desi bit down again harder and went rigid in her arms. "You're so good to me, love," she said as she slowly relaxed against her.

Harry loved that soft voice that sounded lazy and content. "You're the most beautiful woman in the world, and I love being good to you. Especially this way." The joke got her a kiss over the spot Desi had bitten.

"That'll be hard to explain if anyone sees it." Desi took a breath when Harry pulled out.

"Don't worry about that and relax. You need to get some sleep." She lay back and waited for Desi to get comfortable. "I'm sorry this happened on your big night."

"You making love to me?" Desi turned around and pressed her back to Harry's front. "I think it was a perfect end to my perfect night. Thank you for my ring. I can't wait to marry you."

"I have one more to give you, so thank you for saying yes." She took Desi's lead and dropped the subject of Byron and his family. They'd already stolen plenty from them, and if she could help it, they wouldn't take any more.

CHAPTER THREE

Byron didn't think he'd ever experienced the kind of darkness that enveloped the swamp once the sun completely set. But when a little moonlight came through the trees, he prayed for the oblivion of total darkness. The glowing eyes all around them and the...stuff...bumping against his legs were making him want to peel his skin off—he was so afraid. All this, added to the crap he'd gone through after being locked in that fucking place, was on Desi's head.

All he'd done was try to keep his wife in line. He'd worked hard to keep a roof over her head and food on their table, and he'd even taken her fucking sister in. Desi repaid him by throwing him in a pit full of monsters. He'd been railroaded, and he wasn't going to stop until he got his hands on his wife, and she *was* still his wife. It didn't matter what some mouthpiece lawyer said about their finalized divorce.

They'd taken vows, made promises, and he was keeping his end. They'd stood before God and said all the words, and there was no changing any fucking part of that. After years together the simpleton should've known what going against him meant. There were consequences to her actions, and he was going to enjoy showing her what they were.

His weight made him sink into the muck with every step but he stayed close to Tyrell. The man was built like a wall and no one fucked with him in the cell block they shared at the back of the prison compound. It was the oldest and crappiest on Angola and it was the guards' way of showing them how little they thought of them as men.

Tyrell had been the first one over the levee and was moving through this shit like he knew exactly where he was going. Byron didn't know for sure but Tyrell was his best bet of succeeding.

Someone at the back of the line screamed. The scream carried until someone slapped him.

"Get it off," the guy said, struggling to get away.

"Shut him up," Byron said as a guy started punching the alligator that'd bitten down on the guy's leg. The six-foot alligator let go and tried to get a better grip, making the guy scream again. "Come on. Any of you want to get caught before we get anywhere away from here?"

They all started moving faster and the guys toward the back let go of the man, watching him go under as the sight of a second tail whipped around before disappearing under the water with a violent swish and a final watery scream.

As one, they all sped up. There was a clump of trees that made a circle ahead and Tyrell headed for the center. There was a small patch of dirt big enough for them to get out of the water.

"Everybody shut the fuck up," Tyrell said. They weren't being loud, but they all did as Tyrell asked and the only sounds around them belonged there. The crickets, frogs, and some kind of grunting were the only noises. All the sounds seemed to belong there, so it meant whoever was hunting them wasn't close. "We need to split up."

"No fucking way," Byron said. The comment meant Tyrell knew the way through the swamp. There wasn't a chance he was losing the only viable ticket out. "We stick with you."

"I say we sit here until sunrise and wait for the guards. Whatever the consequences for this, it'll be better than getting offed by a gator." Mike stood close enough to him for Byron to feel him shivering.

The temperature was dropping, which made Bryon wonder why there were still so many alligators out. He'd never really gotten out of New Orleans much, but he'd heard that about the swamp creatures. Like the snakes, they weren't supposed to be active in the cold, but tonight proved him wrong.

"I don't want to die out here."

"You want to do that, then sit here or head back, motherfucker." He shoved Mike until he went under the water.

"Both of you shut the hell up," Big Byron said in a whisper that made them both stop talking. He and Mike were grown men, but experience had conditioned them to react to Big Byron's voice.

Their father was totally nuts, which hadn't gotten him out of working every day, but everyone had stayed clear of him. He and Mike hadn't been that lucky. Neither of them had been able to fight off the persistent big guys in their cellblock who'd stripped them of their humanity as well as dignity. He'd dreamed of heaping that kind of humiliation on that dyke Basantes before he cut her heart out as Desi watched. If it hadn't been for Basantes, Desi would've never had the guts to testify against him.

"Quit bitching and pay attention. We gotta make it home so I can see your mama. Woman's gonna pray to die for putting us here." Big Byron broke a stick in his beefy hands.

Once they'd been locked up, his father had convinced himself their mother wasn't dead. She was, in Big Byron's mind, alive and screwing around on him. It was her lies and whoring ways that'd put him in prison. The more days that went by, the crazier he got, and Byron was ready to leave him behind. There were plenty of people to blame for his miserable failure of a life, and a lot of it rested on Big Byron's shoulders.

"Daddy, she's dead. You fucking killed her, so deal with it." He wanted to punch the bastard who'd made it his life's mission to make him feel small. Big Byron knew only one way to deal with the world and that was with his fists. It was the only lesson he'd taught him, and Desi despised him because of it.

"Stop your ly—" His father's voice had risen with each word but he didn't finish when Tyrell slapped his hand over his mouth.

"All of y'all need to zip it before we get caught. You know they're looking for us, so let's not make it that fucking easy for them. I'm not waiting for sunup." Tyrell slid back into the water and let his father go. "If you following me and keep talking, I'm gonna do you right here and walk away. Hell, I'm already doing forty-five years for killing a man, what's a couple more."

They formed a line and followed. There was a sudden splash and they saw two of the guys with them fighting something off but it was too dark to see what. Byron didn't hesitate when Tyrell went faster. This place was worse than prison, but he'd endure it to get his revenge. After that he didn't care if he dug ditches for the rest of his life, he'd disappear and start over. All he had to do was survive this shit.

❖

Desi lay still with her eyes closed, hoping not to wake Harry. The feel of Harry behind her, holding her, eased the tension Serena had caused with her visit last night. It'd seemed like forever since the last time she'd seen Byron in the courtroom. She'd faced him and testified to what he'd done to her and not just that final night. He'd glared at her the entire time, but she'd stared right back with the courage Harry had helped her find. He'd wanted to kill her, but the only thing he did was lead her right back to where she'd always wanted to be.

His guilty verdict should've been the end of it. Bryon and his father had caused enough pain for three lifetimes and had deserved all the punishment the state had meted out, but he hadn't accepted that. Byron screaming he was innocent still knocked around in her head. Now she knew that freedom from Byron and his family wouldn't come from their divorce or his incarceration, but through death. The other truth was that she wasn't willing to sacrifice another thing to him. All that mattered to her was Harry and their family, and she'd do anything to protect all of it.

"What are you thinking so hard about?" Harry's voice was low and rough, and the baby moved under her hand. "How's my little guy this morning?"

"Did you peek? It could be a girl, you know." She turned to be able to look at Harry. It was chilly in their room, and she got as close as she could to keep warm. "Good morning."

"My OBGYN rotation was like a million years ago, but I closed my eyes when Ellie prompted me to since you didn't want to know, so no peeking." Harry rubbed her stomach in small circles. "Good morning, and boy or girl—it won't matter. All I want is a healthy baby and wife." Harry pulled the comforter up higher as if wanting to make sure she was okay.

"Do you think anyone is up yet?" She tried her best to get Byron out of her head, not wanting to waste time on that any longer.

Harry had given her the time to cry for all the things she'd survived and couldn't change, but she was tired of remembering. Those thoughts were like wet bags of sand she'd carried through muck, and it was time to put them down. Forgetting was impossible, she knew that, but it was time to let go and embrace what she had now.

"Mona's probably getting breakfast ready." Harry kissed her forehead before moving to her lips. "Do you need anything?"

"Just you. That sounds sappy, but I need you to promise me again you'll be careful. I can't lose you." She couldn't imagine the hatred Byron had for Harry and how it had built in the time he'd been locked up. If he got a chance to hurt Harry he'd definitely do it.

"You have to promise the same. We didn't talk about it last night, but you don't take any chances." Harry's expression was serious tinged with concern. "You don't need to make any sacrifices because you think you're keeping me safe. Facing everything alone isn't something you have to do anymore. We're a team and nothing is going to change that."

"I still don't understand how all of them could've gotten away, but don't worry, I'm through running. You taught me the way life should be and I'm not giving that up." It was raining outside, making her glad it was Saturday. Harry was off and not on call. A lazy day at home was all she wanted.

"You can get mad at me now, but I'm going to kill him if he steps into the yard."

She shook her head and caressed Harry's cheek. "I know you'll protect us, but I don't want that. I don't want to lose you again, and I don't want that on your conscience. You're wired to preserve life, not take it." She had to close her eyes to get her emotions under control. "God this isn't fair."

"Listen, nothing's going to change. He isn't going to take anything from us. I'll get the guards back until those bastards are back where they belong, and it sounds like the police are on this." Harry held her and they talked a little more before sharing a shower. The rain wasn't letting up, so they dressed casually and sat together in front of the fireplace. It wasn't cold enough to light it, but she loved sitting in the chair she'd chosen with Tony's help. Having Harry next to her only made it better.

She moved to Harry's lap when Rachel knocked and joined them. "I refuse to give that bastard another thought so let's talk about the wedding. We can still have a small party right?"

"Whatever Desi wants. All I want is for her to say I do, and then we could take a short trip somewhere." Harry kissed the side of her neck.

"You're crazy if you think she'll say no." Her sister's sense of humor hadn't changed even after everything they'd survived. "We both say yes, and as the maid of honor, I should've gotten a ring too. It's tradition."

"I'm not familiar with that particular one, but I haven't forgotten you come as a pair. A wedding isn't going to change a thing, and the house is big enough for all of us. You aren't going anywhere." Harry hadn't changed all that much when it came to standing up for both her and Rachel. "But if it takes a ring, I'll see if they still make those mood rings and get you one."

"It's diamonds or nothing, stud." Rachel pointed her finger at Harry and squinted at her.

"Maybe you all can come to stay with us until all this craziness is over," Rosa said when she entered without knocking.

Desi made a mental note to lock the door before getting naked for any reason. She shook her head and Harry stayed quiet. "I appreciate you offering, but I'm not letting Byron run us out of our home."

"Both of you think about the baby."

Rosa sounded reasonable but this was important to her. Backing down would mean Bryon winning. It was probably prideful and stupid, but she didn't think it would get to the point of having to defend their home. There was no way Byron would ever get close to them again.

"Then Francisco and I aren't going anywhere. It won't be long before the baby arrives, and you'll need help."

Rosa wasn't anyone you wanted to argue with, so she nodded and pinched Harry where her mother couldn't see until she did the same.

"Thank you, Rosa. I'd love for you to be here to help with the baby."

"I'm sure Harry will disagree with you," Rosa said, laughing. Their reunion had been rocky considering Rosa was no fool. Harry's mother knew exactly who'd broken her daughter's heart, and forgiveness hadn't been easy to earn.

She loved Harry for standing up for her when Rosa hadn't been exactly welcoming the first time she'd seen them together, and Harry's overprotectiveness had kicked in. Granted, most of whatever Rosa had said to Harry was in rapid fire Spanish, saving her from the brunt of it, but she'd placed her hand on Harry's shoulder and asked her to give her and Rosa a minute.

Having Harry fight all her battles for her wasn't going to work if she wanted a relationship with Rosa. It was important to her because Harry's family was important to her, so she'd do whatever it took for Harry's sake as well as the baby's to smooth things over. She wanted Rosa in their lives because Harry's mother was a strong woman who'd made her childhood so much better than it would've been with only Clyde.

She'd talked to Rosa alone and told her everything, even though she knew Harry had spoken to her mother in generalities about what had happened. Rosa deserved not only the truth, but to hear it from her. They'd cried together and it paved the way forward for them. Francisco, Harry's dad, had been much easier, but now she had a true ally in Rosa.

"I want our baby to know its grandparents, and you and Francisco will be it for them." She felt Harry tighten her hold when she said that, and she held her hand out to Rachel. "Family is something you taught me about, Rosa, and both Rachel and I are grateful for all you did from the day you met us. I want that for our baby, so I'd love for you to stay as long as you want." They'd finally made it back to the family she'd always loved, and she cried along with Rosa when she hugged her.

"Good," Rosa said wiping her face. "Let me go help Mona."

"You made her day," Harry said.

"She made mine too. I don't remember my mom well enough to have clear memories of her, but there are those thoughts that are as hard to grasp as fog. I never know if they're real, but I'd like to think so, especially now. When the time comes, I want you, Rachel, Mona, and your mom close by."

"You're going to get everything you want, so prepare yourself for spoiling."

"I can't wait." Having all these people care about her and Rachel was like having every wish she'd ever had come true. Harry was the person she'd loved above all others, but Harry had given her so much more than her love. It might be old fashioned, but Harry had also given her a home and a safe place to be herself. Some people might not understand that, but her experiences had taught her it was a precious gift not ever to be taken for granted.

CHAPTER FOUR

W hy can't they leave us alone?" Desi asked. She and Harry were sitting in the sunroom, watching it rain. It had taken some convincing to get Rachel to go to work and not worry about Byron and his family, but she'd continued to call and check in throughout the day. Roger and Serena had called too, but there'd been no updates, so all they could do was wait.

"I need you to not dwell on this, sweetheart." Harry rubbed Desi's abdomen and kissed the side of her head. "There are too many people who love you and will do whatever they have to in order to keep you safe."

Rachel joined them and sat on the other side of Harry, lifting Harry's arm so she'd hug her. It was wonderful how much Harry loved her sister. "You're home early," Harry said, kissing Rachel on the head as well.

"Your mom called and said they wanted to take us out to dinner, so I freed up my afternoon." Rachel reached up and threaded her fingers with Harry's.

"How's it going with Serena?" Harry asked. "We haven't babysat in a while. Did you two give up on dating?"

"Serena's parents have been taking care of Butch, and Serena's been busy." It was the same story Rachel had told Desi, and the undercurrent of anger was still there. "So I'm guessing it's not that we've given up going out, but given up going *out*."

"You can talk to her, you know." Harry rested her head on Rachel's, and it made Desi wish Harry had a younger sister who was as nice and loving as Harry. She'd be a perfect match for Rachel. "Sometimes busy is simply that."

"I'm not begging, studly. Besides, it's not like we made any promises." Rachel kissed Harry's cheek before standing and kissing Desi's cheek as well when the doorbell chimed. "I'm going to take a shower, so call if you need help."

"I can almost hear all those heavy thoughts clanking around in your head," Harry said, tapping Desi's forehead. "Don't worry, they'll eventually figure it out."

"Do you have that much faith in Serena?" She didn't have bouts of jealousy often, but Serena could make anyone feel inadequate. That counted double now that she was eight months pregnant.

"I have faith in the Thompson sisters. If she follows your lead, she'll be fine." Harry leaned in and kissed her until they heard someone clear their throat.

"No wonder you're pregnant," Tony said in his usual droll tone. "Harry, give the poor woman a break. If she gets enough rest, maybe the baby will be born with all the fashion sense you lack."

"Harry, I don't need any breaks," Desi said, giving her another kiss. "Give us a minute to change. Get everyone a drink, please," she said to Tony.

"I live to serve you, and please put on the patterned dress we found the other day. It's really cute, so find something for Harry that kind of matches. It'll look good for the Instagram pictures I'm posting to help you mark your territory. I doubt Harry would agree to the forehead tattoo or for you to pee on her in public."

"Ew." She and Harry held hands up the stairs, and she stepped into the closet after she handed Harry a shirt and a pair of pants. She was starting to feel like she'd never be attractive again, so she changed in the closet. "Could you zip me up, please?" She turned her back to Harry and waited.

"How about you sit for a minute." Harry pushed the new dress off her shoulders, and it fell in a pool at her feet. The urge to pick it up was hard to fight, considering the enormously unflattering underwear that was revealed. "Let me look at you." Harry draped the dress over one of the chairs to keep it from wrinkling and sat Desi in the other one.

"Honey, everyone is waiting." She smiled at Harry, now kneeling between her legs as she ran her hands up Desi's thighs to her hips. The way Harry kissed her made her moan, and it reminded her of all the months she couldn't get enough. That was an all-the-time thing normally, but pregnancy had ramped up her desire for Harry to the point of it being embarrassing. The cotton of Harry's sweater felt soft under her hands as she gripped Harry's shoulders, keeping her close even after the kiss ended. "How do you do that?"

"Do what?" Harry ran her finger along the elastic of the most unflattering panties she'd ever owned.

"I look like I have a spare tire strapped to me, and you still want me." She pressed her forehead to Harry's and tried her best not to get carried away. "You make me feel beautiful."

"It's easy when you *are* beautiful, baby. I've always thought so, but now I have a hard time keeping my hands to myself." Harry moved her fingers and stroked from the opening of her sex to her clit. "You're the one person I crave, and I'm glad you get this wet for me."

"Did you lock the door, honey?" She spread her legs as much as she could and started to close them again when she thought of being rude to their guests. "We really shouldn't. Everyone's waiting for us."

"You think they're going to leave without us?" Harry was gentle as she touched her and kissed the side of her neck. "I look at you sometimes and I *need* to touch you. It doesn't matter what's going on or who's waiting." Harry pulled back enough to see her face. "Unless you don't want me to."

"I do...I always love your hands on me." She ran her fingers through Harry's hair and smiled. "Do you promise not to mess up my makeup?"

Harry smiled and slipped Desi's panties off before stripping her shirt and sweater. "I promise to keep my mouth and hands away from your makeup."

She sat back and sighed when Harry spread her sex and licked her clit with a flat tongue. "God, honey, that feels so good." All she could see was the top of Harry's head, so she closed her eyes and concentrated on the feel of Harry's mouth. "Baby, put your fingers in. I need you to go inside."

Harry sucked her in and touched her but didn't give her what she'd asked for. It made her love Harry more—Harry wanted her but was always gentle because of the baby. The need to move her hips was strong, but it was getting harder to do things she wanted. She pulled the hair at the back of Harry's head and gasped when Harry went slow but finally buried her fingers inside, exactly the way she wanted.

"Right there, honey—right there." Desi was trying not to be loud, but all she wanted was to scream at how good this felt. "Harder, baby." It was always the same. Harry had a way of making her crazy and in need of relief. "Like that, like that."

Harry sucked and stilled her hand. Desi dreamed about that mouth when she was away from Harry. She'd learned to make love with Harry, and that time in her life had been so special. It was like that again now, and she was in love and happy. It was all she could think of as the peak came, and she grabbed Harry's head. "Yes, yes…oh my God, yes."

She had to pull Harry's head up as she tried to get her breathing under control. This baby was something they both wanted, but it was hell on her stamina.

"You okay?" Harry asked as she pulled out. "I didn't hurt you, did I?" Harry looked panicked.

"You overwhelmed me by making me a happy woman. Trust me, the tears are a good thing." She combed Harry's hair back and smiled. A nap sounded better than going out to dinner, but there was a crowd waiting on them, so canceling wasn't an option. "Want to grab me another pair of the sexy underwear?"

"It's the granny panties that got me in the mood, so don't knock them." Harry used her shirt to wipe her face, then kissed her.

"You want me to throw all the sexy ones out?" She laughed when Harry stopped and frowned. "I didn't think so."

"It's the beautiful woman in them, love." Harry got another pair for her and helped her into the bathroom.

"Good save, Dr. Basantes. It's no wonder I'm ready to marry you."

❖

Rachel glanced at the closed door and sighed. The noises she heard made her walk to the other side of the hall and try to imagine anything but what was happening in that room, though she was happy for Desi. After years of watching her sister being killed slowly, having Harry back in her life was a miracle. Her problem now was that Desi had her knight and protector back. Desi didn't need *her* any longer, and she was having a hard time imagining her life without Desi constantly in it.

"Geez, I'm being such a selfish bitch." She opened the door to her room and stepped into her closet. She'd have to pick something to wear on her own. The truth was Harry kept telling her she was welcome to stay for as long she wanted, and Rachel knew she meant it. When the baby came, that would become awkward, yet where the hell would she go?

"Hey, sorry," Serena said, closing the door behind her. "I knocked, I promise."

"You were finally able to leave work?" Sarcasm was her norm, usually with humor, but Serena's stuck-in-the-office excuse was getting old, so she didn't mind sharpening her sword. "Does that mean you have information about Byron?" Having Byron come back now terrified her. She'd rather worry about that than whatever was on Serena's mind.

"The prison and other authorities have search parties out, but nothing yet. From what they keep telling us, the area they're slogging through should kill them." Serena appeared tired, and she exhaled as she sat on the bed. "I know it won't make a difference, but I *have* been slammed at work—that's not a lie. My boss is retiring, so the DA asked me to take over the department."

They'd had months of dinner dates and fun nights, and that should've been enough. Hell, it always had been before now. The problem with that didn't hit her until Serena disappeared on her. She'd fallen for someone for really the first time ever, but it was completely one-sided. Serena had never acted like she wanted anything more.

She could hardly blame Serena. She'd gone along, thinking it would only take time, but they were no closer to being more than they were right now. This promotion was the perfect example. That Serena was taking on even more responsibility was something they should've talked about if they were, in fact, a couple.

"Congratulations," she said, stepping back in the closet to get her emotions under control. "I'm sure you'll do great."

"Rach," Serena said, "please come back here. I want to talk to you."

"I've wanted to talk to you all week, the last couple of weeks, actually, but you were swamped. Too swamped for a quick chat, but hey, I get it. I'm not anywhere near your league career-wise, but I'm not a book either." She came back out after taking some deep breaths and opening and closing her hands to bleed out the tension. All she needed was to keep her cool, so she wouldn't ruin the night.

"A book? I don't understand." Serena stood and started toward her, but Rachel put her hand up to stop her.

"You can't put me on a shelf and pick me up when it's convenient to read a page. Look, I get it," she said and laughed, even though her heart was aching. "It was fun, and you're ready to move on, but be honest. Just tell me, and stop all this bullshit. This total radio silence is beneath you. We're not in high school."

"That's not what this was about." Serena stepped closer and took her hand.

"Don't play me, Serena. I may not be as educated as you, but I'm not a fool. You aren't one for long-term anything except Butch, and I'm not going to beg you to go against your nature. Hell, I know some of the women you've been with, and if they couldn't convince you, I'm not going to be able to do it." The real ego crusher was that Rach knew that Serena *had* been ready to settle down, but her true love only had room in her heart for the girl she'd fallen in love with in grammar school. Harry had loved Serena, still did, but she'd never been *in* love with her. Rachel pulled away from Serena and put her hands behind her back when Serena reached for her again.

"I don't want to lose you."

"No, I'm sure that's true. Good old dependable Rachel," she said, just wishing she could get out of this room. "Always waiting when you have time."

"That's not true," Serena said, wincing.

There was no way she was putting up with revisionist history to make Serena feel better. "I'm not going to argue with you, so drop it. No matter what, we'll remain friends, but don't come up with some story now. You've been busy—I get that. I offered to take care of Butch, and you turned me down." This was ridiculous. Serena wasn't even her type, but they did have something in common. They were both waiting for their own version of Harry. "He's your kid, it's your life, and I don't have a place in it. I'm only a stylist, but I can pick up on all the clues."

"You don't understand." Serena turned her back on her and cocked her head back as if fascinated by the ceiling. "What I went through with my ex made me—"

"Stop before I really get angry. Your problem isn't the past, honey—it's honesty," Rach said. "You can lie to yourself all you want, but leave me out of that."

"What's that supposed to mean?" Serena faced her again, and from her expression she'd hit a nerve.

"It means you'd be wearing Harry's ring if she'd asked. The kink in that little fantasy is Harry was already taken, even if my sister wasn't here. There wasn't room for anyone else. If it'd been any other couple, what they shared as kids shouldn't have lasted, and yet both of them were stuck. Neither of them could move forward." Saying it out loud was cathartic, but she didn't get any pleasure from Serena's pained expression. "There isn't room for me or anyone else in your life because you haven't gotten over that Harry turned you down, and you need to be honest about that."

"You're wrong. I love Harry, that's true, but I'm not in love with her. I was at one time, but she's as good at getting her point across as you are." Serena sat back down and put her hands on her stomach as if she was in pain. "I'm sorry for making you think you aren't enough, that you don't fit."

"Your job is important to you, but Desi's show was important to me." She'd given Serena enough credit to realize how far Desi had come and invited her to celebrate that with them. She'd been wrong about that too. "Knowing you can sit there and expect me to believe you couldn't return one phone call is insulting. I'm not waiting any longer, Serena, so go do what makes you happy without guilt." There was no reason to pile on and mention Serena had already done that. Her decisions weren't made with Rachel in mind at all. "Are you ready?" She slipped into her pumps and pointed to the door.

"What can I do to change your mind?" Serena said. "I care about you, and while this week was horrible, I didn't mean to shut you out." Serena stayed seated on the bed, and that's where Rachel was prepared to leave her.

"This isn't the time for this, so let's go." She walked out, smiling when she saw Harry and Desi headed for the stairs. Her sister's gait had become more of a waddle, which made her wonder if she'd soon have more than one little one to spoil. She'd seen the ultrasound, though, so Baby Basantes was just big. That certainly wasn't from their side of the gene pool.

"You okay?" Harry asked putting her free arm around her shoulder.

She was being ridiculous, thinking Harry and her sister didn't want her here. No one could fake love like this. "I'm perfect, and I can't wait to be an aunt." She pressed closer to Harry when Serena stepped out of her room and just stared at them. "Let's get going. I'm starved."

The way Serena looked at her made her hurt. It was as if Serena did care, but she wouldn't allow herself to do anything with her feelings. As much as she wanted Serena, she wasn't going to gamble on what-ifs any longer. She deserved more, and if her sister was any example, waiting for the right person was worth it.

❖

They made it down and heard voices in the den, but they stopped when Butch came running toward them and stopped as if unsure of himself. Desi had noticed the little boy's skittish behavior as she'd started to show. Butch had never said it, but a new baby meant he wouldn't be the center of Harry's world any longer.

"Hey, sweetie." She ran her hand through his hair and glanced at Harry to pick him up. "I've missed you."

Butch kissed her cheek then Harry's, all his hesitancy gone. "Aunt Desi, I missed you. I started school, and I've been staying with Papa and Granny. I'm so happy to see you." Butch rambled as if he had a time limit on getting all the news in his life out. He went from Harry's arms to Rachel's, and he seemed to hold her with all his strength.

"I missed you, sweet boy," Rachel said, not sounding like herself.

The doorbell rang, and Desi wondered if Kenneth was running late, but everyone seemed to already be there. Mona waved Harry off and went to answer the door, and Desi turned her attention back to Butch and his stream of kindergarten information.

Mona came back in, and the expression on her face told Desi something was up.

"Who is it, Mona?" She leaned back against Harry, needing her close and hoping it wasn't about Byron. The only thing she wanted to hear was they'd been caught and were locked up. Two women stepped in behind Mona, and all she could do was stare at the shorter of the two until it felt like her brain seized from the total impossibility of what she was looking at. When she opened her eyes again, she was on the sofa with Harry and Rachel hovering over her, appearing frantic.

"Don't move, and tell me if anything hurts." Harry sounded winded, and the way her hands moved over her didn't make sense.

"What happened?" She started to sit up and thought better of it when Harry stopped her with a hand to her shoulder.

"Honey, no don't."

The tears in Harry's eyes made her chest ache. Her big guy didn't cry often, and she hardly ever appeared scared. Now, though, she appeared terrified.

"You passed out," Harry said, and Desi could tell she was trying to get her emotions in check. "Sorry, I'm probably overreacting."

"Francisco," she said to Harry's father as he took her pulse, "could you excuse us a minute, please?"

"Sure, and I'll come get you when the doctor calls back." Francisco took Rachel's hand, and her sister looked reluctant to go, but she did.

"There are three of them in the house already. How many more do we need?" Desi tried joking to break through Harry's tension.

"What happened?" Harry knelt and took her hand. "I've known you all my life, and I've never seen you faint."

"Those people," she said, remembering the petite woman. "It's so strange, but I saw her and shut down. I'd love to tell you why, but the only thing that I thought before passing out is what I was seeing was impossible. It's just *not* possible."

"What's not?" Harry held her hand against her chest.

"Clyde wasn't the sentimental kind, so there were never many pictures of us as babies or of our mother. She died before I started school, so my memories of her are fuzzy at best. I remember only one picture of her." How many times had she opened the drawer in the hall closet and stared at the picture of the blonde with her big smile, holding her as a baby? Until the day Clyde caught her and snatched it away to rip it to shreds.

"She's dead," he'd screamed before throwing the pieces at her. "*She's dead.*"

"I remember you telling me that. I wish she hadn't died and left you with him." She knew Harry hated Clyde for what he'd done to them, but really for the way he'd hurt Desi. That Clyde had put his hands on her in anger enraged Harry, and there was no outlet for it.

Clyde had died after the cancer had ravaged his body to the point that he appeared weak and small. Desi hadn't visited him in the hospital and hadn't seen the point of planning any service to honor him. He'd had no honor, no compassion, and no love for her or Rachel, so he'd killed anything she felt for him except her hatred. Byron wasn't going to pay to have Clyde buried, so it'd been a pauper's grave for him—it was all he deserved. He was gone, and no one wanted to remember him. All she knew was that he was in the ground at the end of Canal Street and out of her life.

"Once I got to know you, I didn't understand why you and Rachel couldn't come and live with us. I used to ask my mother all the time."

"We wanted that too," Rachel said, coming back in. "Sorry. I didn't want to interrupt you, but you don't often drop like a sack of potatoes, and I was worried about you. Thank God you picked the stud to catch you, or all of us would still be on the ground trying to get you up."

"Is that a joke about my size?"

"As if," Rachel said, stepping behind Harry and placing her hands on Harry's shoulders. "Want to tell us why you look like you've seen a ghost?"

"The woman—the short one, I mean." She glanced between Harry and Rachel before taking a deep breath. "She's an older version of the woman in the picture."

"What picture?" Rachel asked, but Desi saw the recognition in Harry's eyes.

"The one of our mother." She'd told Rachel the story of why the photo didn't exist. Both of them had known better than to ask Clyde anything about her. The subject of their mother was the quickest way to light the fuse of his very violent temper. "Maybe she's our mother's sister, our aunt. If she is, she's years too late."

Francisco walked in and handed Harry the phone. The call had to be Ellie or Sam Casey, her doctors, from Harry's side of the conversation. "Sorry to mess up your movie night, but it'll make me feel better."

"Honey—"

"Don't argue," Harry said. "You fainted, your pressure is a bit low, and your color's off. Humor me and let's get Ellie to take a look at you."

"I'm not saying no, but I want to talk to that woman." She lifted her hand and pressed it to Harry's cheek.

"I don't know if that's such a great idea," Rachel said.

"I don't mean right this second. Could you get her contact information for us? I'm sure you'd like to talk to her as well." There was a buzzing in her head from the anticipation of doing just that. If she could, she'd get up and run back into the other room to confirm what she knew couldn't be true. Their mother was dead. Any fantasy she'd had as a little girl of her coming and saving them from Clyde always died at that very hard truth. Their mother was dead.

"I'll do it if you promise to call me," Rachel said. Her fingers were white on Harry's shoulders. "Let me deal with her, and you go with Harry."

Harry picked her up and cradled her. "I can walk," she said, and Harry shook her head.

"Humoring me, remember?" Harry went through the kitchen to get to the car. She held Harry's hand as they drove to the clinic where most of Harry's private patients went.

She remembered the first time they'd made this trip to see Sam and Ellie. They'd wanted to start trying to get pregnant before her divorce, and it'd taken three cycles for it to work. The joy of sharing this child with Harry had been everything she'd imagined from the time she'd daydreamed about their future together.

Harry was the kind of partner she wanted to have a family with, and they'd been enjoying everything surrounding her pregnancy. They'd decorated the baby's room together, picked furniture, and seeing Harry's face when Ellie had done the first scan was enough to want more children.

"Boy or girl, do you think?" The question was meant to bring Harry's mood up. They'd deliberately not learned the gender, but they enjoyed the speculation. She studied Harry's profile and warmed at Harry's smile. "Which would you prefer?"

"I'm going to love him or her, so it doesn't matter. Though I've dreamed of a little girl with your beautiful green eyes and blond hair, making little bowls with you."

"I doubt you'll get that if your nephews are any indication. Jill is as blond as me, and those guys don't look like her at all." She shifted to open her door when they arrived but stopped when Harry held her back. "Harry, you're not carrying me all that way."

"If everything's fine, I'll let you walk back." Harry came around the car and picked her up, and she put her arms around her neck. The solidness of Harry was something she'd always counted on, and now was no different. She hung on, confident everything would be fine.

"Hey, you two," Sam said, with an alert two-year-old little girl in her arms. Emily was a favorite at the clinic. "Head on back."

"Em, did we mess up your movie night?" she asked as Harry placed her on the exam table.

"Yes, our thirteen hundredth viewing of *Frozen* is a real tragedy, but there's always tomorrow," Ellie said, kissing her daughter's cheek. "Lie back, Desi, so Harry can tell me what happened."

They listened as Harry spoke, but all Desi concentrated on was the baby moving around. The craziness of the night hadn't done anything to calm the hyperactive kid she had a feeling was going to be Harry in every way. She closed her eyes and enjoyed the cadence as the sound of the rapid heartbeat filled the room. Their baby, the start of their family, was the most important thing to concentrate on.

"Everything's fine," Ellie said after a thorough exam. "I'm not thrilled you passed out, but you're okay, and Baby Basante is fabulous." Ellie wrote something down and handed her an appointment card. "Come back in a week, but call if anything else happens. Now is not the time to stay quiet no matter how trivial you think it is."

"Thanks for this, Ellie." She took Harry's arm when she was on her feet. "I'd have waited, but my honey bear worries."

"That's what bears do," Sam said and growled, making Emily laugh.

Desi couldn't wait to see Harry with their baby like this. Rosa and Mona were in the waiting room when they were done, and Ellie answered all their questions. The only problem Desi had now was that she was starving.

"Let's call the restaurant and ask if they'll still take us," Harry said when Desi's stomach rumbled.

"You have the best ideas." The shock of seeing someone she really thought was a ghost was still running around her head. Whoever the woman was who'd shown up at their house looked so much like the picture of her mother that it made her want to run out and find her so she could ask questions. The first one would be *why*. Why leave her and Rachel behind with Clyde? She feared the answer as much as she had Byron all those years.

"Unless you want to order in and talk about what happened." Harry held her hand as they headed to the car.

"Maybe tomorrow I'll be ready for a long conversation, but not right now. I'm sure there's a reasonable explanation, and I want to know what it is, only not tonight." She gladly fell into Harry's arms when she stopped to hug her. "That might make me a coward, but I can't deal with anything else right now."

Chapter Five

Rachel went back to the front room and studied the two women—the two women who were keeping her from going with her sister. The shorter of the two was blond and gave Rachel a clue as to what Desi would look like in twenty or so years. "Now that the drama is over, what can I do for you?"

"I'm not sure where to start," the blonde said, and the other woman took her hand. "I had no idea she was pregnant." Her voice seemed to fade to nothing. "All I wanted was to explain."

"I don't have time to figure out what your game is, but think before you say anything to make this night any worse. You hurt my sister, and I'll hurt you back until you bleed if you think of doing it again."

"You're Rachel?" The woman's smile was back but now there were tears in her eyes. "I'm so sorry."

The defeat sounded so familiar. She'd heard it for years from Desi as she gave up, one slow and agonizing day at a time. It was scary sometimes how close Desi had been to finally giving in and letting go. As traumatic as the day had been, and how worried she was about Desi, she couldn't turn her back on this woman. And if what Desi said was true…

Throwing good things into the universe got you good things back. She'd believed that all her life, but still. Sometimes the universe took a long-ass time to return all those good things, but it was no reason to change how she lived her life. If their mother was alive, that would be what she'd wished for since she had the sense to wish. The flip side was, if it was true, the universe was a true bitch since the news was years too late.

"What do you have to be sorry about?" Part of Rachel wanted to shrug off Serena's hand from her shoulders, but she was oddly grateful for the touch.

"I'd love to talk to both of you at the same time," the woman said. "You're both so beautiful."

All words out of this woman's mouth were strange, and she was having a hard time getting over how much she looked like Desi. "Like I said, I'm Rachel, and this is my friend Serena. Who are you, and why are you here?"

"Rach, maybe this is enough for tonight." Serena squeezed her shoulders and stepped closer. "Let's go check on Desi."

"Not yet." She shrugged Serena off because she needed to face this, whatever this was, alone. Her gut told her that whatever this woman's story was, it would change something fundamentally important. Chaos wasn't always the harbinger of horrible things. "Who *are* you?"

"I'm...June Fontaine." Tears started sliding down the woman's cheeks.

It was like a bomb going off in her stomach. Desi's reaction now seemed reasonable. This was the biggest fucking joke anyone had ever pulled, and it made her angry. "That's impossible, and it's evil to be that cruel. I can't even imagine why you'd say something like that, or who put you up to it." She pointed, coming close to poking the woman in the face. "You'd better pray my sister's okay. If something happened to her or the baby, Harry will make you pay."

"We'll be at the Piquant," the other woman said. She handed Rachel a card and led June Fontaine, sobbing, to the door. "This isn't a joke. If you have any compassion, you'll give her five minutes to explain. She's waited a lifetime."

Rachel stared as they left, then looked at the card the woman handed her. The heavy linen paper with raised lettering had the names *Dr. Bobbie and June Margolis* along with their contact information. All her life she'd been quick to anger, especially if it was in defense of those she loved. She'd stood up to Byron, as well as for her friends through the years, but she'd done it gladly because she couldn't stand the injustice some people were subjected to. It was a job she'd gladly handed over to Harry when she was sure she still loved Desi.

The sight of June Fontaine, though, had gutted her, and there would be no easy answers June could give that'd unravel the fury in her chest. Yes, June had plenty to answer for, but she wasn't sure she wanted to hear it. If this woman really was their mother, she was years too late to make everything okay.

❖

Byron was starting to get cold, and his hands and feet were numb, but he willed himself to stay at Tyrell's back. All he could make out in the distance was more of the same. It was water, cypress trees, and mud. That shit had to end eventually, and the only good thing about the cold was it seemed to have thinned the reptile population.

"I'm hungry," Mike said. His brother hadn't stopped complaining and held on to their father, assuring he kept up.

"Stop thinking about it. We're all hungry, but we gotta get outta here." It was starting to lighten, which only served to highlight the clouds that completely blanketed the sky. The dark matched his mood, and he shivered as the temperatures steadily dropped. "You think we have a lot to go?" he asked Tyrell.

"Rumor is, there's fifteen miles of swamp, but we're circling it instead of going straight." Tyrell had a soft voice for such a big dude.

"Why the hell we did that?" one of the others asked.

"That's where they'll probably be looking for us, but they gonna fan out eventually, so we keep moving. You got a better plan, go 'head. I ain't keeping you here."

"Just keep walking, and let's hope we all last that long," the guy said.

They kept slogging single file in silence. It was as if they could all sense the freedom they were headed to and didn't want to fuck it up. There was a clearing up ahead, with a shack, and Tyrell stopped and put his hand up. The shack had a generator humming and a boat with a push pole, a common kind of transportation used in the swamps. Tyrell pointed at them to stay put. He ducked down until all Byron could see was the top of Tyrell's bald head.

It was obvious there was someone inside, but no one came out as Tyrell untied the boat and started back to the thicker tree line. They all climbed in, glad for the chance to sit as Tyrell stood and used the long pole to move them forward. The rain started, and it shrouded everything around them in its intensity. It was freezing, but the storm was also a way to stay hidden from the cops on their ass.

"What you in for, Tyrell?" another guy asked.

No one had ever asked Byron that from the time he'd been sent to that hellhole, and it was an unwritten rule you didn't ask anyone else either. Eventually most of the guys gave it up, and that's when you could ask questions. The only ones who had problems worse than what he'd faced were the child molesters, but Tyrell didn't strike him as one of those.

"I beat an asshole to death."

"What the hell for?" Big Byron asked.

Byron glanced at Mike and let the conversation go on since he wasn't going to help his father out of a jam caused by his big mouth. Tyrell stared at Big Byron but didn't answer his question. It was obviously as dead a subject as the man he'd beaten.

The boat made much better time than they'd been making on foot, and they did their best to bail as the rain fell. When they jerked to a stop, it almost didn't seem real, but he kept up with Tyrell as he walked slowly up the levee in a crouched position. It was only a shell road at the top, then a river. Where they'd go from here was a mystery, but their one chance was still with Tyrell.

"We wait until dark," Tyrell said, heading back to the swamp. He pulled the boat and left it under the lone tree on the batture.

"Then what?" he asked, sitting next to Tyrell.

"You ask a lot of questions, boy. They gonna have the roads around here locked up tight, so we need to go down the Mississippi for the night and see where we end up. That's the only shot we got."

They spent the day huddled under the trees, out of sight of the road. Most slept, but Byron couldn't. He was practically counting down until they could move again.

They waited an hour after sunset before running across the road and down the levee. Tyrell did his best to keep them close to the shore in case of helicopters, and after what seemed like hours he beached them and headed to the other side of the levee.

The area was lined with pine trees, so they started walking again. The rain was a steady downpour, but it would hopefully throw off the dogs if the cops let them loose in the area. Tyrell slid down a pine tree as if finally feeling the exhaustion of their second day of running and stared at the cluster of houses up ahead. Only one of them had a car out front with no one outside. Though no one would be out in weather like this.

"Stay here and I'll be back. Follow me and I'll kill you." The threat was as chilling as the weather, and they watched Tyrell strip off his shirt, leaving only the white undershirt. He went around the back to the first house and peered through the windows.

Byron wasn't sure what he was doing, but he disappeared inside and came out in different clothes. The pants were too short and the jacket didn't zip, but he looked like a guy ready to go out hunting, in full camouflage.

"Let's go," Tyrell said. He walked back into the trees and seemed to know where he was going.

It didn't take long for them to reach another road, but this one had steady traffic and a few businesses. There was no more talking until the sun set again, and Tyrell stood as if waiting for something. A delivery truck with a produce company logo painted on the side pulled off the main drag onto a dirt access road with *No Trespassing* posted on it. The driver got out and hugged Tyrell before handing him a bag.

"Find something that fits and leave all your clothes here. If you coming with me, get in the back when you done." Tyrell changed and was the first one in. "After this, you all on your own."

Byron's body felt as if there wasn't a warm spot on it as he stripped off the last of Angola, and he tried to keep his teeth from chattering when he dropped the last of his wet things. The dry clothes and sweatshirt felt almost as good as the thought of seeing Desi again. It wouldn't be long now.

❖

The Velvet Cactus restaurant was one of Desi's favorite date night destinations, and she was starving by the time they sat down. Rachel sat next to her and held her hand tightly. By silent assent they didn't bring up what had happened, knowing there was time enough later. Harry had her hand on her thigh as if she was reassuring herself Desi was fine.

"Bring us three of the appetizer platters, a beer for me, a water for my girl, and whatever everyone else wants," Harry said.

They ordered after the drinks came, and she was glad the conversation centered on their small wedding and not what had happened. This time around, marriage sounded blissful. She couldn't wait to tie herself to Harry and the life they were building together. If she had to dwell on something, that was a good subject.

"It's a small affair," Rosa said, "so it only took me and Rachel an afternoon but I think everything is done, so we can relax for the rest of the week."

"Thank you, and with any luck I'll be able to make it through my vows without having to go to the bathroom. Unlike now." She laughed as she stood with her hand on Harry's shoulder to keep her steady and to keep Harry in her seat. "I'll be right back." Harry glanced up at her, and Desi knew Harry was about to stand to go with her, so she shook her head and kissed Harry before Rachel led her off. "I saw Serena coming out of your room earlier."

"Babe, we have plenty to talk about before we even get to that subject. Serena's the person everyone should use as an example when it comes to the whole having-your-cake thing." Rachel took the stall next to hers, and the door slamming wasn't a good sign.

"You've been upset for days, and it's not all Serena." When they were both out of their stalls, Desi put her finger up when it was apparent Rachel was going to protest her statement. "When we get home, be prepared to talk. No more excuses." They washed their hands side by side, and Rachel finally smiled.

She put her hand on the bend of Rachel's elbow and headed back, walking through the restaurant dining room. It was hard not to notice the woman at the bar was staring intently at something. Desi's curiosity made her follow her line of sight since the woman's expression was unreadable.

"Ah," she said softly when she found Harry.

This had happened more than once, and as usual, she was gripped by jealousy that seemed to slither through her guts and squeeze the reason right out of her. The woman in the beautiful dress with the gorgeous face and spectacular figure was openly staring at Harry. Her Harry, who was oblivious to the attention as she said something to make Butch laugh as he sat in Harry's lap.

"Can I get you anything?" the bartender asked absently when she and Rachel stopped at the bar.

"A margarita on the rocks for my sister, and a glass of water with lemon for me, please." Her voice broke the woman's trance, and she took a sip of the drink in front of her. "Are you okay?"

The woman nodded. "Sorry. I saw a ghost from my past." She gave Harry another long look.

"Is that good or bad?" She squeezed the lemon in her water and ignored Rachel's chuckles.

"A little of both, I guess." The woman glanced at her watch and sighed. "It didn't take me long to figure some people are a bit too self-absorbed to see a good thing and hold on to it. Actually, that's not totally true. She was nice about it, but after a couple of weeks she stopped calling. Wasn't meant to be, even if *I* thought it was a good idea." The woman laughed. "Listen to me dumping all that on you."

Desi had run into a few of Harry's exes when she was out with Tony. He'd always explained most were dates to high-profile functions and nothing more. None of them—well, with the exception of Serena—was blond, and Tony had the simple explanation for that as well. He'd told her that if Harry couldn't have her and couldn't replace her, she didn't want to add to the torment. The funniest part of all these encounters was the blatant envy reflected back at her when Tony introduced her. Harry was hers, and that wouldn't change.

"No problem, and I can't blame you. Harry is someone I don't mind staring at, and I'm glad she thought *I* was a good idea." She left her glass and walked back to the table. Harry stood and met her halfway with an easy smile and beautiful eyes. *Petty* wasn't something she did often, but it never hurt to stake her claim.

"I thought you got lost or you ditched me." Harry sounded much more relaxed, and she almost wanted to gloat at how Harry held her before lowering her head and kissing her.

"As if." She stepped closer to Harry and placed her hands on her chest. She loved that citrus scent that was all Harry.

"Friend of yours?" Harry tilted her head in the woman's direction.

"No, no one important." She held Harry's hand, feeling more beautiful than she had in months. It wasn't that Harry wasn't great about remembering who she'd dated, but Harry said she'd forgotten every one of them once Desi had come back into her life.

They ate and laughed until Harry drove them home. Harry kissed her at every red light, and thankfully no one stopped them as they went up to their bedroom. The way Harry touched her, made love to her, gave her a sense of place. She belonged to and with Harry, and the feeling was mutual. The level of Harry's devotion was the cornerstone of her life.

"God, you make me feel so good." She turned on her side and smiled when Harry pressed against her back. "You make me feel sexy when I'm anything but."

"You're crazy if you think you're not sexy. Your breasts alone are enough to make me not think about anything else." Harry kissed her shoulder as she pressed her hand to her midsection, getting the baby to kick.

"Ah, don't get use—" She closed her eyes when Harry's phone rang. Midnight calls were never good. "Answer it, honey. They'll just keep calling."

"Basantes." Harry listened as Desi got up to use the bathroom and was already off the phone when she returned. "I have to go to the school. We'll talk about this when I get back, but I think once the semester is over, I want to resign my position with the medical school."

"Why?" She knew Harry loved the work.

"I'll still do some cases there as a consultant, but I want to be home more. The only reason I took the post in the first place was to keep my mind off my crappy social life." Harry put the shirt she'd thrown on the floor back on and zipped up her pants. "Now, I want to concentrate on other things that are way more important."

"Yeah? What's that?"

"In a few days I'm going to marry the girl I've loved all my life, and I must've done something right to have gotten her back. A few weeks after that we're going to have a beautiful baby, so it's someone else's turn to take all these late-night calls." Harry kissed her before helping her back to bed. "I've enjoyed my time doing that, but my private practice will keep me busy enough."

"Are you sure? I know you complain, but you love your students."

"I *love* you, and I'm sure they'll do fine without me." Harry pulled the covers up and went to put her shoes on. "Right now, let me go talk someone through a surgery they don't really need me for. I won't be scrubbing in." Harry stepped out of the closet and kissed her one more time.

"I love you. Be careful." She touched Harry's face and smiled. "I need my backrest if I want to sleep."

"I'll be as quick as I can." Harry blew her a kiss before closing the door softly behind herself.

Desi closed her eyes, listening to the house creak around her as she finally allowed herself to think about the woman from earlier and the fact that the sight of her made her faint. The impossibility of it made her want to shut down again. She took some deep breaths and ran her hand in a circle, trying to calm the baby. Hopefully, the late-night activity that was the norm was only a womb thing. "Once you get here, you have to sleep."

"Are you awake?" Rachel whispered from the door.

"Come in." She opened her eyes and held her hand up. After they'd moved in with Harry, they'd been able to go back to their late-night talks when Harry had to go out. They'd done it a lot when they were children and she still missed all the good times with Rachel without a guillotine of fear hanging over her.

"Why'd you pass out?" Rachel, as always, cut right to the center. "You already said, but I want to hear you say it again."

"That woman—she looked like an older version of that picture I found. Remember I told you Clyde ripped it up when he caught me with it? That was a long time ago, so I have to take into account that I was young, and my memory might be trying to make up a scenario that isn't there at all."

"She said her name is June Fontaine," Rachel said. "Really, it's June Margolis, but Fontaine must've been her maiden name. No matter what it is, that can't be right." Rachel held her hand and sounded as if she was unsure of herself. "Can it?"

"June Fontaine Thompson was our mother. If she's not dead, then where the hell has she been all this time?" What kind of mother left her children with Clyde?

"She left Clyde—totally get that. Leaving us behind, that I'm never going to understand, much less forgive. She had to have had some idea of what he was like." Rachel sounded angry, raw emotion in her tone. Desi couldn't blame her at all, considering that's how she felt too.

"Why now? Why come back now?" Desi wasn't expecting an answer. The fantasy of growing up with a mom who loved them was one she had often. Rosa Basantes was as close as she and Rachel had gotten growing up, and they'd been lucky she'd been so kind not only then, but now. They weren't really a good fit in the Basantes family, but Rosa hadn't ever cared about all that. Gaining Mona's love as well had given them a sense of place in the family they'd been a part of for so long.

"Should we care?" Rachel pressed against her and sighed. "I don't remember her, and I didn't hate her when I thought she was dead. That might change now."

"Where'd she go after she left? Did she say?"

"I didn't really give her a chance to talk, to be honest, and she apologized. She wants to talk to us, together I mean, so she's staying in town. If she's really our mother, we all have something in common. Whoever Bobbie Margolis is to her, she's as protective of June as Harry is with you. What do you want to do?" Rachel sounded sleepy but didn't seem ready to let this go. "I'll go along with whatever you want, but I don't want anything to happen to you. You don't need to be stressed out."

"I want to talk to her. At least we'll know one way or the other." She scooted down to get more comfortable. "Remember who it was she ran from. Clyde wasn't anyone who should've ever had children or a wife."

"You're too forgiving sometimes."

She kissed Rachel's forehead and took a deep breath. "I'm not saying whether I'll forgive her or not. I just want to know what happened. Clyde took more than sixteen years from me by forcing me into something I didn't want—he stole our childhood as well. It didn't take a genius to know he never really wanted us. If she's our mother, then she's got plenty to answer for."

"You want me to call her?" Rachel didn't sound eager.

"I want Harry here with us, so wait until I know for sure she's not on call." She was going to need Harry to lean on. They both would.

Chapter Six

H arry!" Rachel's voice screamed from Harry's phone.

The panic made Harry stop and shiver like she'd been doused in cold water. She was between the hospital and the parking garage after observing the surgery she'd been called in for, and all she wanted was to go back to bed with Desi. "What's wrong?" She couldn't get her voice above a whisper.

"We're leaving for the hospital with Desi. She woke up with contractions, and she's freaking out."

Harry could hear Desi moaning, and she started running. Damn this day and all the shit that'd gone wrong. If stress had caused this, she was going to hunt their mystery guest down and arrange her own trip to the emergency room. "I'll meet you there. Take care of her. Make sure you take my father in case you need help."

She didn't remember the trip to the hospital, and one of the nurses pointed to the right room the moment she stepped inside. Desi started crying when she saw her. "I'm so sorry, Harry." She held her stomach and gritted her teeth. Rachel was wincing and seemed relieved to see her.

"Breathe, baby." Harry put her hand over Desi's and turned to the nurse. "Get either Ellie or Sam Casey here now."

"They've been paged, Dr. Basantes, and Sam is finishing up a case and will be here soon." The nurse's tone wasn't exactly cordial. "You might not remember working with me, but I followed procedure."

Harry didn't have time for attitude and glanced down at the woman's name tag. *Mindy Lyons*—it took her a long stretch to remember exactly who she was. This was one of the nurses the day they'd brought Desi to her private room, only she'd been more interested in getting

Harry to call her than making Desi comfortable. "Listen," Harry said, but another contraction started, and she turned to deal with Desi.

It passed and Desi fell back into her pillow. "I did something wrong, didn't I?"

"Honey, you need to take some deep breaths and try to calm down. I know that's the most ridiculous thing to tell you, but this isn't your fault." Harry stood behind Rachel and kissed the top of her head. She knew Rachel was probably as torn up about this as Desi. "Both of you breathe for me. I promise it's going to be okay."

"I just want this so bad—I want our baby." Desi was getting more upset, so Harry reached over Rachel and placed her finger over Desi's lips.

"Listen to me." She let go of Rachel and got on the bed with Desi so she could put her arms around her. "Everything is fine. Babies are temperamental little people, and they have their own timing. You didn't do anything wrong. Our baby is just ready to be out in the world."

Desi exhaled against her chest and didn't seem as tense when she held her closer. "Are you sure?" Desi looked at her with a silent plea to make it okay.

"I'm positive."

"Do you want me to go?" Rachel asked.

"Stay," Harry said, knowing Desi would feel better with her sister close by.

The nurse came back in and frowned when she saw where Harry was, but she kept her mouth shut. Harry moved for a minute as Mindy set up the equipment to monitor the baby's heart rate. Once she was gone, Harry turned the volume up and smiled as she got back on the bed.

"Listen to our little one chug away," she said and smiled. "You've done everything right—you have to believe that."

The cadence was almost like a tranquilizer to Desi. She closed her eyes and held Harry's hand as if enjoying the sound. "I can't wait, love."

"Me too," she said as Sam walked in.

"Hey," Sam said as she closed the door and headed for the sink to wash her hands. "I know you two love me, but our date isn't for another four weeks or so." Sam was in scrubs and appeared tired. "We want this kid to sit tight a little longer. We already know Harry's half-baked, and look how that turned out. Let's take a look."

Harry wanted to kiss Sam for making Desi laugh.

Sam did a thorough exam and gave them good news—Braxton-Hicks contractions. Baby Basantes wasn't going anywhere. "Our only decision now is whether to admit you for the night for observation, or to send you home with Harry."

"What do you think?" Desi asked her. Whatever Sam had ordered pushed into the IV had gotten Desi to relax.

"We're not that far away, so how about we go home, and Sam can leave orders to have you brought right to a room if anything else comes up." She held Desi's hand and smiled. "You'll be more comfortable in our own bed. It's been over twenty minutes since your last contraction, so you might be done practicing for the night."

"That's a good way of putting it, and you have our cell numbers. Don't be afraid to use them. It's what I'm shamelessly planning to do when my kid breaks something." Sam kissed Desi and Rachel on their cheeks and hugged Harry. "I'll put you down for an appointment tomorrow, so I'll see you at the office."

"Thanks, buddy." They had to wait a half an hour before the nurse came with the wheelchair and their discharge papers.

Desi smiled at the group in the waiting room as Harry sent everyone back home and to bed. The worry still in Rachel's expression when they got home made Harry point to the other side of the bed, not having a heart to tell her to leave. She was exhausted but she held Desi and kissed the top of her head.

"You two want to tell me what's going on?" Harry asked. Despite exhaustion no one was sleeping.

"The woman who came here—" Desi started.

"She's our mother," Rachel said.

Harry thought she'd misheard. "I know you said she looks like the woman in the photo, and there's a family resemblance, but how is it possible? Your mother's deceased."

"That's what Clyde told us. The only one of us who would've had any memory of her is Desi, but she was too young to remember exactly what happened."

"Baby," Harry said, tightening her hold. "Did you recognize her?"

"Not from any memory of her. She just looks like an older version of that picture, and strangely like me. Clyde told us she was dead, and that was the end of that discussion. He never said how she died. His reaction if we asked about her was always anger, and I didn't know why." Desi only ever sounded this haunted when she spoke of her years with Byron. "Rachel and I talked about it, and we don't understand where she could've been all this time."

"What do you want to do?" Harry placed her hand on Rachel's shoulder. "I'll support you no matter what, but it should be something you both want."

"I want an explanation," Rachel said, sounding just as upset.

"We both do," Desi said. "We want to talk to her, but I want you there."

Harry didn't want another emergency that night. "Let's get some sleep, and we'll come up with a plan in the morning."

The truck stopped, and Tyrell placed his finger to his lips. Byron recognized the sound of someone getting ready to pump gas. Given how long they'd been riding, he figured they were almost back in New Orleans. His first stop would be the house he'd shared with Desi to find the money he'd stashed in the wall of the closet—he'd seen it in a movie once. It'd be enough to get him out of the city once he finished what he had to do.

They were back on the road, and the sound of the radio made him smile as he closed his eyes. He wasn't comfortable, but he wasn't about to complain. It was a hell of a lot better than his cell or the gator-filled swamp. The farther they got from Angola, the closer he was to getting the hell away from his brother and father. The only way he'd stay out for good was on his own. He leaned back and tried to find a comfortable spot.

The sudden quiet and lack of movement disoriented him, and he jerked awake, unsure how long he'd slept. He woke his father. Byron was instantly on edge as to what came next. There was no way to figure out where they were or what the hell Tyrell had in mind since it was quiet outside except for the ticking of the cooling engine. He flinched when the door rolled up and raised his hands when the young punk outside pointed a gun at him and the others.

"This is where we get off," Tyrell said. He jumped down and headed for an Escalade with tinted windows. "Get walking."

"Where the fuck are we?" His shout stopped Tyrell. "You can't leave us in the middle of nowhere."

"You're lucky I brought you this far." Tyrell smiled at him, and the almost-smirk made Byron want to smash him in the face. "Do whatever the fuck you want, but the truck's stolen, so my advice is to walk."

"Where are we?" It was still dark, and all he could make out were the pine trees lining both sides of the road. He was hungry, tired, and—he'd never admit it—scared as well. Fear of his father, his future, and his failures had ruled his life up to now, and he was damn tired of it.

"Mississippi. They'll be looking for us in New Orleans. I did you a favor, so take off and stay out of the city." Tyrell opened the back door of the SUV and glanced back.

"I need to get back," Byron said. "I'll leave on my own time once I take care of business. That ain't up to you."

"What business you got?" Tyrell laughed and made him angrier.

Byron was tired of people laughing at him and treating him like a punk. His father had done it all his life, and he'd taken the abuse because he thought it was his duty. There were plenty of guys like Tyrell, though, who looked at him and saw nothing but a dumbass, willing to take whatever they decided to dish out.

His one chance at changing that dynamic was with Desi. He'd wanted her since high school and had willingly agreed to marry her. No one had told him the little bitch was damaged goods. Every day was a struggle of teaching her how to act, but no matter what he did, he'd never made her want him. Loving him was a stretch he couldn't make either.

He didn't understand why Desi had ever agreed to marry him in the first place. If she was a damn pervert, she should've left him alone. All of it, though, came down to his father and that fucker Clyde. His father had seen the wedding as a way for him to get out of the trouble he was facing with some other bitch, and he'd also get Byron out of his house. His mistake was allowing Rachel to live with them. That slut was like Tyrell and all the rest.

"The people who put me in that place need to pay. It's not like I'm going to fuck your shit up."

"You tried to kill your wife, big man." Tyrell moved toward him, and he stepped back. "If you want it that bad, figure it out, but I ain't helping you." Tyrell cocked his head to the side as if trying to decide what to do next. "What I should do is kill your ass right here. It was an asshole like you that fucked up my sister, so I should've left your asses out there to rot. The three of you are fucked in the head."

"Why are you going back? That's the first place those bastards are gonna go looking for you." If this guy left them there, he'd never make it back to the city.

"That ain't your business, so start walking before my friend's finger gets twitchy on that trigger. You're going to do what you're going to do, but you made it this far. Let that shit go. You try to follow us and I'm going to fuck you up so bad, you're going to wish for Angola."

"Look," Byron said, "I'll do whatever you want, but I need to get back." He ran his hand through his hair, grimacing at the oily, dirty feeling of it.

"I could give a good fuck what you do from here on out. You begging makes me regret not killing you and doing your old lady a favor." Tyrell moved toward him again, and getting out of his way made him trip over a branch and fall on his ass. "I'm telling you to head east. You go back and I find out, you gonna pray for those alligators. You understand me? I know you're not too bright, so don't make me say it again."

Byron nodded and clenched his fists when he heard the others laughing at him. Tyrell got into the car, and they watched the taillights disappear. Now all they had to do was figure out where they were and how to move without getting caught.

His father glared at him, and he didn't have to say a word to know the disgust he felt toward him. "Let's see if there's any gas left in this thing." The inside of the truck was clean, and the little fucker who'd come for Tyrell had taken the keys. "Fan out and see if you find the keys."

The guys spread out, but his father and Mike didn't take the bait and stayed close to him as he reached under the steering wheel and hotwired the damn truck into starting. There was shouting behind them as he gunned it, hoping there was a way off this road without having to turn around and go through the guys they'd left behind. He wasn't about to travel with a bunch of escapees begging to get caught. Tyrell was right. It was time to split up.

"Where we going?" Mike asked. "I think Tyrell had a point. We need to keep heading east or north and find some kind of cash job on the Gulf Coast."

"I thought you only had a few years left on your sentence and wanted to go back?" He often wondered if he and Mike were even related. They looked nothing alike, and Mike was afraid of his fucking shadow.

"You screwed that up for me like you screwed everything else up with your big ideas. I know you've been dreaming of going back and facing Desi and that woman again, but you're only going to get fucked up like you did last time."

"Sit there and keep your damn mouth shut." He drove until he saw a small farm to the left. It was dark, but it was still the middle of the night, so that didn't mean anything. He cut the engine and got out. "Wait here and I'll be back."

"Try not to get the law on us again," his father said.

He walked around the side of the property, not hearing any animal sounds coming from the small barn, and the grass in the yard was high and unkempt. There were no signs of life in any of the windows he looked through, so he broke one out with a rock and ran off. He waited, but nothing happened, so he climbed in through the broken window.

There was no electricity or running water but all the furniture was still there, so he went out and motioned for Mike and his father to come inside. "Take a look around and see if there's another car, and I'll find us something to wear."

It took them two hours to get the ancient truck in the barn to turn over. He wanted to be out of this town before the sun rose and anyone noticed the truck they'd stolen was missing. There'd been forty dollars in small bills in the house, and it'd have to be enough to make it back.

The road back the way they came was clear, and he wondered where the guys had gone. They'd have to ditch the truck he was driving if the cops caught the rest of the escapees and found the produce truck they'd hid in the barn. All he needed was a little luck before he disappeared forever, but he wouldn't be at peace until Desi, Rachel, and Basantes were in the ground.

He dreamed of his new life as he drove. He'd find a girl who loved him, and they'd have a baby. It's what he'd wanted with Desi, but she couldn't even get that right. It was just one more thing in a long line of them that he blamed her for. His life had been fine before Desi and her fucked-up family got tangled up in it. Maybe leaving for Florida wasn't a bad idea, but pride kept him from turning around.

There'd be a fresh start, but not before the past was put to rest.

CHAPTER SEVEN

Rachel opened her eyes and saw Harry was gone, but Desi was still sleeping. She moved carefully, not wanting to wake her sister after last night. The scare had taken a toll on all of them, but Rachel had a feeling it was Harry who'd been the worst off. Harry's expression when she'd walked into that room was one she'd never forget even if she'd tried to shield her sister from it.

The shower came on, which explained Harry's absence, and she left to give her some time with Desi when she woke up. It was a blessing Harry understood her fears when it came to Desi and her need to be close. Byron would've rather castrated himself than let her stay last night if this had happened during their marriage.

She went back to her room and lay down, wanting to have a few minutes to think as she stared at the business card with those names on it. This was the last thing she would've ever thought could happen. "Shit." The knowing was something she desperately wanted, but she had to also think of Desi.

Growing up, she'd only ever had Desi. From her first memory it had been Desi who'd tended to her, taught her how to handle Clyde, shielded her from him, and she'd been the only mother figure in her life. Rosa had been wonderful, but it was Desi she'd run to when she needed comfort, and her sister had never failed to give it. That had been their reality because their mother was dead. Nothing was as permanent as that.

"Hey," Harry said from the door.

"Good morning. Desi still sleeping?" She waved Harry in and moved so she could sit on the side of the bed.

"Yes, and I wanted to talk to you before she wakes up." Harry accepted the card from her and shook her head. "What do you think this is about? If she's really your mother, then of course I want you both to meet with her, but I don't want a repeat of yesterday. If we lose our baby, Desi will never get over it, and neither will I."

"I was just thinking that before you got here. Not that I compare you to Byron often, but I can't imagine her being pregnant with that nutjob."

"Why in the world would you do that?" Harry laughed, a small victory. Last night Harry had smiled for Desi, but Rachel could tell she was worried.

"I see how you are with her, and it's not because of some obligation you took on but didn't really want. She dreamed of you for so long, and she'd convinced herself you'd hate her if she ever got to see you again." She placed her hand on Harry's forearm and squeezed. "You make her so happy, and I love seeing that. He only ever treated her like crap, and he wouldn't have cared for her like you did last night. Hell, we probably would've been at the hospital because of something he'd done to her."

"The years we were apart were hard," Harry said, "and I never did learn to be without her. That's kind of pathetic when you think we were in high school when she disappeared, but what happened—at least what I thought had happened—broke something in me." Harry took a deep breath and held it. "When she told me everything, I was so ashamed of myself."

"You don't have to be, and you're anything but pathetic. Desi has the life she's always wanted, and you love her despite the scars, both mental and physical. And to answer your question"—she sat up and pressed her back to the headboard—"the way I see it, the dominoes that fell and landed on us with the force of an avalanche started not with Clyde or Byron but with the death of our mother."

Harry nodded. "She wasn't there to protect you, but she was dead so she couldn't help it. Only she was standing in our house yesterday, and it was a shock."

"I'm not sure how much Desi told you about Clyde, but he was a horrible father as well as a horrible person. He used his hands only sparingly when we were growing up, and not because he was mellower back then, but because he didn't care. He dropped us at his mother's, and she wasn't bashful when it came to hitting. We spent our days with her until Desi was old enough to take care of me, and then you came along."

Harry nodded. "You know I would've done anything to change all that, right?"

Rach smiled, but she was so cold inside. "I know that, honey. When it came to Clyde, it changed later on—the hitting, I mean. When we were kids, it was mostly verbal." She turned to the window when she heard it start to rain again. Stuff like this was easier to get out when she didn't have to look someone in the eye. "It's like he was punishing us for something we had no clue about. We were convenient punching bags."

"You and Desi are remarkable people for surviving that, and I'm only sorry that you didn't tell me or my parents. I should've figured it out." Harry was always so quick to take blame.

"We were embarrassed and didn't want to mess up the small bit of normalcy and happiness we had. Trust me, you made a difference, and the rest wasn't your responsibility. You were, and still are, wonderful." She reached for Harry's hand and loved the smoothness of Harry's skin. Harry was everything she thought of when it came to strength, loyalty, and love.

"Do you think it's a good idea to talk to June Fontaine? To see her again, I mean."

"I think I want her to answer for a lot of things, and I also think Desi needs to hear what she has to say." She nodded, glad Harry understood the magnitude of the situation. "Last night was a shock. I was in that same boat when I looked at her and saw an older Desi. It's out in the open now, so I doubt Desi's going to want to wait until the baby comes."

"This weekend we're getting married, and after that, well, the initial shock is done, so a conversation can't hurt." Harry stood and held her hand out. "How about some coffee?"

"I'd love some." She put her hand in the bend of Harry's elbow on the way down the stairs and couldn't help the small dose of jealousy that ran through her heart. Desi deserved everything Harry had brought into her life, but damn. Why the hell wasn't there another one just like her who was willing to fall in love with her?

"You want to talk about it?" Harry asked.

"I thought we just did." She wanted to stall, not ready to talk about the stupidity of her broken heart.

Harry laughed gently. "You're good at evasion when you set your mind to it. You know exactly who and what I'm talking about."

She stood on her toes once they reached the quiet kitchen and kissed Harry's cheek. "I do know who and what you're talking about, and while there's nothing I love better than talking to you, I'm not sure about spilling my guts when it's someone you dated."

"Can I be honest?" Harry prepared the coffee maker and also put on the teakettle.

"That's your usual way of going about things, so sure." She worked with Harry to get everything they'd need, and the tea meant they were headed back upstairs.

"When you started dating Serena, I thought it was a bad idea." Harry put her hands up when Rachel frowned. "It has nothing to do with you, sweetheart, but everything to do with her. I've known you since you were in kindergarten, and I watched you grow up. There isn't anything in the world I wouldn't do for you, but I draw the line at choosing who you spend time with."

"Then why'd you think it was a bad idea?" When you considered careers, education, and social standing, she and Serena didn't make much sense. She just didn't think Harry would bring up the fact that they were polar opposites so blatantly.

"Like I said, we might have had that long break, but I've thought of you as my family for most of my life. When you love someone like that, you want what's best for them, and Serena isn't the settling-down kind. She isn't what's best for you." Harry hugged her when she noticed Rachel's hand shaking. "I'm in love with Desi, and I want the same thing for you. I want you to be in love with someone who understands how spectacular you are and is willing to show you. Don't ever settle."

"Thanks, and I want that too, but I think you're right. She totally ghosted me this week, and even before that it wasn't that great. Now she's sorry, and I'm supposed to forget and forgive her ignoring me and say it's okay." She enjoyed being in Harry's arms because of the security it gave her. In a strange way, Harry had been almost like her second parent.

"That's not okay, and you'll survive it if you decide to move on, but maybe you should hear her out. Like I said, I thought it was a bad idea, yet there's always an exception to every rule." The coffee finished brewing, but Harry didn't let her go. "When I told Desi what I thought about this situation, she thought it was because Serena is my friend." Rachel leaned back so she could see Harry's face. "That's not it at all. For once I think she *is* ready for something more, and I believe it's also scaring the hell out of her."

"Come on, Harry, she can have any woman—or man, for that

matter—she wants." It was nice to be convinced. Thinking that Serena was frightened of a relationship with her, though, would take a Mount Everest climb of convincing.

"Sometimes it takes someone completely different than you to make you get out of your head and start thinking with your heart." Harry squeezed her before pouring their coffee and preparing Desi's decaf tea. "With Desi, it was a gradual thing. You don't fall in love with the woman you're going to spend your life with in grammar school, but I think I did. The way I felt about her kind of programmed me for what my life was supposed to be. We'd get married, have children, and share this life. Does that make sense?"

"Totally, but that's you, Harry, not necessarily Serena."

Harry nodded and started back up the stairs. "I can't prove it, but the same thing has happened to Serena, only later on in life. She's used to dating people who are career oriented, and not that you aren't, but you two are like me and Desi. Serena's work, like mine, is more analytical. Maybe that's the wrong word." Harry shook her head on the landing and seemed pensive. "What I mean is there's only so many variants of doing what Serena and I do even if we have two very different careers."

"Don't worry, I understand." She started the rest of the way up.

"I don't know about Serena, but my job is stressful at times. The best parts of my days now aren't fixing what's wrong with people but talking to Desi at the end of all those days. That artistic, carefree job she's chosen for herself makes me as happy as it does her." Harry smiled. "Probably more so because I love listening to her telling me about it. People might have certain perceptions of who I'm supposed to be with, but the last thing I want is someone just like me. Desi is perfect for me simply because she's Desi."

"I totally get that too, but like I said, you're not Serena." They stopped at the door of Harry and Desi's bedroom, and Rach was grateful for the conversation even if it didn't solve anything.

"You and Serena are good for each other because you're complete opposites. I haven't known Serena as long as I've known you, but you've rocked her view of her world. She can't stay away from you even if her head is telling her that's the way to go." Harry smiled and kissed her cheek this time. "You're going to say last week proves me wrong, and I could be, but her heart will win out. The only thing that will derail a path forward is you."

"So I should say fine, I don't mind when she ghosts me?" she asked, incredulous.

"No, you should set some ground rules, like not leaving wet towels on the floor, only with a bit more punch. It's up to her to make whatever's wrong up to you, and if you decide to do that, don't be afraid to be demanding."

"How'd you get so good at this kind of thing?" She opened the door for Harry so she wouldn't spill her drinks.

"Your sister gives me lessons when she's not fussing about me leaving towels on the bathroom floor."

Rachel sat and talked to Harry and Desi until she had to get dressed for work. "Whatever and whenever you decide, just text me."

Harry nodded as Desi got up to use the bathroom. The three of them had come to the agreement that they'd call June Fontaine and her friend and invite them to the house. Desi hadn't wanted to go out in the horrible weather, and Harry had agreed. Harry didn't know for sure, but she figured Desi and Rachel also wanted the comfort of being home when they talked to June.

"I don't know what I'm going to do with my day when I don't have to go to the bathroom every three minutes." Desi came back to bed and turned slightly so she could lean against Harry instead of the headboard. "Do you think it's going to stop raining today? Tony offered to help me find a dress. I'd like to marry you in something other than sweats and a flowy top."

"If it means shopping, he'll put you in a bubble to keep you dry." She made Desi laugh. "And you can wear your nightgown if you want. All I need is for you to show up."

"Don't tempt me, but I want to look halfway decent in the pictures." She put her hands back on their child. "This baby is going to be all you, I think." The baby was constantly active. "Junior doesn't react to the sound of my voice like they do for you."

"I don't know about that. Maybe the baby's excited about going shopping." She kissed Desi's temple and enjoyed the quiet morning. She'd taken the week off to make sure everything was ready for the wedding. They'd only have a few friends and family when Albert, Serena's father, married them on Saturday.

Once their baby was born and they had the little one baptized to make her mother happy, they'd get the priest to bless their marriage, which would also make her mother happy. She'd felt married from the moment Desi had confessed her feelings. If God really did perform miracles, that—as well as a healthy baby—were the only ones she'd need in this lifetime.

"I doubt it, but maybe the next one." Desi ran her fingers lightly over her forearm and sighed. "I guess we can't put this off forever," Desi said, glancing back at her.

"Do you want me to make the call?" They'd made the decision, but Desi didn't have to be the one to do it. "I'll be happy to do it if you tell me what's bothering you."

"It's not that anything's wrong." Desi spoke slowly and Harry gave her the time she needed to express herself. "I don't understand why she came back. Wouldn't it have been better if she'd stayed dead? She was dressed well, and that card she gave Rachel means she hasn't been destitute this whole time. She gave us up and chooses now to come back?"

Desi stopped moving, and Harry had some idea of what she was thinking. Even after the crappy things that Desi had lived through, she still didn't like to think ill of others. How she'd been able to hang on to that part of herself boggled Harry's mind, but Desi was a pure and good soul. "I'm going to tell you the same thing I told Rachel this morning when we talked about Serena."

The way Desi turned and stared at her made her want to talk fast. "She talked to you after I've been asking and asking?"

"Let me finish and then you can fuss." She kissed the tip of Desi's nose and waited until she got comfortable again. "I explained to Rachel that she had to either cut off whatever she and Serena have going, or she'll have to take a chance. If she chooses to end it, we'll eventually get back to all being friends. It's up to her to pick."

"What kind of chance?"

"The kind that's scary because you don't know what's going to happen and you don't have a guarantee of success. That kind of gamble might break your heart, or it might give you something precious." She had no idea what June Fontaine's story was going to be, but it sounded like one worth hearing. "The same can be said of your mother."

"I wonder if she has any idea what she left behind?" Desi sniffled and wiped her face with impatience. "I have a hard time believing that Clyde was any different when they were together and only became the bastard he was because he was bitter."

"No one is saying you have to forgive, my love. Listen, then decide. Either way you'll both have closure." She wiped away the rest of Desi's tears and kissed her slowly. "I'll be right there with you, and I think it'll be a good thing, so you can stop wondering."

"You're right, and you're brilliant if you got Rachel to talk." Desi moved so they could look at each other.

"It's all those sensitivity classes you've been giving me." She waited until Desi moved around some more so she could get comfortable. "She's going to be okay. I just told her to wait, be demanding, but go for it if that's what she wanted. Broken hearts mend, especially if you have people who'll help you. The flip side of that is she might get all those things she wants if she simply doesn't give up."

"Do you have any idea how much I love you?" Desi kissed her and fisted the hair at the back of her head tightly. "I'm so lucky."

"That's a circular argument since I think I'm the lucky one."

"You have no idea the difference you make, and I'm always in awe of how generous you are. I'm embarrassed to ask you for anything else." Desi pressed her lips to the side of her neck and ran a line of kisses to her shoulder.

That was an interesting thing to say, and Harry couldn't concentrate on what Desi was doing. She didn't want to ignore Desi to have an internal dialogue with herself, but that comment stuck with her. "What did you want to ask for?"

"Nothing," Desi said way too fast. "Sorry. It's hard to forget that I don't need to mind my place, as Byron used to say." The way Desi said his name was always the same. It was a mixture of disgust and emotion born of fear. "I was going to talk to you about it, I promise."

"Honey, if you want to skip this for some other time, that's okay, but remember a few things. This is your home, I'm in love with you, and you have the right to ask for the things you want."

"Tony and I were talking…"

Desi spoke as if words were steps through a minefield. It was the one thing she hated about Desi's experiences. Byron had conditioned Desi to always expect the worst and that nothing she wanted or valued mattered. Her opinion had never counted with him, and Harry was trying her best to show her things were different now. No matter what was going on in her head, she never wanted to lose patience when it came to leading Desi out of those dark places in her head.

"Can I say something before you tell me what's on your mind?" Desi tensed at her question, and she didn't have to ask why. Even if Desi knew in the deepest part of her heart she'd never hit her or punish her for anything, that's what she was waiting for. It was a learned response, and it wasn't going to completely disappear overnight. "It's something I've said before, sweetheart, but this time I want you to listen with your heart as well as your head."

"I'm sorry," Desi said, and the defeat in the words made Harry wish she could turn the clock back.

"There's nothing to be sorry about. You're the woman I've loved since before I understood what loving someone other than my family was. What you did to protect Rachel and me, that isn't something I can undo even if it's like an ice pick through my eye when I think about it. Now, though, we're here, and we're going to navigate all this together. This is our home, you're going to be my wife, and this is our family," she said, with her hand on Desi's middle. "You have every right to say what you want, ask for whatever you want, and no one, especially me, is going to hurt you because you do."

"I know," Desi said softly.

"I know you do, but I want you to believe it with your whole heart. That sounds sappy, but that's what I want." She held Desi and wanted to cry with her. "Now tell me what you want."

"Tony and I were thinking of opening our own gallery. Nothing big, and as soon as I save enough, we'll decide, but I wanted to ask you first." Auctioneers had nothing on Desi when she was nervous about saying something, so she got through it with speed.

"Is that something you want, or something Tony's trying to ramrod you into doing?"

"No, I'd love it. We could sell our stuff but open it to other artists, like the show I just had. I'd be able to bring the baby too, if we owned it." The subject seemed to relax Desi enough into talking about it more freely.

"That sounds like a good idea. What's the problem?"

Desi moved her finger in a random pattern on Harry's arm. "There's no problem. Like I said, I need to sell a few more pieces before we can make any plans. I wanted to know if *you* thought it was a good idea."

"If you think it's a good idea and something you'd like to do, then that's good enough for me." She kept talking when Desi shook her head. "Listen, you're the one who's going to have to work to make the pieces to fill it, meet with artists you'd like to display, and put up with Tony. So if you want to do it, then do it."

"Thanks, honey, and I'll think about it once I have enough for my half."

"Can I ask you something else?" She waited for Desi to nod. "Did you happen to spend all the money in our joint account?"

"No," Desi said, almost yelling. "I haven't touched your money, Harry, I swear."

"I see. So if I asked you if I could use some of the money you made the other night, you'd tell me no because it's your money?"

Desi appeared mortified at the question. "Of course not. You can have it all if you need it. I want to pay you back for all this."

"You have a hard head, my love. What you so willingly offered goes both ways." There were times she wanted to pull Desi out of her timidity, but that wasn't the way to go about it.

"Are you sure?" Desi didn't look convinced.

"Tell me what you two have in mind." Her question started Desi talking, and it didn't take long to get her animated—until Desi's stomach grumbled. "What are you hungry for?"

"How about some chicken salad?"

"This kid is going to be born with feathers," Harry joked as someone knocked on the door. Mona came in with a tray and shook her head when she found them still in bed.

"Harry, are you bothering Desi again?" Mona gave Desi a plate with a sandwich and all the foods Desi craved during her pregnancy.

"We were talking about the gallery she and Tony are opening soon," Harry said and Desi smiled as she chewed.

Mona picked up the clothes on the floor, glancing at the bed every other step. "Don't you have an appointment today?"

"In a couple of hours, so she's got plenty of time to eat some chicken salad." Harry laughed at Desi's look of contentment as she ate, but deep down, she continued to worry. Byron was out there somewhere, a loose cannon waiting to create chaos. Desi's mother was back from the dead. And all Harry wanted to do was protect the people she loved.

CHAPTER EIGHT

D o you want to go shorter?" Rachel asked the woman in her chair. She was trying her best to get home early to be there when the police came over to give an update on Byron and his loser family. Desi also had a follow-up appointment with the Caseys, and she wanted to go to that too if she could manage it without having to cancel anyone. "I think it'll frame your face beautifully."

The woman nodded, and she got to work, her mind still on the conversation she'd had with Harry that morning. She'd lived with Byron and Desi to keep her sister alive until they could both escape the asshole, and she'd dated some during that time, but not as much as people thought. The few dates she had been on were the highlight of Byron's conversations the next day since he loved hurling slurs at her.

In a way her social life made Desi's life harder, so she'd tried to forget that part of her life and concentrated on doing for Desi what her sister had done for her from the time she had memory. All those lonely nights listening to the horrors Desi was living through made it easy to fall for Serena, who was the absolute opposite of all she'd watched Desi go through. She was kind, attentive, safe, and fun. They laughed at the same things, argued about silly things that then made them laugh, and there was no denying the sex was explosive. The best part was Serena understood her better than anyone she'd ever met because she'd lived through the same experience with her ex-husband. There'd been no reason for her to have to explain.

They'd had fun, and Rachel had loved how special Serena made her feel. It didn't matter if it was a quiet night at Serena's place, playing in the park with Butch, or a work event for Serena—Rachel had felt wanted. That was the one thing she'd never had, and it'd been intoxicating. That's what also made the pain so acute when it stopped.

"Rach," the receptionist called out.

She looked up and saw the delivery guy holding a beautiful bouquet of roses. "Rachel Thompson?" the guy asked. He put them on her stand when she nodded.

"Read the card," the woman in the chair said, sounding more eager than her. "My hair can wait."

"That's okay." She kept cutting as she answered the client's questions about the flowers and who she thought they were from. She had two more clients after this, and it wasn't until she was finished with them that she reached for the card: *I'm an asshole—there's no need for a jury to render that verdict. I'm also very sorry for being an asshole, and I promise to do better if you only give me a chance to talk to you.*

She had to give it to Serena—she could write an apology that actually made her smile. This was the gamble Harry talked about, and she wasn't completely sure if she was willing to have her heart broken. She was already feeling the effects of losing Serena, and they'd never even mentioned love. Serena was great, but she wasn't willing to play the role of bed warmer whenever Serena got an itch. She had more self-respect than that.

Her coworkers all waved as she headed out to the car. She'd taken Desi's this morning since it was blocking hers, and if she made it home now, she'd be in time to go with Desi and Harry to the doctor. She wanted to hear from Ellie or Sam that Desi was indeed fine. When Desi had moaned the night before, so loud it woke her, she'd completely panicked.

She searched through her purse for the key and jumped when she looked up to find Serena there. "Shit!" She was holding a single rose the same shade of pink as the bouquet she'd sent.

"Sorry," Serena said, appearing unsure and nervous. "I thought we could get lunch or a cup of coffee if you had a few minutes."

"Thanks for the flowers. Totally unnecessary, but they were lovely." Coffee or lunch meant no to going to the doctor. "Tell me one thing before I agree to go anywhere with you."

"Sure," Serena said, handing her the flower.

"In a very short sentence, tell me why." So far Serena hadn't really said anything but sorry. Sure she'd been busy, it was her job, her maybe promotion, but that really wasn't the why of it all. "And I mean short."

"You scare the crap out of me is the best explanation I have." Serena rubbed her hands along her jeans, which made Rachel think her nerves were real.

"So after months of dating I suddenly scare you?" The answer was sincere, she had no doubt about it, but it also didn't make sense, even though Harry had said as much when they'd talked about it before. Serena went to court every day and slayed dragons to keep women and children safe. There was no way she was afraid of her.

"I can tell you why, but it's going to take a little longer than the short explanation you asked for." Serena shrugged and it made her look adorable.

"One coffee, so make it good." She followed Serena to a local place and sat outside as Serena ordered for them. They were silent as they added sweetener, and then Rachel made a rolling motion with her hand. "Tell me why you're scared because that answer makes me think you might be slightly full of shit."

"When I met Patrick, I was surprised at how attracted to him I was. He was so different than anyone else I'd dated, and he was relentless in pursuing me. I should've realized right then it was stalkerish, not sweet." Serena ran her hands through her hair and shook her head. "He was also one of the only men I've ever dated in my entire life. Before I knew it, I'd agreed to marry him. I didn't think—I just accepted because he made me believe I couldn't live without him. I *needed* him in my life."

"And I remind you of Patrick?" That was the most ridiculous thing she'd ever heard, not to mention insulting as hell.

"No, no, that's not what I mean. I haven't experienced the crushing need to be with someone all the time until you. Patrick was the only other person I felt that way about. I woke up about a month ago to watch you sleep, and it scared the hell out of me how much I felt for you—*needed* you, really. There's no way you'd hurt me like he did, in the way he did, but you also have the power to break me if you leave." Serena was blushing by the time she finished talking.

"Honey, why didn't you just tell me? I would've understood." She couldn't help but reach across the table and take Serena's hand. "That you just shut me out really hurt."

"I know, and I feel like an ass, but I couldn't help myself. After Patrick, it was about having a good time, no strings attached, and no complications."

Rachel smiled and shook her head. "Until Harry."

"Yeah, until Harry. What you said about her, I understand that. Why you would worry, I mean, but you don't have to." Serena didn't let go of her hand, but she did lean back in her chair. "Harry was special to me, and I love her. She was there when Butch was born, and she helped me get over the hurt of what had happened to me, and not just the physical part. I think my broken jaw had just healed when my mother dragged me to that fundraiser where we met."

"She's good at comforting people," Rachel said. "I'm sure you've heard the story of the day we first met her, and she's only grown more protective. My only fear is that Harry is who you're waiting for, or someone like her."

"Harry isn't in love with me, and I'm not in love with Harry. I'm actually in love with you. You're not at all who I pictured myself with."

Rachel pulled her hand back. "What an interesting thing to say. I would've thought that you'd have practiced exactly what you were going to tell me, and saying you love me in the middle of a semi-insult wasn't what I was hoping for. That what just came out of your mouth is what you went with means you're a bit of an ass."

Serena laughed. "I don't mean it in a bad way. You're not at all who I thought I'd end up with, but you've shown me what my life could be."

"Serena, maybe you'd feel more comfortable with someone who's more like you. Someone who understands your job, fits in with your family, is from the right pedigree." None of those things were her.

"That's where you're wrong. You have this picture in your head that I'm embarrassed by you, but I'm not. I love everything about you, and it took nearly losing you to realize I *am* a fool for not saying this before now. My problem has been that you fit me the way I thought Patrick did, and in my head, I know that's wrong. You're nothing like him, but my heart seemed to recognize the feeling, and my first instinct was to run." Serena slid her hand, palm up, to the center of the table.

"You thought I would hurt you?"

"No, but I don't think I'd survive the kind of heartbreak I had with Patrick. A second time isn't in me."

She took Serena's hand again, lifting it to kiss the back of it. "You *are* a fool."

"Does this mean you'll give me another chance?"

"Maybe, and I do accept your apology." She remembered her conversation with Harry that morning. It was time to set some ground rules, be demanding, and prepare herself to walk away if that's what it took.

"You can't forgive me?" Serena went to pull away from her again but Rachel held on tight.

"I've already done that, but it's not going to be that easy this time around. When I first met you, I think I got caught up with your pretty face and all the new experiences you gave me. It left me wanting more, and the more I got, the more I didn't think I had the right to ask for everything I wanted. In my head I thought if I did, I'd lose you." She'd always felt sorry for people who completely lost their minds when they met someone. It didn't matter how intelligent or accomplished they were—they were willing to change fundamental things about themselves to meet someone else's expectations. That's what she'd done with Serena, and she didn't feel good about it.

"What is it you want?"

"I'm not asking for a kidney. All I ask is that you make me a priority. For the last couple of months, it's like I've been an afterthought in your life. You kind of made me feel like a booty call whenever you got around to returning a message from me."

Serena laughed and she glared at her. "Sorry, and you're right. I should've talked to you about all this before now."

"You have to understand a few things before we make any kind of decision going forward. I understand you haven't been with someone on a regular basis since Harry, but doing something like taking a job without talking to me about it first isn't going to work for me if we're going to be a real couple. I get that it's great for your career, but you already work crazy hours, and a promotion isn't going to help matters. We'll be right back in that whole ignoring thing you do."

"I haven't accepted the promotion yet. That's something we have to decide together." Serena motioned between them. "I also apologize for not leaving Butch with you. He loves you, and he didn't understand any more than you did." She bit her lip. "I guess maybe I was trying to protect him from my decisions."

Serena was saying all the right things, and she did want to hear them, but she wasn't jumping back in without making her needs clear. "This last week hasn't been one of your best, at least when it comes to decision-making. I get that you were scared. Is not talking about it going to be the norm going forward?" She threaded their fingers together and leaned in, putting her other elbow on the table. "If it is, that's not going to work for me either."

"I'm here to ask you for another chance. There's no guarantee I won't screw up again, but I can promise I'll do better." Serena leaned in as well and repeated her move of kissing her hand.

"I'm not going to dwell on how much you hurt me, and if we're going to do this, it's got to be a fresh start. If you do agree to that, just remember one thing."

"What?" Serena said, appearing like she'd do anything.

"You do this to me again, there won't be another chance. As much as it'll hurt, there'll be no going back. Flowers and heartfelt apologies aren't going to change my mind." She let Serena's hand go and grabbed her purse. "Like I said, I'm not a book you can read a page at a time when you feel like it."

"Are you sure you want to try again? You sound pissed." Serena twirled her coffee cup as if to have something to do with her hands.

"I am pissed. You treated me like shit, and I didn't appreciate it. The next move is up to you, so think about what I said before making it." She stood and motioned for Serena to stay put. "I want you to be completely sure."

"Thanks for talking to me, and I promise you won't be sorry." Serena stood and threw both their cups away. "All I'm asking is that you pick up the phone."

"Don't worry about that. Now, tell me if there's anything new about Byron's case. Desi doesn't like bringing it up, but I know she's nervous. If you're dropping a bomb of bad news on us, then let me try to prepare her."

"I'll call the house this afternoon and work out a time I can bring Roger with me and give you all an update on what's happening. They still haven't been found, and I need you all to understand that Byron isn't a threat just to Desi. You need to be careful too, and know that this is our top priority until he's caught."

"Thanks, and I'll see you." She walked away without giving Serena a good-bye kiss, feeling better than she had in days. Maybe she'd send Harry flowers for giving such good advice. Serena was worth taking a chance on, but Rachel needed to feel respected. *If anything, I might have a date to the wedding in a few days.* But she wanted more than that. She wanted forever.

CHAPTER NINE

Harry sat next to Desi in the waiting room of Ellie and Sam's office and held her hand. Trying to leave the house without her mother and Mona was impossible, so they were sitting across from them along with the guards Harry had ordered. The nurse called them in, and she pointed to her mother and Mona to keep them in their seats, to save Ellie from the barrage of questions they had at the ready.

The best part so far was that Desi hadn't experienced any more contractions. "Do you need a wheelchair?" she asked Desi and got an eyeroll in response. They both turned when they heard a door open, and a little boy came running out.

"Dr. Harry, I heard you. I told my daddy it was you."

Harry smiled at the man in the doorway trying to shield the woman waiting to get an ultrasound. "Hey, Charlie." She squatted down to be at eye level with the boy and accepted his hug. "What are you guys doing here?" She knew, but she enjoyed the excitement Charlie displayed when he talked about his soon-to-be sibling.

"We came to see my little sister on the TV, Dr. Harry." Charlie hung on when Harry stood with him in her arms. "Do you want to see?"

"That's okay, little buddy, but you'll have to bring her to see me once she's born."

Charlie nodded, then seemed to notice Desi. "Hi, my name's Charlie, and I'm four." He held up the right number of fingers and his smile was proud.

"Hi, Charlie, I'm Desi. Are you excited you're going to have a little sister?" Desi appeared charmed by him as she took his hand. "I think you're going to be the best big brother ever."

"I wanted a little brother to play with, but my daddy said we can't give her back."

"You'd better get back in there so you don't miss anything. I'll see you guys tomorrow." Charlie had become one of her patients when an accidental fall from the top of his bunk beds had done significant damage to his left shoulder. She'd fixed most of the damage, and now they were taking a break to see if any additional surgery was necessary.

"Hey, Harry. I don't mind if y'all come in," Charlie's mom called out. "Anything that saves me from getting dressed and leaving the house is something I appreciate. You can take a look at him now." She waved them both in. "I'm sure your partner totally understands the staying in your pajamas all day goal, and I figure you guys have seen all this before."

Harry sat on one of the stools and flexed Charlie's fingers. "Okay, buddy, now you do it."

Charlie appeared to be concentrating as he opened and closed his hand. "I can't too good yet, Dr. Harry. It still hurts a little. Will my digitals always hurt?" He'd heard her referring to his fingers as digits early on, and he'd called them *digitals* ever since.

"You're doing great, and it won't be too long before your digitals don't hurt at all." Harry probed his arm and the area around his shoulder. "You promise to keep doing the games we showed you every day, and I promise you'll be ready to climb in no time." She accepted another hug from Charlie before putting him back on his feet. "Take care, you guys, and I'll have one of the nurses call you in a couple of weeks. If Charlie keeps being the awesome guy he is, he might be done with me."

"Is Dr. Harry taking care of you too?" Charlie asked, gazing up at Desi. He was obviously done with her and had moved on to making new friends.

"She is, and she's doing a great job. We're going to have a baby like your mom, and maybe you can come over and play, if it's a boy."

"Really? I can't wait." Charlie pressed his hands together, and Harry was pleased from a clinical standpoint. She hated when stupid accidents turned into a lifetime of problems, but Charlie wasn't going to have to worry about that.

"Thanks for everything, Harry," Charlie's mom said. "It's great meeting you, Desi. Harry talks about you nonstop, so it's nice to put a face with the stories. Good luck with the baby, and my advice is to buy a race car bed. Skip the bunk beds," she said, smiling adoringly at her son.

They made their way to their room, and when the nurse left

them alone and Desi hopped on the exam table, she looped her arms around Harry's neck and kissed her. "You're better than chicken salad sandwiches, my love, and it was great meeting Charlie. I can't wait to see you with our children."

"He's a great little guy, and I'm putting a race car bed on order," she said, winking. "After your promise of a playdate, I almost want to know what we're having."

"Let's ask while we're here. We have enough other suspense in our lives, and I'd like to start thinking names." Desi kissed her again and enjoyed the press of the baby between them. Last night reminded her of the fragility of life, and she never wanted to take it for granted.

Ellie walked in while they were kissing again and cleared her throat. "It's good to see you not giving Harry too hard a time. By this time in my pregnancy, I almost made Sam move out. Her breathing and lying next to me in bed were really getting on my nerves." Ellie read the chart then pointed to the exam table. "Just slip your underwear off so you don't have to completely undress, and let me take a quick look."

Harry helped her then draped the sheet over her waist. "She's not dilating, is she?"

"Give me a minute," Ellie said as she continued with her exam. "Any more contractions?"

"Not since last night," Desi said. "I'm not sure what happened, but I was sleeping and the pain woke me."

"Everything looks great, so I think it was just a warmup for the big day. Try and get plenty of rest, but I'm not confining you to bed unless it's absolutely necessary. Besides, it'll be crowded in the bedroom if you have to get married in there. I don't want to be bumped from the proceedings since I've been waiting to see Harry get fitted for a nose ring and collar for the leash you own. If you need pointers on how to properly train her, give me a call." Ellie made Desi laugh, and the good mood made Harry happy.

"Thanks, Ellie, and we'll see you on Saturday." Desi accepted Harry's help to sit up. "Should I be doing anything else?"

"Just be careful and try not to stress. Sam told me what happened, and it sounds like you couldn't have avoided the shock of this woman appearing at your house. If you're going to meet with her, and I'm sure you are, then try to keep it to a dull roar." Ellie made some notes in her chart and smiled at her. "If you don't have any questions, I'll see you in a week. And don't forget what Sam said. Don't be afraid to call even if it's just to say hi."

"Actually, we have one more question," Desi said, glancing at her. "Boy or girl?"

"At least until Baby Basantes tells us differently, a boy."

The thought of a little boy took a minute to sink in for Harry. She really didn't care what the gender was, but a small part of her had hoped for a blond little girl who'd remind her of her mother. Desi, though, appeared thrilled.

"A boy? Really?" Desi pressed her hands to her middle and her eyes got glassy with tears. "Oh, Harry."

"And he's going to be gorgeous like his mother." She wiped Desi's face, not caring that she was crying as well. "I can't wait to meet the little guy."

"Congratulations, and I'll see you soon," Ellie said.

"Thanks again," Harry said, and Ellie hugged her.

"Can I interest you in a nap?" Desi asked on the way home. They'd answered all of Rosa's and Mona's questions again like the night before, but they kept the baby's sex to themselves for now. She knew Desi, and the first person she'd want to tell was Rachel. That was fine with her.

"You want to eat anything before we lie down?" She helped Desi into her nightgown and stripped down to her underwear and a T-shirt.

"I'm too excited to eat anything. I'm happy, but I'm also tired, so let's go to bed."

"Let me make a call, and we'll be set."

Desi handed her the card Rachel had left with her, and she stared at the names for a moment before dialing.

"June Margolis, please," Harry said when a woman answered.

"This is June." The woman sounded hoarse and emotional. "Desi?"

"I'm calling on her and Rachel's behalf. I'm Desi's partner, Harry Basantes." She stopped to see if June had anything to say, but all she heard was her breathing on the other end. "We'd like to invite you to come back tonight for a drink. I don't want Desi upset, so please keep that in mind. How about seven?"

"We'll be there, and thank you, Harry. You probably would rather us disappear for another thirty years, but I promise I don't want to hurt either of them."

"I hope so." She ended the call and put her arms around Desi.

"She's coming?" Desi pressed the side of her face to Harry's chest.

"She is, and it'll be okay. Close your eyes and know I'll be there. Nothing bad is going to happen." They fell asleep and everyone left them alone. Harry woke to Desi running her fingers along her forearm as she spooned behind her.

"Are you awake?" Desi asked softly.

Harry could hear the rain outside, so it was a perfect time to stay in bed. "I am, and I'm beginning to see the allure of afternoon naps. What can I do for you?"

"Nothing. I know it'll be a shock to you, but I have to go to the bathroom again. I didn't want to wake you." She helped Desi sit up and waited for her to come back, smiling at how beautiful Desi looked.

"You get more gorgeous every day." Her mother kept mentioning how important it was to tell Desi everything that was on her mind.

"I love you even though you're a little delusional." Desi lay as flat as she could and faced her. "I have, though, enjoyed this process with you. Do you remember when I told you I was pregnant?"

"It was the anniversary of our first kiss, and I remember crying through the appetizers." The sight of that pregnancy stick in the box Desi had wrapped would be forever one of her favorite memories. "I know it's too soon to talk about it, but I'd love to do this again. You really do look beautiful. That glow people always talk about isn't a myth."

"Don't worry, we have time for maybe one or two more." Desi smiled and reached for her hand. "I love you, and it's sometimes surreal to think I'm back with you, but I remember waking up one night when you had gotten home late. You were exhausted and fell almost instantly asleep after kissing me. I'd just started showing, and you placed your hand over our baby. That one night made me believe all this was mine, and nothing could take it away from me."

"Sweetheart, you're never going to lose me. I'm yours, and I always have been." She pressed her hand to Desi's side and laughed at all the kicking. "What made you think about all that?"

"I had a dream once about our baby, a little boy who looked just like you. I dreamed about how much we loved him." Desi threaded their fingers together and kept it on her middle. "And it really is a little boy."

"I can't wait to meet him."

"Me too, and it also made me think of June Fontaine and what her showing up means. It doesn't make sense that our mother left us. There has to be a story there, and I'm willing to listen."

"I agree, but you have every right to tell her to take a hike if you don't like what she says. Let me call Rachel and tell her about tonight.

Until then, don't work yourself up into another trip to the emergency room."

"I can't help it." Desi glanced back at the clock and sat up a little. "Rachel should be home soon."

As if conjuring her up, Rachel called out to them, knocked, and opened the door. "How'd the doctor's appointment go?"

Harry gave her a rundown of everything that happened and that her sister was fine.

"We have news," Desi said with a wide smile.

"It really is twins?" Rachel said and laughed.

"I think that's another comment about my size, but no, it's not twins. It's a boy."

"Congratulations, babe." Rachel hugged Desi, then Harry. "Butch will be thrilled."

"That's true, and we have more news. Harry called June Fontaine, and she'll be here at seven. I'm not sure how you want to handle it, but I think we should hear her out and then make a decision—together." Desi stared at Rachel, and they seemed to come to an agreement without uttering a word. "Nothing says that we have to have a relationship with her or forgive her after hearing what she has to say."

"I promise not to lose my temper and throw coffee at her head. And thank God she's coming back. I'm trying to let it go, but I keep thinking about it obsessively. At least tonight we'll have an answer one way or the other."

"Can I ask the question I really hadn't thought about until now?" All the answers had to lie with Clyde, but the bastard never gave up any of his secrets before his death. "Did Clyde ever mention where your mother was buried?" Harry asked.

"Harry, the only thing Clyde did in his whole miserable life was come home and scream at us—to be quiet or to get him something to eat, or just to curse our existence. I think he was secretly relieved when Rosa took an interest in having us over all the time. Trust me, we never sat around and talked about anything." Rachel sat on the end of the bed and shrugged. "His main job was at some dive bar in the Quarter, but he told us about the jobs he did for the Bracato family. That's how he made his money, and Byron took control of what was left when he died."

"The cancer didn't leave much. Clyde spent almost every penny trying to stay alive. It was like he feared death," Desi said.

"Clyde was nothing but a coward and a son of a bitch," she said. All those what-ifs made her clench her teeth.

"Stop it, honey," Desi said. "Clyde knew what he was doing."

"He did horrible things, and he's burning in hell because of every single one," Rachel said.

"All those stories he loved telling is why I believed him when he threatened you and Rachel," Desi said. "Clyde was your complete opposite. He wasn't bound by family or love, and you are, which is why you can't understand what happened. I'd like to believe the way he died was punishment for the way he lived his life." Desi sounded flat as she talked about their father. Clyde was truly evil, but Harry never realized just how rotten he was until Desi had told her everything.

"I'll grab a snack for everyone and wait until tonight for your answers. The only thing to remember is that you aren't alone in this. Not this time. Not ever." Harry stood and reached for her pants. "I'll go do that, so you stay, Rachel, and keep an eye on Desi."

She was glad to hear them talk about the wedding instead of Clyde as she left the room. Desi was right about one thing. How her mother could've left her and Rachel with Clyde was something she couldn't imagine. The scenario had to have been dire, but no mother worth anything would have walked away from her kids. She was prepared to listen, but she'd do whatever it took to keep June out of their lives if that's what Desi and Rachel decided.

❖

Byron beat the steering wheel when the truck choked, sputtered, and died when they ran out of gas on some backwoods road. From the road signs they were still in Mississippi, and he had no clue how close to the Louisiana border they were. That fucker Tyrell had really screwed them up.

"What the hell now?" his father asked.

"We ran out of gas," Mike answered. "We might as well start walking."

"First we gotta push this thing off the road. I don't want to give the cops any clues as to where we are. If we're walking, we're going into the trees again." There was no way they were going to find another house like before, so he'd have to think about what to do next. If Tyrell had left them in the city, this would've been so much easier, but he wasn't giving up.

"I'm hungry," his father said. He'd been nothing but a pain in the ass from the moment they'd run.

It wasn't until this moment that Byron realized all the fear he'd had of his father all his life had disappeared in the face of who Big Byron really was. The asshole had killed his mother, and he'd done everything he could not to man-up to it.

"Daddy, you really need to quit your bitching. It's not like me and Mike are holding you back. If you want to leave, go ahead. If not, shut the hell up. We'll eat something when we find something, so stop talking about it." They pushed the truck as far into the woods as they could and found branches to cover it up. It was getting late, but they'd survived another day of freedom.

"Talk to me like that again, and I'll put you down, boy." His father shook his fist close to his face before turning and stomping away.

"Let's walk until the sun goes down, and maybe we'll find another house." Mike sounded subdued as if he'd embraced the fact that there was no going back. It actually shocked Byron that his brother hadn't left him and his father behind, considering Mike thought of himself as the smart one. "If it's still this isolated, let's get some sleep until morning."

"You think I'm an idiot, don't you?" He didn't raise his voice and thought for a moment how nice it was to be walking over the pine-needle-covered ground. That was something he'd never really done.

He'd struggled through school, never really enjoying it until he'd started playing football. It had been his one talent, and people had praised him to the point that he dreamed of a future beyond his father's garage. He remembered how people treated him after a big game, and how that feeling of superiority had never come again once the opportunity to play had been stolen from him. The girl he'd put his hands on, because that's all he knew, had ended his dreams.

The police had come to his high school, and that afternoon his coach had broken the news that he was benching him. That's when it hit him. His life would be listening to his father, working on cars, and nothing else.

The one thing he got excited about was Desi. It was fun at first trying to bend her to his will, but that had gotten old. He didn't think someone could cry that much, but it didn't matter. She was the first thing that had been totally his, and there was no way he would fucking ever let her go.

He still believed that, so not heading back wasn't an option. "Come on, you can tell me."

"What does it matter what I believe?" Mike walked with his hands stuffed into the pockets of the denim jacket he'd found. "What you never realized was that you didn't have to live the way Daddy did. You broke Desi's leg, did all that other shit to her, and somehow you're the victim."

"You don't know shit." It was like kicking himself in the balls trying to talk to his brother.

"No, you just don't like the truth. What about the fact that she left, testified against you, and found someone else shocks you?" Mike laughed, and it aggravated the hell out of him. "You're a complete dumbass. There wasn't one day that Desi wanted anything to do with you."

"If I'm such a dumbass, what the fuck are you doing here?" Would it kill any of his family to support him? It was like Mike was loyal to no one.

"Don't worry—I'll go my own way as soon as I think it's time. Now shut up and keep walking. It's not like you've given me another goddamn option."

"What the hell does that mean?" He didn't need a fight from all sides.

"Nothing, just keep walking."

Their father stayed quiet and shuffled his feet, leaving a line in the pine needles. At three in the morning, none of them felt like taking another step, so they found the thickest stand of trees and lay down. He was grateful for the jacket he'd stolen as the cold seeped through his pants. It was dark, and he stared in all directions before closing his eyes. There wasn't a light anywhere in the distance.

"Are you thinking about me?" he said softly as he tried to see anything in the night sky. That was the only thing he found joy in. He knew Desi was thinking about him, full of fear as to what came next.

He stared at the stars and tried to forget how cold and hungry he was. Though, as miserable as he was, this beat the hell out of being locked in a building with forty other guys. The moaning at night had been bad enough to make him think about picking a fight so someone like Tyrell would finally put an end to the nightmare of spending two and a half decades locked up. He'd come even closer to ending things himself after two men ganged up on him in the shower and taught him one of the dirty little secrets of jail.

He'd never wanted to talk about it, even though he was sure it'd happened to Mike as well, and when it was over, if he was granted one wish, it was to live to see freedom again. The day he walked out was the day he'd beat Desiree Thompson Simoneaux until she was dead. Once she was, he'd put a bullet in Harry Basantes and one in Rachel before turning the gun on himself because there was no way he was going back to Angola. No way.

Mike had accused him more than once of having no imagination, that his revenge plans were getting stale, yet here they were. They were out and headed back to where he wanted to be. That had been the hardest part of his little fantasy, so the rest would be easy.

"Why is this so important to you?" Mike's voice broke his train of thought.

"Let me ask you something. Why didn't you ever get married or at least fuck a girl on a regular basis?" His brother had always been a loner who worked and sat around drinking beer when he wasn't working. The guy never looked happy about anything.

"Because I didn't want to repeat what I'd seen all my life. I got punched plenty for trying to defend Mama, but it wasn't right." Mike never sounded different, never deviated from his normal. It was like the guy had one way to be and that was calm. "You didn't last a fucking day after meeting Desi before you turned into Daddy. I never understood that shit. What do you get out of beating someone so much smaller than you who can't or won't fight back?"

"I'm nothing like Daddy, but that's easy. When you love someone, and they don't love you back, it pisses you off. They can't love you because they're still crying over someone who dropped them back in the sewer. You try and wake them up to the reality they're living." He turned away from Mike before they got into another fight that wasn't going to solve anything right now. "Your problem is you think I don't love Desi. I do. I have from the beginning." The comparison burned a hole in his chest because he was nothing like his father. He really loved Desi in his own way. He doubted his father had ever felt that for their mother.

"I guess I'll always have a problem then," Mike said, and Byron heard rustling. "Because that's the last thing I think."

"Then shut it. Stop talking about things you know nothing about. I love her, and she threw me away. Unlike you, I have some fucking pride, so I'm not just going to roll over and let her fuck me over. That's never going to happen."

CHAPTER TEN

It finally stopped raining in the late afternoon, and Rachel talked Desi into letting her cut her hair. "You're going appreciate this when you're running around with vomit on your shirt, and Harry Jr. crying in your arms." It was just the two of them since Harry was doing rounds down the street. "And stop worrying. I could shave your head and she'd still love you."

They were sitting outside on the large balcony off Harry and Desi's bedroom so they wouldn't get hair all over the floor inside, and Desi was fidgeting. It was a couple of weeks into January, so the yard was mostly varying shades of brown, but this space had quickly become one of their favorites for spending time together. She'd loved how at peace Desi was here as she gazed out into the large yard full of flowers.

The only green things still visible, aside from the live oaks, were the sweet olive trees planted close to the house. The notoriously slow growers must've been ancient because of their size, and it wouldn't be until spring that the small white flowers would appear with their intoxicating smell. It was elusive on the breeze, but it made you stop and enjoy it whenever you noticed it.

Rachel knew Harry and Desi loved sitting out here as well as on the swing Harry had purchased from the people living in their old house. She'd proposed to Desi on that swing a few days ago, and it was only right considering Harry's story of falling in love on that same swing.

She started cutting, and Desi closed her eyes. "You promise you'll be okay tonight, right?"

"I'll be fine, and I don't want to put this off. I want to know," Desi said, brushing hair off her cheek. "I know you do too."

"I do, but I'm worried about you."

"No need to be. Our days of worrying and being afraid are over.

I know Byron hasn't been found yet, but I'm not going to think about that until it makes me sick. It might be stupid of me, but I'm so tired of hiding and being afraid." Desi twisted the diamond ring on her finger, but she did seem relaxed. "The world is a strange place sometimes, isn't it?"

"I'm glad you're finally living and being happy, but what do you mean?"

"I think about all those nights I dreamed about Harry. I wondered what she was doing, who she was with, and if she was happy without me. It's like I wanted her to be—happy, I mean. It's why I did what I did, after all. But there was a small part of me that hoped she missed me." Desi shrugged and stopped talking.

"Do you promise not to tell on me if I share a secret?" She unclipped a section of hair and started trimming.

"What kind of secret?" Desi turned her face up to look at her.

"Do you remember the first night after we moved in, when Harry was out for an emergency, and I found you out here?" Desi had finally shed her cast and boot, and had healed, and Rachel had gone out to dinner with one of her clients. The weariness that seemed to go bone-deep was starting to fall away because of Harry's love, and Desi had stopped being so skittish.

"I do, but I come out here more than you think. This place is magic, especially at certain times of the year." Desi had that same peaceful expression she'd had that night, and it brought light to all the dark places in Rachel's soul. "Those sweet olives make you want to linger."

"You fell in love with those when you and Harry used to take me to the park on St. Charles. She'd push me on the swings and watch to make sure I didn't go sailing off the damn things. You, on the other hand, watched Harry."

Desi laughed, not denying it. "I spent a lot of years trying to not make it obvious I was watching Harry, so it's nice I don't have to do that anymore. She tells me all the time that I can look all I want."

"True, and that's something you've taken full advantage of."

"What does that have to do with a secret?" Desi brushed at her face again, and she was glad they weren't in front of a mirror or Desi would be freaking out because of how short she'd gone.

"I asked Harry one day while you were in the shower why she'd bought this place. It's way too big for her and Mona, and it was a little on the formal side, which isn't Harry." She ran her fingers through Desi's hair to satisfy herself that it was done.

"She told me she purchased it as a change of pace, even though Tony did all the house-hunting." Desi's response meant she'd asked Harry about it but hadn't gotten the whole story.

"Tony found this place, and another one on Jefferson he thought she'd like better. It was more her style, he said, but they walked through this one in the spring. Tony said she stood against the railing and inhaled that scent you loved so much and told him to make an offer." She'd cried when Harry had told her that story because their stoic protector who'd loved them for years was crying too. At the heart of Harry's stoic exterior was her love for Desi.

"Why have I never heard this story? Why didn't she tell me?" Desi wiped her eyes as if guessing the end.

"Tony said she got the house because if you ever came back, if you ever forgave her for whatever she'd done, she was sure this would be one of your favorite places. Those trees are her way of proving she'd never stopped thinking about you. In her heart, I think, the only woman who'd ever share this place with her was you."

"That's what I want for you too, Rach. I want you to find the woman who's going to love you like that. Thank you for telling me that story."

"I told you because I want you to remember that no matter what, you have a place and a person. It doesn't matter if June is going to crap all over us tonight with some bullshit story—we have a place and people who love us. Harry loves us." She kissed Desi's cheek and spit out a few fine hairs, getting her sister to laugh. "Let me go blow this out so you can get over the shock before Harry gets home."

"Rachel," Desi called out when she stepped into the bathroom. She was staring at herself in the bathroom mirror and pulling on the ends of her hair. "I thought you meant a trim."

"Let me finish, and I guarantee you'll get lucky later." She hugged Desi from behind and pushed her onto the vanity stool. "Once I'm done, we'll show June Margolis that we survived and turned out just fine without her help."

She wondered at times if the people who believed in reincarnation were right, and you kept coming back to fix what you did wrong in your past life. What atrocities had they committed in some distant lifetime that they'd had to pay for so heavily in this one? The horrible years they'd survived weighed on her, but not as much as on Desi. It was enough to make her want to scream up to the heavens because if there was some supreme being, they'd never bothered to listen to any prayer she'd ever said.

She'd follow Desi's lead. Forgiveness was hard after the years they'd survived, but she wasn't so hard-hearted that she couldn't listen. June, though, had to come up with one whopper of a story.

❖

Rachel stood behind Mona as she opened the door for June and the woman with her.

"Welcome to the Basantes residence," Mona said.

"Thank you," June said.

Rachel glanced toward the grand staircase and watched Harry carrying Desi down. Harry was the definition of a gentlewoman, especially with her sister. Rachel joined them once Harry placed her sister on her feet, and she took Harry's other hand. No matter what they heard there was no doubt Harry was their protector, and from the set of Harry's shoulders it was a job she took seriously.

"Thank you for coming back," Desi said with a neutral expression. "We didn't have the chance to do this before, but I'm Desi and this is my fiancée, Dr. Harry Basantes. Why don't we all sit and talk." Desi led them to the den and chose the sofa across from two wingback chairs.

"Thank you for the opportunity to talk to all of you. I'm sure the last day hasn't been easy, and you probably have many questions." It was the simplest way of putting it. Their mother seemed to know the fastest way for this to go to hell was if she tried to sugarcoat it. "Like I mentioned, I'm June and this is my wife, Dr. Bobbie Margolis."

"Where the hell have you been for twenty-seven years?" Rachel did nothing to hide her anger, bringing the calm of the family reunion to an end. "I mean, what the fuck? Are you really our mother?"

"Rach," Desi said softly. "That won't get us anywhere." Desi pressed to Harry's side and placed her hand in Harry's lap. "Please go on."

"I'm not making excuses, Rachel, but sometimes you have to do things to keep the people most important to you safe."

"Yeah, like leaving them behind with a sadistic asshole who almost ruined our lives. Way to go, Mom."

Rachel said the title with enough sarcasm that June wouldn't misread her anger. She liked to attack with the precision of a prizefighter.

"Hey," Desi said, "come over here." Rachel sat next to Desi and Harry put her hand on Rachel's shoulder. "How about if we promise to let you talk? Once you're done, we'll ask questions."

"So many years have gone by that sometimes I think it'd have been better to let you believe I'm dead. There was no easy way of coming back and explaining what happened."

Desi nodded and placed her hand on Rachel's leg. "None of this is easy, but start at the beginning."

Their mother took a deep breath and nodded. "I was fifteen when I met your father. He'd quit school and was always hanging out at the diner where I worked." She stopped and rubbed her temples as if it pained her to get the words out. "My family was poor, and I started working when my father threatened to make me quit school, so I could start bringing money in."

"That must've been tough," Desi said.

"All I wanted was an education, so I could get something better than waitressing. When I was sixteen, though, I got pregnant, and according to my parents there was no other option except to marry Clyde."

"Jesus, that's not much of a choice," Rachel said.

"I was afraid of my father and naive enough to think it'd be okay. And, well, that's how things were done then. Clyde was twenty and went along with what my parents wanted. He was working as a bartender, and once we moved into that little house he had, I barely saw him." That seemed to be the only part of her story that didn't carry the weight of pain. "I had no clue what he was really doing, and I didn't push."

"I totally understand that," Desi said. "We didn't push either. It wasn't worth it."

"The day you were born, all that didn't matter. You were so beautiful, and when they laid you on my chest, I knew I'd do anything to try and give you a better life than I had." June wiped her face, and Rachel rolled her eyes. "You were a girl and that didn't thrill your father, so he wasn't around much after your birth. Three years later you were born, Rachel, and I loved going through the process even more since Desi loved helping me take care of you. She treated you like one of her dolls."

"I'm sure Clyde wasn't thrilled with the fact that I was a girl too," Rachel said, and June nodded. "That guy really was a bastard."

"He came home even less after that, saying he didn't want to hear crying kids all the time. I didn't mind, and he gave me enough money to take care of you both, and to keep the house. It was a place he came to shower, demand things of me, and eat. I'm sure anyone would've thought it was a pathetic existence, but I had the two of you." June smiled even though she was crying. "I wasn't lonely, but it sometimes hurt when I saw how other people lived. Marriage, a partner, and a family are what most people strove for. But not in the way I had mine."

"I'm sorry he treated you that way," Desi said. "Clyde never struck me as a man who sought that out."

"He wasn't, but complaining or expecting him to change wasn't something I was willing to do. His reactions to any kind of suggestion like that were extreme, and I didn't want either of you hurt."

"What changed?" Rachel asked, calming as the story unfolded.

"A young doctor moved in next door before I gave birth to you, Rachel. I was about seven months pregnant." June smiled up at Bobbie and squeezed her hand. "We'd waved to each other, but I didn't officially meet her until three weeks later."

"I was in the city for a yearlong fellowship," Bobbie said. "After all those long nights at Big Charity, I loved watching your mom with Desi on the porch of that old house. I'd never talked to her, but I could tell she loved you."

"It was you, Desi, that got her to stop one day. You saw her walking home from the bus stop and ran to the fence and yelled hello." June stopped and took a breath.

"We talked for an hour while you ran around with a doll," Bobbie said. "You were a beautiful child, and your mom was starting to really show with you," she said to Rachel. "Those morning talks became the best part of my days."

"It was nice to have someone in my life who treated me like a human being, and even nicer that Bobbie didn't care that I hadn't even graduated from high school. She stopped by every morning, and it was nice that she played with you, Desi, and she started bringing me to all my doctor's appointments." The way June gazed at Bobbie showed the deep devotion they had for each other. "Bobbie showed the kind of interest Clyde should've given his daughters."

"It was impossible not to," Bobbie said. "I fell in love so easily that I didn't realize it until it was too late."

"Did you not want to?" Rachel asked. It was as if they'd carried the stigma of no one wanting them from the day they were born.

"The eventual outcome is something I blame myself for." Bobbie put her arm around June and kissed the top of her head. "But loving your mother is something I'll never regret."

"After a month of visits, I found myself waiting for her," June said. "There was nothing back then aside from Desi and my due date that made me happier than seeing Bobbie come up the street. It wasn't hard to imagine a life with her and you two."

"I was working when she went into labor, and I wanted to hand out cigars when you were born, Rachel." Bobbie smiled as if conjuring up the memory. "It was a special day, and I wanted nothing more than to commit to you two and June for life."

"What about Clyde?" Desi asked with compassion. She seemed to know where this story was going.

"We brought Rachel home, and two months later I was pregnant again." June covered her face with her hands. "I was in love with Bobbie, but Clyde still showed up whenever he wanted, doing whatever he wanted—well, taking what he wanted really. The reality of another baby wasn't something I dreaded—it was telling Bobbie that scared me. Denying Clyde, though, was a dangerous thing. My fear was that if Bobbie left, I wouldn't survive it."

"I was paged to the emergency room early one morning," Bobbie said as she held June while she cried.

"Clyde came home and beat me badly enough that I had to go to the hospital." June shook her head with more force and started crying until she could hardly breathe. Her history with Clyde, like theirs, was a minefield of bad memories with the ability to blow up and inflict pain even after all this time. "I lost the baby, and that was the catalyst to make me want to run with you two. Bobbie had been pushing me to go with her—away from Clyde. New York was miles away, and I thought it'd be safe."

"Why didn't you?" Rachel couldn't help but warm to her mother. The story wasn't new or surprising, but it didn't negate the trauma of surviving what should've broken all of them.

"Your father threatened me," Bobbie said. "I wasn't worried about it, but then he threatened what we both loved above everything in this world." Bobbie held their mother as if she was shielding her from the reality of what they went through. "We almost made it, but Clyde beat us to the neighbor's place where your mom had left you while she headed to the emergency room."

"He held a gun to your head," June said, staring at Desi. "I believed him, and while it killed something in me, I left to save you—both of you. There's nothing I can say that will make you forgive me, but I did what I thought was right to keep you alive."

"We've dreamed of this day for years, and we stayed away to keep you safe." Bobbie sounded so miserable. "I realize it makes us seem weak and uncaring, but this wasn't something you could just share with the police without consequences."

"He would've killed you both and gladly done the time to hurt us," June said. "Making me leave you made it almost worse than death, though, and I've never forgiven myself for what happened."

"You're here now, and you have to believe us when we say we understand," Rachel said, holding her hand out to her mother. "All that matters is you came back—both of you."

"See, my love," Bobbie said as she wiped the tears from June's face before worrying about her own. "My rabbi's been preaching about justice all these years, and it was ages in coming, but we've finally gotten it."

"You have, and it's time to look forward," Rachel said. Hell, if she couldn't find love, she'd at least found more family. That was something to celebrate and be happy about. Glancing at Desi, though, brought the high back to earth.

CHAPTER ELEVEN

Desi was glad Harry had her arm around her. Listening to June's story made her feel like she'd get sucked into the chasm the words opened in her chest. Her heart and head were in agreement that it was all the truth. June had described the type of man Clyde was in a few sharp, hard sentences. She'd not only had the experience of having Clyde as a father, but Byron as a husband. Only someone who'd lived through the same thing would understand completely.

"Oh my God," she said, burying her face in Harry's chest. "Now I understand his reaction when he caught us on the porch graduation night."

"What do you mean?" Bobbie asked.

"It's a long story, but our father was the most homophobic man ever to breathe," Rachel said. "Having a gay kid, much less two, was something he tried beating out of both of us."

"I'm so sorry," June said. "I guess he never forgot the insult of losing me to Bobbie. Did he punish you for choosing Harry?"

"That's how I ended up in a marriage to a man who didn't treat me much differently than Clyde treated you. I lost Harry when I gave her up for the very same reason you gave us up."

"You have to believe we wanted to come back sooner," Bobbie said because June appeared too emotional to speak. "From the day we left, twice a year—and it always came as a surprise—we'd get a visit from different thugs reminding us that giving in to the desire to seek you out wouldn't be good for either us or you."

"What thugs?" Rachel asked. Her voice was now soft, making her sound vulnerable.

"They never introduced themselves, but your mom knew Clyde

worked for a man named Giovanni Bracato. I researched it and learned the threats they made weren't empty. Every visit they warned us to keep quiet and stay away from the city." Bobbie rubbed June's back the same way Harry was rubbing hers. "We never forgot either of you, but the sacrifice of not being in your lives and remaining as dead to you as Clyde wanted us was something we did to keep you safe."

"What made you decide to come back now?" Rachel asked and Desi nodded.

"It's been two years since anyone came spouting all the old threats, so I hired someone to see what'd changed. We wouldn't come back until we knew for sure there'd be no threat to either of you." Bobbie stopped and wiped her face. "These people who've ruined our chance to be a family are all dead. In Bracato's case, he's presumed dead along with his children. All we wanted was for you to know that what we did wasn't easy, but we did it because we love you."

"Clyde is really dead?" June finally spoke.

"The bastard died in the most painful way possible, and I pray he's treading in pig shit up to his mouth for the misery he sowed while he was here." Rachel reached over and held their mother's hand as she spoke. "He begged the nurses to call us so we'd come before he died, but there was no way either of us would give him the satisfaction."

"He died, but he left so much destruction behind," Desi said. It was amazing how one conversation could change her life. This wasn't what she'd expected when she sat down, and she hated her father even more than she had. How one man could be so cruel was beyond her comprehension, but his whole life had been about inflicting pain on the people he should've loved.

"You and Rachel seem happy," June said, her tears still falling.

"That's been a recent thing," Rachel said.

Desi told their mother the story of what had happened and of her marriage to Byron. She watched the pain morph June's expression into one of horror, and she wanted to comfort this woman she'd only just met but who had given birth to her. The story also reminded Desi that Byron was waiting, just like Clyde had done for so many years, to take away all the good things in her life. In so many awful ways, Desi's life paralleled her mother's. As Harry squeezed her hand, she knew that cycle had finally been broken.

"So he's escaped?" Bobbie asked.

"Along with his brother and father," Harry said, having to clear her throat. "I'm sure they'll be found before they can get to us, but we're still waiting for news. I also think we should get something to eat. What do you think?" Harry asked, glancing down at her.

"I'd like that," Desi said, rising. "What you did for us," she said, taking June's hand, "I understand. It's not something I can condemn you for since I did the same to keep Harry and Rachel safe."

"You forgive me?" June swallowed a sob as she squeezed her hand. "You don't hate me?"

Desi closed her eyes when June got to her feet and gave her a hug, and her tears began to flow when Rachel joined them. "When I first saw you, I had so many questions, but I could never hate you. We need to look at this like I look at what happened with Byron. I can't change it, but if I dwell on only that, then I'm not celebrating the fact that Harry loves me. That I got out, and I'm free."

"I feel the same way," Rachel said. "If we stay angry, then all we're doing is letting Clyde win, and he's gotten away with too much for too long. I hope you stay so we can talk some more."

"How about I go pick some food up, and we can stay in?" Harry offered.

Desi blew her a kiss. She watched Harry go, glad they'd have the night to relax and get all the bad memories out of the way.

"She's very devoted," June said.

"She is. I fell in love with Harry when I was a little girl. We grew up together and started our relationship in high school. Clyde robbed us of sixteen years, but Harry literally put me back together when Byron beat me and broke my leg. Like Bobbie took care of you when Clyde put you in the hospital." Desi sat back down, closer to June and Bobbie, and smiled when Rachel took her hand. "We're actually getting married in a few days."

"That's wonderful." June smiled for the first time, and Desi could see what Rachel was talking about. Her resemblance to her mother was uncanny.

"That is wonderful, and we're happy for you," Bobbie said.

"So, you made it after all that happened?" Rachel asked. "It's good you had each other."

"I was lucky the second time around, but I tried to talk her out of staying." June looked at Bobbie, and she kissed the side of her head as if this was a practiced response to this subject. "She took me in when I had nowhere to go, and I helped her heal from the beating she got that night," June said, running her fingers over the scar along Bobbie's jaw.

That also seemed like a move she did often. "Bobbie was just starting out, and I didn't want her saddled with my problems. And I was a wreck over having lost you two."

"There was no way that was going to happen. I fell in love with your mother, and almost thirty years hasn't changed that. We tried our best to make a happy life, and there's plenty of foster kids who've come through our doors who have a better life because your mom loved them. That was her outlet for the love she had for you." Bobbie kissed June's temple and squeezed her to her side. "Never in all that time did I lose hope that we'd see you again and try to explain what happened."

"This is so surreal," Rachel said, her smile back. "I used to pray that you'd help us go live with Harry and her family, that you were some kind of angel watching over us. When I was a kid, I'd get mad thinking you didn't hear me."

"This might sound contrived, but I would've gladly let Clyde kill me if he'd let Bobbie raise you both. The time we spent together sharing stolen moments was the happiest I'd ever been, and she treated you two like you were her own. Believe me, she's suffered as much as I have," June said. "I hope we can be part of your lives, but if tonight is all we get, I'm happy you forgive us."

"You can't believe we wouldn't want you in our lives," Rachel said. "I know Desi feels the same way, but we've lost out on too much already. Please don't go. If you have to go home, then let's make plans for you to come back. The wedding is going to be small, but both of us want you there." She looked at Desi, who gave her a loving smile in return.

"I'm semiretired, and we were planning a two-week stay, so not to worry. And we'd love to come to the wedding if there's room for us," Bobbie said.

"That would be wonderful," she said. "I was willing to wait, but Harry wants to be married before the baby comes." She rubbed her stomach, sighing at all the tumbling the baby was doing. "What kind of medicine do you practice, Dr. Margolis?"

"Please call me Bobbie, and I'm a pediatrician. It's been a life full of runny noses and upset tummies, but I've loved every minute of it. How about Harry?"

"Harry's an orthopedic surgeon like her father and brother. If our baby turns out as hyper as Harry, we have the medical side covered." They talked until Harry came back with the food, and Desi just sat and listened while June and Bobbie answered all of Rachel's questions.

The way June looked at them, barely blinking, made her think that her mother feared they'd disappear if she closed her eyes even for a second.

Rachel answered all of June's questions about her life and whether or not she shared it with anyone special. That Serena wasn't there made Desi regret not inviting her. No matter what Rachel said, there was something between them, and not having her present the day they met their mother was a missed opportunity.

"It's late, so we should let you get to bed," June said. "Would it be okay if we came back tomorrow?"

"We'd like that. There's a few more things to get done before Saturday, and it'll be nice to have some extra help." She glanced toward Harry, unsure what to do, and mouthed *guest room*.

Harry picked up the thread. "How about if I go and check you out of the hotel, and you can stay with us?" she offered. "It'll be hard for you all to get to know each other if your visits only last a few hours."

"We don't want to put you out," Bobbie said, holding June's hand. June's eyes were wide, her lips trembling.

"Please," Desi said. "This is our home, Rachel and I both live here, and Harry's parents are staying with us as well. The ceremony we have planned is for family and our closest friends. You certainly qualify."

"If you give me a ride, I'll take care of it, Harry," Bobbie said.

"Take it easy on the stairs, and we won't be long," Harry said, kissing her.

"She certainly loves you," June said, watching Bobbie and Harry go. "Let's get you upstairs, if that's okay."

"Sure, we'll give you a tour of the rest of the house," Rachel said, walking on the other side of June. They ended up in Desi and Harry's bedroom, and June seemed drawn to the picture on the mantel.

"That was the last day we were together before Clyde made me leave her," Desi said. "I was married to Byron four months later, and I'm still amazed that I survived it all." She sat in her favorite chair, and Rachel sat next to her on the arm.

"I'm so sorry all that happened to you. You can't know how much."

"I've made peace with it, and in reality, if I had to do it over again, I wouldn't change anything except finding Harry sooner. That she still loves me is all I concentrate on." She took the hand June was offering her, and the first touch made her cry.

"I'm so sorry," June said. "I failed so horribly."

"No, you didn't, and we're glad you came back to us. I doubt any of us would've done anything differently if we'd been in the same position. He would have killed us all. Clyde was a horrible man, and a terrible father, but he's dead." Rachel placed her hand over theirs and cried with them. "We need to bury him permanently."

"You're right, and this is like a dream," June said.

Desi nodded and realized why Harry had left. June had gained confidence and opened up more once she was alone with her and Rachel.

"And your doctor is a smart one," June said, obviously figuring it out as well. "I'm glad to know you're as lucky as I am."

"Harry is one of a kind, and she's crazy about my sister," Rachel said. "It's been one of the best things in my life to watch them fall in love, and in a month it'll only get better."

"Yes it will, and it'll be even better now that you're here." She tightened her hold on her mother's hand and thought about life going forward. Her mother was here, and her child would have more than Harry's parents to rely on. "It's a gift."

Byron was exhausted from the shivering that'd made it impossible to sleep and had him aching all over. If they accomplished anything today, it would be to find a warmer place to camp for the night that would provide some kind of shelter to get out of the cold. He'd started coughing, and he could hear the rattle in his chest that usually landed him at the doctor's office. There was no time for that, considering it was an impossibility. Escaped felons couldn't just walk up to a doctor's office.

"Where the hell did he go?" Mike's question made him lift his head, then lower it just as fast when the pain in his skull made him close his eyes. What a fucking time to get sick.

"Who?" he rasped.

"Daddy, who the fuck did you think I meant." Mike stood over him and stared him down with disgust. "Did you hear him get up?"

"No, and he can't have gone far. Give me a minute." He took a breath and sat up. Every part of his body hurt, but his head was like a drum stuck on a constant beat. The area was shrouded in thick fog, and he could see his breath as he exhaled. There was nothing but trees and quiet in every direction.

"Stay here and let me go look," Mike said. He disappeared into the mist quickly, so Byron leaned back against a pine and concentrated on getting motivated enough to move. There was no way to gauge how long Mike was gone, but it seemed like hours when he finally made it back. The weather had cleared some, but the sky was still overcast, meaning the temperatures wouldn't climb much with no sun.

"What?" he asked when Mike stood quietly, not looking at him.

"He's gone." The news didn't surprise him, and he wasn't sorry. Whatever had happened to their father's mind after he'd killed their mother wasn't going to change. It was like it'd severed the connection that tethered him to reality, and it wasn't going to repair itself. Their mother had died without Big Byron's permission, and the anger had driven him crazy.

"We can't spend another night out here, and we can't wait for the cops to come and get us if he leads them right to us." He rolled to his knees and stood slowly. "Did you see anything?"

"There's a truck stop about two miles up the road, but that's it. It looks like the road we were on angles back toward the interstate, so we aren't that far off the highway." Mike pointed to his right. "Place seems busy since it's the only damn thing out here."

"I wonder how far from the state line we are." He followed Mike, prepared to spend the day on the lookout until it was safe to move.

"Worry about finding Daddy first, and then you can get on with the fantasy you have of seeing Desi again." Mike sounded condescending as always, and it pissed him off.

"If you think I'm such an asshole, then why not take off like the old man?" He bent over in a coughing fit, surprised Mike waited until he was finished. Mike was younger than he was, but they had very little in common besides being related.

In school he'd gravitated to sports, girls, and a good time while Mike was a loner who barely graduated. They worked together every damn day, but at night Mike went home to read. The guy acted like he was allergic to people. It bothered him that he couldn't figure his brother out, and that Mike was never on his side. Blood should come with some form of built-in loyalty.

"I have my reasons, and we need to find him. Daddy's out of his mind, and he's an asshole, but he doesn't deserve to be shot down like a dog."

They walked in silence after that until he saw the place Mike was talking about. There were plenty of pumps and a garage advertising tire and engine repair. It wasn't a huge business, but it did seem to be busy.

Them walking up and trying to hitch a ride would be noticed, so there was no way he'd chance it.

"Think Daddy found this place and caught a ride with someone?" he asked. The guy was crazy but could hold on to lucidity a bit at a time. It should have been easy to find him, since he couldn't have been that far ahead, but there was no sign of the old bastard.

"Either that or he's in the back of a squad car helping them find us," Mike said. "Might as well stop looking for him. You want to keep walking?"

The walk had cleared his head a little, but he was ready to catch a break. He was exhausted and walking for another whole day wasn't in him. But what the hell choice did he have? "Let's keep going but keep the interstate in sight. We have a better chance of finding something like that truck we stole if we move."

His feet were numb from the cold, and his breathing was getting labored from the exertion of walking for hours. He squinted into the distance and saw the highway sign that informed them the next exit was in five miles and New Orleans was still a hundred and eight-five miles away. If they had to walk the whole way, it'd take them a year.

It was almost dark by the time they saw the exit, and this town had more than a gas station. He smiled when he saw Burger King and a line of other fast-food places. If the restaurant was open twenty-four hours, they might have a chance of stealing one of the employee cars from the back lot, as well as getting something to eat.

"Let's wait until it gets busy, and we'll walk down there," he said to Mike, surprised when he only nodded. Hunger was a good motivator for getting his brother's cooperation. He told him his plan, and they had enough cash from the first place they'd broken into to buy a couple of meal combos.

He sent Mike in to order while he checked in the back for cars that hopefully wouldn't be missed for hours. They ate in the woods they'd been in all day and watched as the night shift came on and the drive-through window started to slow. Nothing in his life had tasted better than the hamburger and fries Mike had brought out for him. His head was still stopped up, but he'd enjoyed the simple pleasure he'd always taken for granted.

A guy came out with four garbage bags on a cart and headed to the dumpster, and they waited for him to go back inside. The parking lot connected to the cheap motel next door, and once the area had grown quiet again, they tried the doors on the crappiest car in the lot. The back passenger side door was unlocked, and he rigged the starter to get them going.

Lucky thing, it was full of gas and didn't sound like it was about to die, so driving it close to two hundred miles might be possible. It stank and was ugly as sin, but it was warm and dry. It didn't take long to find a state highway heading west, and there was enough traffic to let them not stand out. He drove until he was too tired to go on, then Mike took over. They had to push the car off the road when it ran out of gas—of course the gas gauge was broken, so much for luck—but he was that much closer to his goal. Sitting inside would be warmer than heading back into the night, but getting caught in a stolen car would be stupid.

"Now what?" Mike asked.

"Walk until we get some distance between us and the car, then we sleep." It was still dark and the trees had thinned, so there'd be no moving during the day. "With any luck we're close to home."

"Don't count on it."

Mike's sarcasm was starting to get on his nerves. "If you think I'm giving up, then you really don't fucking know me." However long it took, he was going to get back home to the stash he'd hidden, so he could start over. He had a list to check off, and it started with that. "Look, let's put this behind us for good. I know you think I'm stupid for trying, but I can't leave it like this. You and me going to jail—she dumped that on us, and I can't let it go. What happened to me in that hellhole is not something I'm going to let go." The shame of prison life made his chest burn with embarrassment, and someone was going to have to pay for that.

"Wouldn't it be better to run and make her wonder? To me that would be the cruelest thing. Leaving her hanging, always waiting for you to show up, is the way to go. She'd never stop looking over her shoulder."

Mike had a point, but sometimes you needed the satisfaction of sticking a knife in something and watching it bleed.

"She left me for some big dyke, and that bitch she's creaming her panties over has always been there from our very first night together. That's all she thought about since that sick bastard left her for bigger and better things." How many times had he come home and found her staring out the window, not seeing a goddamn thing? All those daydreams wasted on some woman who hadn't given her another thought because she was done slumming.

"You really are stupid if you think Clyde didn't have something to do with making Desi stay with you. Him and Daddy planned the whole thing, and it always hit me wrong." Mike laughed, more at him than with him. "And you. All you saw was that pretty face and you were all-in. You never cared a damn thing about what she wanted." Mike tightened his grip on the steering wheel.

Killing Mike now would leave him to do all this alone, and he wasn't ready for that. "You would've done the same damn thing—don't lie. Desi was a sweet piece of ass, and she was wild for me at first."

"Yeah, right. Now who's lying. I may not know everything, but I do know all that girl ever wanted was away from you. Think about that before you sacrifice your entire future for someone who's been running from you ever since she laid eyes on you. The only reason she stayed was because you chained her in that house, and she had nowhere to go." His jaw clenched. "Just like Dad kept Mom locked up."

"Shut the fuck up and let me think." The road had become deserted and darker, but sleep was the only option until they could start walking again. He glanced at Mike, glad he'd closed his eyes and rested his head against the window. Yeah, it wouldn't be long now, and the cops wouldn't be any wiser. The assholes were probably still covering the swamp and woods around the prison searching for them, if they hadn't already assumed the gators had gotten them.

He wondered where Tyrell had ended up and thought about shooting him in the head for leaving him out in the woods with the losers who'd run with them. The only thing Tyrell had going for him was friends still on the outside willing to help him. Even if Byron found a phone, there was no one to call. He might be on his own, but he didn't and wouldn't owe anyone shit. Owing meant you were that much closer to someone stabbing you in the back.

"And I hope it happens to you sooner than later, you bastard," he said to Tyrell, hoping he'd somehow hear him. He knew the guy didn't owe him anything, but he'd really fucked them by dumping them to get caught that much quicker. And what he'd said about doing Desi a favor and offing Byron before he could make it to her set a fire in his chest. What did he know? "You deserve whatever you got coming."

CHAPTER TWELVE

Harry stood to the side of the kitchen as the last-minute details of their wedding were being discussed. She smiled at Bobbie, who seemed as confused as she did as to why a short ceremony in front of a federal judge took this much discussion.

All that mattered to her was that Desi looked happy, and it'd be Desi who she'd be marrying. The rest was fluff, as her father liked to say. The new haircut Rachel had given Desi was also distracting her to the point she wanted to tell the lot of these people to get out of her house so she could be alone with her future wife.

Mona pointed to the front door when the doorbell rang, and she saluted before going to get it. Seeing Detectives Roger Landry and Sept Savoie outside brought the reality of Byron and his screwed-up family back into their orbit. There was no hiding from it, and that'd bring the happiness happening in her kitchen to an abrupt halt as reality set in.

"Harry, sorry to come so early, but we thought you might appreciate an update," Sept said, rubbing her hands together and blowing on them.

Sept had been the one called to investigate the home invasion at Jude Rose's house the night Byron and Mike had broken in, thinking they'd be hauling Desi away. After Monica Rose broke Byron's nose, the two geniuses figured out they had the wrong house. Jude was not only an old family friend of her parents, but a respected judge. Roger had been the detective assigned to Desi's case from the night of Byron's initial assault, and he'd done a great job of reassuring Desi every step of the way.

"Hey, thanks. I was beginning to wonder when you'd come by. Did they rope you into helping, Roger?" She shook hands with Roger before accepting Sept's hug. "Please tell me you have all the assholes in custody and are here to help me celebrate."

"I wish, but let's talk about this with Desi as well in case she has any questions." Sept followed her to the kitchen as Roger brought up the rear. "Hey, Desi," Sept said, kissing Desi's cheek. "You look beautiful."

"Don't you have your own girl?" Harry asked. She smiled at Rachel when she moved so Harry could sit next to Desi and take her hand.

"Thank you, and it'll be good that we'll have you and Keegan to call for our first playdates." Desi took a few deep breaths and held Harry's hand tightly. "How is Keegan?"

"It's not an easy thing to be nauseous all the time and be a chef. I'm about to go through acne again if I eat another peanut butter sandwich, but it's the only thing that doesn't make her ill." Sept's expression completely changed when she talked about her partner, the head chef of Blanchard's

"Ooh, I can't imagine morning sickness lasting that long, but it's a good thing Harry loves peanut butter since that was my go-to while I was sick. Now I think I've eaten my weight in chicken salad."

"That's so strange. You have the same cravings I did," June said. "With Rachel it was Cheetos, of all things."

"We might be related," Desi deadpanned. She stood and paused as if enjoying the levity a moment longer before moving to the cabinets to take out two coffee cups. "I hope you being here is good news."

"I wish," Roger said. "A few of the men who escaped after what happened to the guard were recaptured. It's where they were found that has changed the scope of our search."

"They're in the city already?" Harry asked. She'd have to get the guards back in bigger numbers and think about how else to keep her family safe. The sudden panic was a foreign concept. Her life before all this had been about work and fleeting relationships. This was different. With Desi it was her future, her love, and the dark thoughts of what-ifs completely paralyzed her. How Desi had been able to live this way for years made her admire her for her strength.

"No," Sept said, standing and taking the cups from Desi and walking her back to Harry. "Sit and I'll get it." Sept poured two cups and nodded toward Roger so he'd start talking.

"Five of the guys were found in Mississippi. They were walking together on a road outside of Hattiesburg. Their story was that Tyrell

Lagrie, one of the other prisoners, had one of his crew come and get them." Roger read from his notes. "They got into the back of a truck, thinking they'd end up in town. Tyrell double-crossed them and dropped them in the middle of Nowhere, Mississippi, although it's a damn shame he even took them that far."

"Byron and his family weren't with the group?" Desi asked.

"No, sweetie, they're still at large," Sept said. "But the guys we captured have confirmed that the three of them were part of the group in Tyrell's van, so they definitely made it out of the swamp. The good news is, now we have confidence about where we need to search."

"Why Mississippi, do you think?" Desi asked. "Why would one of them do that to the others?"

"One of the guys said Tyrell wanted to give them the chance to run from a place we wouldn't be looking for them," Sept said. "That does make sense, but I still don't understand why go that far east. All that matters is it made sense to Tyrell, so maybe he thought he was doing them a favor."

"So what happens now?" Harry asked.

"We're actively covering the places Lagrie might run for help and putting both Mississippi's and our state troopers on alert." Sept slid her hand across the table and flattened it over Desi's. "This case is a priority. Roger did an excellent job last time, and he's assigned to your case again, but my partner and I will also be involved. We're taking precautions so the Simoneaux family doesn't pose a threat to you or Jude and Monica Rose."

Harry said, "I called the same service we used before to watch the house, and I'll tell you the same thing I told Serena and Roger when all this started. If he gets anywhere near Desi, it'll be the last thing he does." This was ridiculous. How much did Desi have to take in this lifetime? She'd paid in pain, humiliation, and fear for years, and it was time for it to stop. That she couldn't do anything to prevent what she knew was coming was making her chest hurt.

"Harry, I need you to listen to me. Both of you," Sept said. "There are no guarantees in life, so I'm not going to sit here and tell you that we'll be able to stop something bad from happening. I *can* promise that we'll do everything humanly possible to keep you, Desi, and the baby away from this guy. If it comes down to you and him, then I expect you to protect your family, but don't say things like that in front of us. We feel you, but we're also sworn to uphold the law."

"That's true," Roger said. "All we're asking is that you allow us to do our job and don't go looking for trouble." He paused. "But if it finds you, and we're not here…"

"And the guards are a good idea, but we're going to beef up patrols around you, and either Roger or I will check in with you daily." Sept smiled and let go of Desi's hand. "I know we dumped a lot on you today, but try to enjoy your time, and we'll see you guys tomorrow. I'll be here to make sure you say your vows right, and to make sure nothing goes wrong." Sept pointed at Harry.

"Thanks, Sept, and I'm not angry with either of you. It's the situation," she said, putting her arm around Desi.

"You're a lot calmer than I would be, so don't sweat what's not important." Sept slapped Roger on the arm and stood. "Call me no matter the time. The most important thing is that you're taken care of, Desi. Those are Keegan's orders, and she passed along that she can't wait to see you guys tonight."

They were having a big family dinner at Blanchard's before the ceremony tomorrow, and Sept's visit seemed to have put Desi more at ease. "Can you let Keegan know to add two more?" Harry glanced at Bobbie and June. "I didn't get the chance to introduce you, but this is Desi's mom, June, and her wife, Bobbie."

"I'll drive over there now. Remember, I don't care if you think it's trivial—call me," Sept said, pointing at Desi.

"I will and thank you. You're a good friend, Sept." Desi joined her in walking Roger and Sept out, where they found Serena walking up the sidewalk to the front door. "She's in the kitchen," Desi said.

She stood with Desi in the foyer with her arms around her and kissed the top of her head. "Are you okay?"

"I will be, love. There's nothing he can do to hurt me more than he already has. The difference now is that I have you."

"That you do, and it's a lifetime commitment." There were times when she had to stop and think about how much she had to lose. Byron was as determined to hurt Desi as she was to protect her, and she was prepared to do whatever it took to make sure they had a chance at living without any threats hanging over them.

She'd had a burning in her gut from the moment Serena had informed them of Byron's escape. It was a combination of anger and fear, and she'd done her best to let that go. She couldn't let her guard down, and Desi deserved better than her constant list of what-ifs.

❖

Rachel turned from placing things in the dishwasher and found Serena standing in the doorway. Everything that had been on her mind when it came to Serena changed when she saw her. Serena was lucky that her good mood from having her mother back spilled over to her, and she'd consider being more understanding. "Hey," she said to put Serena at ease.

"Do you have a few minutes?"

She glanced at June before taking Serena upstairs and didn't feel bad leaving them when June winked at her. There'd be no big introductions until she knew where she and Serena were headed. "If you had anything to do with getting Sept and Roger over here to talk to Desi, thank you." The click of the bedroom door seemed loud when she closed it behind her before she sat on the window seat. "It's scary to think about, but I think it helped."

"They really are working hard. Not that Desi and Harry aren't important, but Jude and Monica's weird involvement has the police in overdrive to get this done." Serena walked to the other side of the bench and sat down. "I'm glad they stopped by, but that's not what I wanted to talk to you about."

"What is it?" It was like they were strangers who'd had a history of sex. Perhaps that's what conclusion Serena had come to, and she was there to finally put an end to this.

"I keep thinking over everything and wondering what the hell went wrong. You and what you brought into my life were incredibly special, and then it was gone." Serena was nearly whispering. "When you disappeared, I wanted to blame you so I could prove to myself why relationships aren't a good idea, but all of it was on me."

"I think Harry is right that we have a lot in common," Rachel said. "We've dated plenty, and no one was special enough for us to stick around. Until you, that is," she added, vowing to herself to be honest. "You made me consider what it'd be like to share a future with someone, but you aren't in love with me."

"Wait," Serena said, but Rachel shook her head.

"No, be honest. I've asked you that before, and that's all I want from you. Honesty. There's plenty of things and people in your life that are important. You love your job, Butch, and the life you've created for yourself. I'm not saying you don't care about me, but I'm way down on your list." She reached over and took Serena's hand. "That's not something I'm asking you to change, but I'm not going to accept being an afterthought."

"I don't want you to." Serena stared at their joined hands. "All I'm asking is for what we talked about yesterday. I want a second chance. After our talk, I spent the rest of the day and night thinking. I screwed up, I'm not denying that, but the one thing you got wrong is Harry."

"Honey, it's okay. I get it, and I've been in the same spot. Harry is who everyone wants to be in love with. My sister floated through high school because Harry swept her off her feet. It's like she imprinted on Desi's heart, and there was no one else. In a way it was epic." She smiled, promising herself she was over the anger. "Harry's easy to fall for, but you need to move on. My sister is in no way a violent person, but if you still have feelings for Harry, you're going to lose."

Serena pinched the bridge of her nose. "I know you don't believe me, but I have moved on. What I shared with Harry happened when I most needed someone like her. I don't have to explain what it's like to be in an abusive relationship. Mine didn't last as long as Desi's, which makes me admire her strength. My love for Harry turned to friendship when we both realized there was no future for us except as two people who loved Butch." Serena let her go and stood up to pace. "Harry and I didn't work as a couple, and I accepted that way before you and Desi got here. There's a difference, though, between what I feel for you and what I feel for Harry."

"I'm not a tall, good-looking orthopedic surgeon?" she said with a slight smile.

"I need you to understand that I want you in my life. If we talk about it, I'm sure we can make it work."

"That's true, but you haven't shown a propensity for including me in any conversation about your life, much less your decision-making process. Your job, Butch, and your time are all in your bracket of what you don't share. Where does that leave me?" On second thought, maybe she was still a little pissed.

"I told the DA I was going to think about the promotion because I wanted to talk it over with you. Butch isn't happy with me because you aren't around anymore and he's convinced I'm to blame, and my time is empty without you in my life." Serena knelt in front of her and took her hands. "We can go as slow as you like for me to prove to you that I'm serious."

"Please, I'm not a big fan of the over-the-top gesture. I said we can be friends." She leaned in and kissed Serena's forehead.

"I think friendship is important to any long-term relationship, but I want more than that. All I'm asking is for you to start listening to what I'm saying. I'd like you to be as committed to trying as I am. I'd like to start by asking you out. Do you have a date for the wedding?"

She had to give Serena credit for not giving up. "I'd like to think so." The way Serena's face fell in disappointment touched her. "I meant you, honey."

"Good, I don't think I could handle seeing you with someone else. And I know it's short notice, but is there anything you need me to do?"

Jealousy on Serena's part was new, and it frankly surprised her. And, maybe, made her a little happy. "How about coming downstairs and meeting my mother?" She didn't resist when Serena moved closer and kissed her cheek before placing a chaste kiss on her lips.

"I guess that worked out, huh?"

The question softened something in her, and she pressed her lips to Serena's with more intent than was normal for friends. "This will shock you, but I was pissed until she told us what happened. Do you know anything about some guy named Bracato?" She didn't let go of Serena's hand when she stood and sat next to her.

"Big Gino Bracato, you mean?"

"I think so." Having someone in the DA's office would come in handy for this kind of thing.

"Bracato was a player in the drug business until he went up against Cain Casey, the alleged Irish mob boss. From what little I've heard of him, he was trying to set up his sons to continue the business until the day they disappeared. I mean completely disappeared." Serena closed her eyes as if it helped her remember. "Once the sons were gone, Big Gino was frantic, and then he vanished. The feds think Casey is to blame for that, but there's no way to prove it. If she is responsible, whatever she did to them, they haven't been found."

"Would the people who worked for him have gone to someone else?" She wanted to understand how Clyde had evolved. Was there any chance that side of Clyde's past could continue to haunt them?

"Some of Bracato's men went to work for some of the gangs coming up, and some of them did their own contract work. You have to understand that some of the old guys aren't about to take orders from some of the young punks taking over. It's not really my division, but I can ask around if you want more information. What you don't want to do is become a blip on Casey's radar." Serena had become more animated as she spoke about all this, proving Rachel's point of how much she loved her job.

"I'm not looking to bring down organized crime in the city." She told Serena June's story and how long they'd been harassed. "They haven't come before now because they thought Desi and I were in danger. We're already in danger from Byron and his Neanderthal family, and we don't want to compound that, but I need to know if getting to know our mother will turn into something else. I don't think either of us wants to give up on a relationship with our mom, but I want to be prepared."

"Once Clyde died, I think whatever favors these guys owed him died with him," Serena said. "To be on the safe side, please be careful until this is over. If Clyde's thugs stopped visiting, that would fit with the timeline of when Bracato and his sons disappeared. Don't take any chances, though." Serena turned and faced her. "Let the system work, and I'll start researching what happened to make sure there isn't a problem we haven't identified."

"The system can fuck itself. It was supposed to lock Byron up until he was too old to care about us, but that didn't work out."

"Angola itself is unique. It's is built on old plantation land, and some of it doesn't have to be fenced because nature built in deterrents. Breaking out of there is next to impossible, but the guard having a massive coronary and his partner leaving him alone wasn't protocol. If they'd followed the rules, Byron would be fish food along with anyone else who went over that levee."

"Shouldn't they have been found by now?" She wanted to do her part to fight for her sister. "If they aren't found soon, I'm going to lose my shit."

"It's not going to come to that. Like I said, I don't have any guarantees, but Byron and his family aren't that smart."

Rachel nodded and went with it when Serena hugged her. "The offer's still good. Would you like to meet my mother?"

"I'd love to." Serena held out her hand, and she took it.

Bobbie and her mother were sitting with Rosa, Francisco, and Mona but turned their way when they walked back into the kitchen. "This is Serena Ladding," Rachel said, and Serena squeezed her hand. "She's a good friend and helped Desi with her case."

"Thank you for all you did for our girls," Bobbie said, and Rachel's chest warmed.

It was like she'd been stuck in the cold for years, and the kindness of inclusion made her feel as if she'd been given a warm blanket and hot chocolate. She'd always belonged with Desi, but this was different. Bobbie and June represented the parents she'd always wanted and been denied.

"Yes, ma'am, we're doing our best. I'm so glad you made it for the wedding," Serena said.

"I'd like to think it's our reward for having to stay away so long. Are you coming?" June asked.

Serena lifted their linked hands. "I'm Rachel's date, and I'll be back in a few hours to help with anything that you need from me."

"You're working today?" Rachel asked, her stomach dropping. So much for being a priority.

Serena winced slightly. "Just the daily briefing on Byron and the others still at large. I'm sure Sept and Roger gave you a status update."

She couldn't hold Serena's work against her when it had to do with their safety. "Okay. Don't forget to ask about what we were talking about." She walked Serena to the door and closed her eyes when Serena held her.

"Call me if you need to, and I'll report anything new when I get back." Serena seemed to hesitate before finding her bravado and kissing her. "And I will be back."

"I'll be waiting." It was strange to have so much hope on so many fronts, considering there was a real threat lurking on the shadowy horizon. She kissed Serena again and smiled against her lips. "Don't forget to bring Butch."

"I'm not going to forget anything we talked about."

Progress wasn't impossible. She just had to find a way to believe she could have the fairy tale too.

Chapter Thirteen

The family dinner at Blanchard's was surreal to Desi. It was a good example of how drastically her life had changed. There were so many people who were happy about the wedding the next day, and they accepted what Harry meant to her. Harry was talking to Jude and Monica, but she gazed at her often enough for her to know she was on Harry's mind.

"Are you feeling okay?" Keegan asked. The head chef of Blanchard's wasn't working that night but had been giving orders since she and Sept arrived. In the months Desi had been with Harry, Keegan had become a good friend and had invited her to dine in the kitchen often. She and Rachel had come without Harry for lunch, and she enjoyed Keegan's friendship. Keegan got the credit for inviting some of the people who'd attended her show.

"I'm excited enough that I'm trying to ignore my aching feet tonight. Thank you again for doing this for us." The dinner for everyone attending tomorrow was Keegan and Sept's wedding gift.

"Please, I'm having children with Sept, and if I've learned anything from the Savoie family, it's that having someone who can set bones on speed dial is a good thing. Besides that, we love you guys, and I'm so happy for you both." Keegan was a beautiful woman who, like Harry, could've had anyone. She'd picked Sept, who was a cop from a cop family, and they made it work. She thought of them when she was insecure of her place in Harry's life. She didn't need to be a doctor or any other high-flying professional. She could just be herself.

"Sept mentioned you were still having morning sickness." She knew Keegan was having twins. Sept reminded her a lot of Harry, and she was worried about the size of her baby, so she couldn't imagine having two at once.

"That's the worst name for that since it's all-the-time sickness," Keegan said and laughed. "It's getting better, but work has been a bear."

"You should teach Savoie to cook something to give you a break," Harry said, putting her arms around Desi from behind.

"Savoie knows how to cook plenty. If you ask her, she could teach you a couple things." Keegan winked and excused herself to talk to the staff.

"I love you," Harry said when they were alone. "Tomorrow I'm finally going to get what I've wanted all my life."

She leaned back against Harry and smiled. "What's that?"

"I get you, and I get to call you my wife." Harry kissed the back of her neck, making her shiver. "That we don't have to wait much longer for the baby is a bonus."

The baby was active and Harry's hands on her seemed to rev the gymnastics. She put her hands over Harry's and really leaned back into her. This was her safe place, her person, her home. "Who knew I was that smart in high school."

Harry kissed the back of her neck again. "Thank you for saying yes, and for loving me."

"I never stopped, you know. There was never a time, no matter the consequences, that I stopped loving you. I couldn't because of all the promises we made to each other." She turned around and fisted her hands in the lapels of Harry's jacket so she'd lower her head. The kiss was sweet and held all the happiness she'd come to expect from Harry. "I can't wait to marry you, and have you be mine."

"Well, this proves this is going to be a good match. It bodes well for the future when you can't keep your hands off each other," Kenneth said with Tony at his side. He tapped a spoon against his glass to get everyone's attention. "As the best man, I wanted to get my toast practice in." The staff came in with champagne and sparkling grape juice. "I've known Harry all my life. We were best friends back in kindergarten, and I know there isn't anything she wouldn't do for me if I asked," he started once everyone had a glass. "We survived medical school and residency together, and we found love together with two incredible people. Tony and I were lucky enough to be there when Harry and Desi fell in love, and it's been an awesome thing to watch grow."

Desi smiled when she saw Tony's face soften. Her best friend, aside from Rachel, had been the rock she'd needed to ease herself into Harry's life. She'd been nervous about that for weeks, but with each shopping trip and gossip session, those panicky sensations had disappeared.

"Desi, I'm glad you're here to take care of her. My best friend has a new best friend, and I couldn't be happier. It's good to know that love does win and that you both know that it was worth waiting for. Tomorrow starts your life together in marriage, but there's so much more to come. I personally can't wait to see you as parents, if only to gain a patient," he said, winking at them. "So I lift a glass." Kenneth did just that. "Congratulations, and my wish for you is a long, good life full of all good things. To Harry and Desi."

"To Harry and Desi," everyone repeated.

After that the conversations around them centered on the baby and the day they had planned tomorrow. Harry's older brother, Miguel, had come back with his family, and the kids were playing with Butch. This was the life Desi had always wanted. Harry's family had accepted her and Rachel, and they'd be as protective of her and Harry's child as they were of Miguel's boys.

"You look fantastic," Miguel said to her. His wife Kimber held his hand. Desi had loved their time together, getting to know him again with his family. He'd been sweet when they'd asked him to be their donor when they'd been ready to start their family, and Kimber had hugged her, saying it was about time Harry fell in line. "The boys are ready for a cousin, and my sister needs to experience middle-of-the-night feedings and diaper changes. She's had it too good for too long."

"Thanks," she said, watching Dominic and Hugo with Butch. Dominic was older, but he didn't seem to mind sitting with his little brother and Butch. "If this kid gets any bigger, I'm going to force Ellie to induce labor. At this point I'm praying they weigh like twenty pounds, so all this weight is gone right away."

"Been there and have the stretch marks to prove it, but enjoy this while you can. Once they come out, they never stop, sleep, or sit still. It's full speed all the time, and it's exhausting. The only good thing about it is they'll knock the weight off you soon enough," Kimber said. "We really are happy for you. It'll be nice to not have Harry moping during the holidays."

They laughed, and Harry teased her brother about a few things. The staff put out small desserts so folks could walk around and continue talking. She made an effort to take Harry around and talk to everyone who'd come. They left her mother and Bobbie for last. Her mom seemed to be having a good time, and Kenneth and Tony had made a point of sitting with them.

"Did you enjoy dinner?" she asked her mother. Bobbie seemed to be having a good time talking and comparing treatments with Kenneth.

"It was wonderful, and I keep wanting to pinch myself to prove I'm not dreaming." Her mother held her hand between hers and seemed animated.

"About tomorrow," she started and glanced around to find Rachel. When their eyes met, Rachel walked over holding Serena's hand. "Rachel's going to stand with me, so would you consider giving me away? Both of you, actually."

Bobbie turned when she asked that, and Desi felt the weight of Harry's hands resting on her shoulders.

"Are you sure?" her mom asked, clearly in awe.

"It's not something I'm planning to do again, Mama—marriage, I mean. Harry is it for me, and I'd like you and Bobbie to be a part of the day." She smiled as Rachel nodded. "If you're not comfortable with that, it's okay, but I wanted to ask."

"How can you forgive me so easily?"

Her mother's question didn't surprise her. Being on their own so long only to find out their mother was still alive should've pissed her off. Truthfully, she *was* angry, but not at her mother and her wife. They'd been forced into an untenable situation as well, one that had hurt them deeply. Punishing her mother wasn't the answer and would only let Clyde win the game he'd started so long ago. It'd be like blaming Harry and Rachel for her having to marry Byron.

She gazed at her parents, since Bobbie seemed to be as invested as her mother, and smiled. She'd only had vague memories of her mother up to now, but they were starting to come back, and she remembered calling for her mama. That sense of being loved had disappeared when she'd been left with Clyde and his mother, but it was coming back.

"You're my mother but I remember so little about you. I'd like to change that. What happened wasn't fair, but I'm about to give birth, and I'd love for our baby to know their grandmothers. This kid is our second chance to show Clyde how wrong he was, keeping us apart." She moved a little away from Harry and took one of June's hands, then Bobbie's. "It doesn't matter what happened," she said and they nodded. "What matters is that my mama and mom have come back, and Rachel and I will be richer for it."

"We'd love to walk you down the aisle," Bobbie said when June started crying again. "And we love you. That's not something that stopped because we weren't here."

"Good answer," Harry said, making her laugh as she and Rachel embraced their mother.

They stayed an hour more before heading home, and she stepped into the den with Harry. The last thing she wanted was to be separated from Harry even for the night, but Tony and Rachel had insisted. After dropping her off, Harry was going to spend the night with Kenneth while Tony stayed in Rachel's room. That would give her and Rachel the night.

"Don't forget that we have a date tomorrow," Harry said as she put her arms around her.

She loved being held like this. "I'll be there with a ring for you." She kissed Harry's chest and sighed. "And I'm glad that after tomorrow no one can talk me into having you spend the night somewhere else."

"That's true, and we're going to make the most of those nights, so don't let Rachel keep you up too late." Harry pulled her closer and lowered her head. "You are, and have been, the love of my life. I can't wait to stand before our family and friends and say just that." The way Harry kissed her, slow, passionate, and with what seemed to be her whole self, made her knees weak. It was so real and wonderful.

"I love you." She let Harry go and wanted to follow her out the door but was stopped on her way.

"Girl, get your butt upstairs and put your feet up," Tony said. "Harry left us a little something."

She did as he ordered and sat on the bed with him and Rachel, sipping from a glass of champagne after checking with Harry to make sure it was really okay. Leaving her old life behind was only hours away, and Byron would be a distant memory no matter where he was and what he was planning to do.

❖

She woke up with Rachel pressed against her, and she placed her hands on her middle. Baby Basantes was up and active.

"You're going to be one lucky kid once your mom gets ahold of you."

"They'll be even luckier once they meet their mama," Rachel said, yawning.

"If you add their aunt, then it'll be a wonderful life." She kissed the top of Rachel's head and got up to use the bathroom. "Speaking of wonderful lives, should I get my hopes up after seeing who your date was last night?" She pointed to the chairs by the fireplace. It was cold enough for Rachel to open the flue and light the logs Harry had stacked.

"We talked yesterday after Sept and Roger left, and there might be a chance we can date without me wanting to hit her with my car. She told me that I was wrong about how she feels about Harry. The rest of the conversation was about a partnership going forward, along with a lot of apologizing." Rachel blew on the fire and then curled up in the chair once it caught. "Of course I'm paraphrasing, but she sounded sincere."

"But you're still not ready to give in," she said, understanding Rachel like no one else.

"You're lucky, sis. Harry is like the grand prize in a contest for the perfect partner. She loves you, goes through ridiculous lengths to show you, and is loyal to the core." Rachel poked her with the tip of her toe. "You can take her at her word because she's proven herself over and over. Serena I'm not sure about yet. She's really good at saying all the right things, and considering what she does for a living, that's not surprising. The problem is follow-through. She gets wrapped up, and I get shuffled to the back of her mind. I'm not up for a lifetime of that."

"You know I'm here no matter what, so take your time. All I wanted was for you to not write her off without talking to her first."

"I'm not going to be rash for once. Let's go eat something so I can do your hair and makeup after you've eaten. I'm not sure if you remember, but you're getting married today."

"It's been a long time in coming." All those fantasies she'd spun when she was in high school were about to come true. The reality of that made her whole in places she didn't think could ever be repaired they were so broken. Harry, God love her, was the model of all those bible verses about being patient and kind. When she'd been unsure, Harry had been sure enough for the both of them that Desi belonged with her. That love they'd forged when they were young had withstood the test of separation, forgiveness, and drama, and the pure joy suffusing her soul felt like it could burst from her any second, like her body simply wasn't enough to contain it.

Breakfast was full of laughs and teasing from Mona, and her mother gave her some advice once she went up to get dressed. "My life has centered for so long around depression over what I lost, but I was lucky that the woman who chose to love me was Bobbie. She's understood me and gently pushed me to channel what I was feeling into something I'd find rewarding."

"She told me about the kids you both fostered." She stepped into the dress Tony and Rachel helped her pick out and stared at her reflection.

The A-line V-neck ivory silk dress was the fourth one she'd tried on, and they'd all fallen in love with it. The flowy dress accentuated the fact she was very pregnant, but it wasn't clingy, and it felt luxurious against her skin. She'd had it altered so she could wear flats, and she felt beautiful in it.

"It was so much more than that. Bobbie gave me a reason to go on, to live, and to have faith in the future. Our children were never going to be completely lost to us. She's said that for years, and she was right. The best thing about her is how she's loved me, and I see that in Harry. All you can do is love her back and enjoy what you are together." She hesitated and blinked away tears. "What we've both been through, you and I...it can be hard to truly believe in our right to be happy. But it *is* our right, and we can heal. I promise."

"If we haven't said it enough, we're glad you're here," she said, and Rachel kissed their mother's cheek. "With everything going on we haven't had time, but I'd love to sit with you and talk so much more. I'm still amazed that we get another chance without all the baggage."

She held her mom's and Rachel's hands as they went down the stairs, and she kissed Mona's cheek when she made it into the kitchen where Bobbie was waiting. The hug Bobbie gave her made her hang on for a minute, enjoying the warmth of her. Bobbie's cologne struck a chord of remembrance in her, and she kissed her cheek before letting go.

"While we're all here, Rachel and I have something to ask you," she said as the four of them stood together.

"You can ask us anything," Bobbie said.

"It might be too early, and we still have so much more to talk about, but we'd like to call you Mama and Mom. I know I said it last night, and if you think it's too much too fast, that's okay too."

"None of us are getting any younger, though, so don't take too long," Rachel said, breaking the tension.

"I'm pretty sure it's you and Harry who are supposed to receive gifts today," her mother said. "That, though, is better and more special than anything we've ever been given. We'd be honored to take those titles back." She took her hand and Bobbie took Rachel's.

"What she said," Bobbie said, sounding as if her emotions were on overload. "Let's not keep Harry waiting."

"Let's go, Moms," Rachel said, picking up her small bouquet. "I'll be right ahead of you."

It was winter, so the garden wasn't spectacular, but the spot close to Desi's studio always had flowers, and that's where Harry was waiting with their friends and family. There were enough heaters to keep her warm as she braved the chilly morning, wanting to remember this day as the one when all the dreams and hopes of a naive eighteen-year-old came true. Everything else faded away when she saw Harry and how she looked at her.

Bobbie and her mom stood at her sides and walked her between the chairs until they reached the pavers where Harry stood. As cold and rainy as it'd been, the weather had finally cleared to a brilliant blue sky.

She hugged both Bobbie and her mom before putting her hand in Harry's as they faced Judge Ladding. He didn't talk too much before getting to the vows, and all she wanted was to pledge herself to Harry so she could be back in her arms.

"Harry," Judge Ladding said.

"I remember the first day I met you. It wouldn't be hard to describe what you were wearing and what you sounded like," Harry said as she held her hands. "I remember that and everything that came after. Our first kiss, the first time you told me you loved me, and how you said good-bye. As painful as that was, it proved to me that my love for you was all-encompassing. That's our history, and how we made our way back to each other is important, but it's not as important as our future."

The vows Harry had written made her teary, and she wanted to comfort Harry and say it'd be all right like Harry had on so many nights. It was like baring an important part of who they were in front of all these people even if they were their closest friends and family. This was a glimpse of the Harry who belonged solely to her.

"We will build a family, a marriage, and a bond that will only be broken through death. I promise to love you, honor you, and protect you. There will never be another day that you aren't the center of my world. I love you, Desiree, and I can't wait for all that comes next."

"Desi," Judge Ladding said, his smile wide.

She took a breath and gazed into Harry's eyes. "I've told you before that no matter what happened, at the center of me there's always been you. You taught me how to love, how to dream, and how to ask for the things I want. All I want is you and the family we'll build together. You were the person I'd wait an eternity for. I promise to love you, honor you, and protect you. I'm going to love my life because I finally get to share it with you and the children we'll raise together. I also promise that you'll have all of me for as long as I live because I love you and I will for as long as my heart beats."

They exchanged rings and smiled when Judge Ladding said it was okay to kiss the bride. Harry put her hands on her hips and stepped close before lowering her head and kissing her like she never wanted to stop. They did when the applause registered, and she realized that they were married. All those fantasies in high school weren't so far-fetched now that Harry wore her ring.

"There are women crying all over the city." Tony teased her when he hugged her. "You made off with the prize with hardly any effort."

"She *is* a prize, so leave me alone to enjoy the day." She kissed his cheek and held him as tight as she could manage with the baby in the way. Above all else she hoped he knew how important to her he was.

"I know, honey, and I love you too. I'm so happy for you, and I'm glad Harry waited to get it right." He kissed her forehead and dabbed her eyes with a tissue. "Now don't mess up Rachel's beautiful work before the pictures."

They headed back inside to the champagne breakfast Mona had prepared to be enjoyed while everyone mingled—mimosas, coffee, and bite-sized breakfast foods. Her cheeks were tired from her perpetual smile and Harry seemed to be in the same frame of mind.

Kenneth, Miguel, and Francisco all proposed toasts to welcome Desi officially into their family. That Francisco had made his with his arm around Rachel warmed her. She and Rachel finally had what they'd wished for as children, membership into the Basantes family, and no one could take it away from them.

"Are you ready?" Harry asked after a couple of hours.

"Yes." She pulled Harry closer and sighed happily when Harry held her.

"Remember one thing," Ellie said before they could make it out the door. She watched Harry arch her eyebrow in question, and she wanted to laugh. "One strong orgasm and I might get to meet you at the hospital."

She didn't need a mirror to know she was blushing. The heat radiating from her ears alone made her dizzy, but it was their honeymoon, dammit. She'd been waiting too long to go on one with Harry, no matter how short it was. "Are you trying to tell us we should only talk tonight?"

"No, I'm not baiting Harry into filling my car with frogs or something else equally horrific in retaliation," Ellie said, laughing. "I'm just giving you a friendly heads-up because I want another couple of weeks before you give birth."

"How do you feel about a multitude of mild orgasms?" Harry sounded like she was thinking about that frog option. "We know the risks and I'm not going to put Desi in a bad situation. And if we show up at the emergency room because I'm an animal, don't dawdle."

"Are you kidding? I'm as anxious to meet the baby as you are. Have fun." Ellie kissed their cheeks and stepped back to let the rest of the family say good-bye.

"Where are we going?" Desi asked once they were alone in the SUV.

"I wanted at least one night of quiet with you." Harry kissed her and backed out of the drive. "We'll talk and be naked while we do it. Let's see where that gets us without anyone but room service knocking on our door."

"Thank you. It's like when you're a kid and someone tells you something is off-limits. The last week has been crazy, and all I've wanted is to curl up with you." The trip downtown to the Piquant was short, and she exhaled when they were shown to a suite. There was a basket of snacks on the side table, but she ignored it as Harry tipped the bellman and turned to her. That expression on her face was one she'd seen often in the last months, and she took Harry's hand and followed her to the bedroom.

"Well, Dr. Basantes, should we get to the naked conversations?" She turned her back on Harry so she'd unbutton the dress.

"Yes, Mrs. Basantes, that's exactly what we should get to."

Chapter Fourteen

Serena brought a stack of dishes to the kitchen after taking her jacket off and rolling up the sleeves of her silk shirt. Rachel watched her as she stood at the sink with Mona, who shook her head. "Get out of here and put that girl out of her misery. I'm sure dishes are the last thing on her mind."

Saturdays were Rachel's busy days at the salon, and she liked the way the constant work let her get lost for hours at a time. Having the rest of the day free without Desi and Harry there made her anxious, but Serena had promised an early dinner with a friend she thought she should meet.

"That's the last of them," Serena said.

"Good, I have plenty of help, so why not go and do something fun," Mona said, pointing to her two daughters who'd come to celebrate the wedding.

She changed into wool pants and a sweater, so she wouldn't have to come back later. Serena opened her door for her after she'd gotten Butch settled in the back seat and talked to him the whole time she was buckling him in. It was special how many times he'd told her he'd missed her. Her feelings for Serena still weren't solid, but she loved Butch and wanted him in her life.

"Can I come with you and Rachel, Mommy?" Butch asked as if he recognized that they were heading to his grandparents'.

"How about we go for ice cream tomorrow?" she offered and hoped Serena went along with it. "Just you and me, and you can tell me all about school."

"Yes," he said, clearly excited. "I can't wait."

They dropped him off, and Rachel enjoyed the hug Butch gave her. "Where are we going?"

Serena headed downtown. She hadn't said much after they'd gotten in the car. "You wanted to know about Clyde and the people he was involved with. Your father's death should've ended the threats he made to you, Desi, June, and Bobbie, but I want to be sure." Serena made eye contact at a traffic signal. "From what June and Bobbie said, that's probably true, but that's not my area of expertise. I thought we could talk to someone whose job it is to know these things." Serena took her hand, lifted it, and kissed her palm. "I don't want you worrying about something that you don't need to be worried about."

The fact that Serena moved so quickly on this made her stare at her profile once they got going. It was nice to be in the center of someone's thoughts. "Thank you. I didn't expect you to do this so quickly."

"I didn't tell you all I did yesterday to hear the sound of my own voice. Neither the NOPD nor the DA's office is going to be much help with this, so I had to go another route. The city might investigate particular murders that type of criminal commits, but the overall organized crime picture is handled by the feds." Serena pulled into the Piquant, and she had to wonder if she knew this was where Harry had brought Desi for their honeymoon night.

"The feds hang out here?" The place was nice, and she'd come often with Harry and Desi to have lunch when Harry could get away, and at night they sometimes came to have a drink and listen to the music.

"The agent we're meeting loves the piano bar, and the drinks are good, so I thought we could make it a good experience." Serena took her hand and went up to the third floor after the valet took their car. The hotel had been a large department store until the eighties, and when it closed, the beautiful building sat vacant until it was converted into the five-star jewel it was today.

The upscale lounge was off the reception desk, and she loved the large marble bar with the oak top that dominated the left side of the room. Whenever the owner was in town, that's who was at the piano, but when she wasn't, there was a great lineup of talent that kept the place packed. People came to drink, dance, and sing along to the songs everyone recognized. She and Serena had actually come here a few times, and she'd enjoyed being romanced on the dance floor.

Serena waved to a blond woman in a great suit that was both flattering and professional. She was beautiful but looked a bit severe—Rachel was sure the tight ponytail she wore was her professional look.

"Serena, good to see you." The woman shook Serena's hand and turned to her.

"Shelby, Rachel Thompson," Serena said. "Rachel, this is Special Agent Shelby Phillips. Shelby's team was involved in the Bracato investigation."

"Thanks for doing this." She shook Shelby's hand and smiled when the agent held it a tick over what would be considered good manners. The move made Serena tense beside her.

"I've been following what happened with the Simoneaux family on the news and with the marshal's office, so I don't mind at all. When Serena told me the extra wrinkle that you found out this week, I didn't hesitate to meet you." Shelby finally let her hand go and pointed to the chair next to her.

"So, you know about this Bracato guy?" There was something about Shelby that made her want to go someplace quieter to have this conversation. It was strange growing up with a man who terrorized both her and her sister into doing things they had no desire to, then to find out his cruelty went much deeper than that. The answers to questions she didn't even have yet were sitting right next to her in a designer suit.

"I didn't know him personally, but we've been watching him for years. When I say we, I mean the Bureau. The only time he was in my sights was when he crossed paths with Cain Casey. That's my focus of investigation."

Shelby focused on her in a way that Serena should take pointers on. Eye contact was at times unnerving, but at other times sexy. Shelby had the sexy part down.

"Serena mentioned this Bracato guy is missing," Rachel said, glancing at Serena before turning her attention back to Shelby.

"First off, we have no evidence yet to support our theory, but I'd bet my house and savings that Gino and his sons are dead. If your family faced any threat because of him, his family, or the guys who worked for him, that threat is gone." Shelby motioned the waiter over so they could order drinks. "And whatever your late father told you, I can't find any evidence of him being some major cog in Bracato's engine. He was small potatoes, and I think he convinced some of his Tater Tot buddies to visit your mother as a favor."

"Who investigated Bracato?" She tried again, wanting to have the most information possible when she told Desi and her moms all this. "Don't you guys watch around the clock?"

"In a roundabout way, I investigated him when there was a mob war about to erupt in the city. Like I said, my main focus is Derby Cain Casey, who is Teflon when it comes to making any kind of charges stick." Shelby shook her head and took a sip of her drink. "New Orleans has its fair share of crime and crime families, but they are not created equal."

"What do you mean?" She glanced at Serena again but couldn't keep her eyes off Shelby.

"Cain is a surgeon working in a world of butchers. Bracato was a butcher, a man who used a hammer to smash everything he could reach. It's our opinion that Casey brought an end to the Bracato family in a way that was permanent. They've never been found, and I doubt they ever will be."

The waiter put down the glass of wine she'd ordered, and the music started again. It was loud enough to make it impossible to have a conversation, so she sat back and listened.

"I don't want to keep you, but I can give you the whole rundown whenever you like," Shelby said before the next song started. "Here." She handed over her card with a number written on the back. "That's my cell number. If you're free for breakfast, call me."

Serena shook Shelby's hand again, and they watched her walk away. "Do you want to dance?" Serena asked, a frown line showing as she turned away from Shelby.

"Sure." She really didn't, but Serena had been nice enough to set this up, and she wasn't ready to head home. "That's good news, don't you think?"

"What, that Clyde's boss is dead?"

She nodded against Serena's shoulder, suddenly tired. "I hope those assholes that hassled Mama and Mom died a horrible death."

"Karma is a better wielder of justice than I can ever dream to be. If everyone involved with what happened to your moms is dead, it's one less thing we have to worry about." Serena held her closer, and the feel of her was familiar and nice. "Want to come home with me?"

She hesitated but not long enough for Serena to notice. "Sure," she said.

"If this is too fast, it's okay to say so," Serena said. "I'm not going anywhere."

Rachel responded by tilting her head up for a kiss. "Let's go."

She pressed her back against the elevator and kissed Serena when she put her arms around her. This part of their relationship they'd never had problems with. The question was whether to give in so soon. At this particular moment, she wanted to do just that, but she knew it might set them back to where Serena would think flowers and a sorry would get anything forgiven.

Serena's car was waiting when they made it outside, and she smiled when the valet got her door. Serena's house wasn't that far from Harry's, only smaller and off one of the cross streets with St. Charles. It was nice, comfortable, and she remembered the times they'd cooked together when they'd spent the day relaxing.

"I want to hold you." Serena spoke as if she'd read her mind and held her hand as she turned toward the Garden District and home. "I miss the feel of you."

The *feel* of her wasn't what she was expecting to hear. Not that she doubted Serena's sincerity, but she'd wanted Serena to miss *her*. That she couldn't say it meant they weren't quite there yet. Wherever there was "Actually," she said, and it must've been her tone that made Serena flinch, "could you take me home? I'm exhausted, and you probably wouldn't enjoy the feel of me until I have enough sleep. Right now I'll probably be too blunt for your tastes or expectations."

"Are you sure?" Serena didn't let go of her hand. "What I want is to take whatever you want to dish out. It's the only way to move forward."

"No, and we're not getting into that tonight." She was confused about what came next, and that feeling wasn't something she enjoyed. She couldn't just commit, believe, take on faith what Serena was saying. Being burned had been her norm in the past, and Serena was perhaps paying for the mistakes of others, but she wasn't exactly as attentive as she should be. Rachel deserved better, and she wasn't going to settle because she was lonely.

Her life had always revolved around working and keeping both her and her sister alive one more day. That life was vastly different than her reality now, and she had to get a new plan that might or might not include Serena. Tonight wasn't the time to find answers when all she felt was anger. It sneaked up on her, and she was tired of the irrationality of it, but Serena's actions had unhinged that part of her.

"Don't shut me out."

That made her clench her jaws to keep from laughing. Serena had done exactly that, only then it hadn't been a problem. "You're a riot."

"What does that mean?"

Her phone rang before she could answer, and Harry's face on her screen was the last thing she was expecting. "Harry? What's wrong?"

"We're headed back to the emergency room. The contractions started again, and I don't want to take any chances." Harry sounded like she was making an effort not to freak out.

"I'm on my way home, so I'll meet you there."

"I can take you," Serena said.

"I don't want you—"

"Come on, babe. Give me the chance I'm asking for."

She shook her head. "Let me finish. I don't want you to have to sit in the waiting room for hours. I promise I'll call you once I have news."

"You think I mind? How about I come with you, and I'll read files while I wait? If I catch up, then we can have dinner a few times next week. Butch can come if you're not busy." They headed for the hospital. "Isn't this a little early? For Desi, I mean?"

"Yes, and I don't want to talk about that either." She pointed to the emergency entrance. "Let me off here."

"It's going to be okay," Serena said, kissing the back of her hand. "Remember, I'm right outside if you need me."

She stared at Serena and leaned over and kissed her. "I'll hold you to it."

Harry pulled in behind them and Serena promised to park their car so they wouldn't be held up. She held Desi's hand as Harry wheeled her in where Ellie and Sam were already waiting. Desi didn't have any trouble getting on the bed on her own and appeared fine.

"They stopped?" Sam asked since Desi didn't appear in distress. At least not like the first time they went through this. Ellie crossed her arms and stayed quiet.

"I owe you both dinner somewhere nice for getting you out, but two blocks from the hospital everything was fine." Harry rubbed Desi's arm as she explained, and she seemed relaxed. "So to answer your question, yes, they've stopped."

"I don't have to guess that you two totally ignored my advice, but so did we when we were at this point. It's the only reason I'm not fussing," Ellie said as she put on gloves to start her exam. "Let's make sure you're okay to return to your honeymoon and the checkerboard Sam brought you to play with for the rest of the night."

"How many practice contractions does this kid need?" Rachel asked.

"The body's mysterious sometimes, and babies are even a bigger mystery when it comes to timing." Ellie did another thorough exam and declared Desi wasn't in labor. "Go back to the hotel and get some sleep, then take it easy until you're really in labor."

"Are you talking bed rest?" Desi asked.

"Not complete bed rest, but no work, no strenuous activity, and not a lot of moving around." Sam wrote in the chart while she laid down the set of rules Desi and Harry were supposed to adhere to.

"Sorry, guys," Desi said, appearing somewhat embarrassed. "You're going to stop coming if we have any more false alarms."

"Harry offered dinner, so no problem," Sam said. "That's our job, so don't sit at home if this happens again. Believe me, you don't want Harry delivering this baby. Leave that to the experts."

"You make it appear easy enough," Harry said as she moved to hug Rachel. "You doing okay?"

"These trips to the ER get my blood pumping, but that's good for the soul, I guess. You do keep life interesting, sis." She hugged Harry before helping Desi off the bed. "Are you going back or home?"

"We're going back, but we'll be home tomorrow so I can plan things I can do in the bedroom." Desi kissed her cheek and blushed.

"I can't be sure, but I'm pretty sure that's what got you in here tonight." She followed Harry out the ambulance entrance after texting Serena to bring the car around. "Behave, and I'll see you guys tomorrow."

Serena drove her home, and she waved to the guards Harry had hired. For now they were at the gate and patrolling the perimeter of the fence, but that would change if there was news about Byron. When Serena put her car in park, Rachel's exhaustion hit her like a freight train.

"Thank you, and I'd like to pick Butch up tomorrow for ice cream." She held Serena's hand as they walked to the door and she yawned. "If that's okay with you."

"You can pick him up from my parents' and bring him home. I'll cook for you guys." Serena took both her hands and got closer.

"Thank you for that and for going slow." She pulled her hand free and pressed her palm to Serena's cheek. No matter her jumbled feelings that vacillated from anger to want, Serena was a beautiful woman who inspired thoughts of conquest.

"You're important to me, so I'm not going anywhere." Serena kissed her, and it was nice. "We'll go as slow as you want. If we move at the right pace, we'll find something we can build on."

Rachel walked on autopilot to her room, realizing no one else from the family had come to the hospital. That meant she'd been the only call Desi and Harry had made, so there'd be some pissed-off people at breakfast in a few hours. Breaking the news to the family wasn't her job, so she stripped and closed her eyes. Her phone dinged, and she was expecting it to be Serena.

How about breakfast to finish our talk?

The number wasn't one she knew. She dug the card Shelby had given her out of her purse—the numbers matched. She hadn't given Shelby her number, but the woman was an FBI agent. Rachel laughed when she thought how easily Shelby had found her, so maybe she'd go to breakfast to get her interested in finding Byron and his family.

I'd love to.

She typed and sent it before second-guessing herself. The wording, though, now that she looked at it, might've benefited from a bit of second-guessing. "It's only breakfast, and then it's ice cream with Butch." Talking to herself wasn't new but it wasn't helping.

Impulse control wasn't something she had a problem with, and she doubted Shelby Phillips was going to tempt her. "Breakfast, that's it." She had to admit, though, that Shelby was good at the follow-through. It was something else Serena should take note of.

The inside of the car was cold, but Byron was hot. They'd pushed it off the road and as far into the woods as they could, and he'd stupidly thought this would be better than sleeping outside. He was sweating, and everything from breathing to blinking hurt. There was no way he had enough strength to get out of the car and stand next to it, much less walk for hours. Mike was still sleeping next to him, so he drifted as he let his mind wander. The daydreaming lulled him back to sleep.

It was the train whistle that scared him awake. The damn thing sounded so close he sat up to make sure they weren't on the track. He spotted the Amtrak cars at a full stop as another commercial line crossed the intersecting track in front of them. The direction the idle train was headed gave him an idea, and he hit Mike in the chest to wake him.

"Come on." He opened the door and tried to bury his misery. The early morning light rain and heavy fog weren't helping his cold, but it would give them the cover they needed as they ran. The Amtrak train had about fifteen passenger cars followed by a string of commercial cars. "Go for the cargo cars," he yelled.

The train started to roll, and he pushed himself to be able to reach the edge of the car covered in graffiti. This was the best way to cover miles without having to worry about gas or getting stopped by the cops in a stolen car. Mike sat next to him in the small space they shared, and he could feel him shivering. He'd grown up in the city and didn't remember this kind of cold. When he was a kid it'd snowed once, but he didn't remember these sink-into-your-bones kind of temperatures.

"Are you sure about this?" Mike's fingers were white on the edge he was hanging on to, and there was snot draining out of his nose. Letting go to wipe it meant falling, so his brother was smart enough to ignore it.

"We've never been there, but the commuter trains stop by the Dome. No more searching for a way to get back. All you got to do is not fall off."

They sat as close together as they could for a little warmth, and the car at their back broke the wind, but they could still feel it. He couldn't tell how long they'd been moving when they stopped, the sudden silence jarring his nerves. The ache in his body was concentrated in his hands so he stretched his fingers while he could as he prepared to run if they were the reason they'd stopped.

"They're picking up people," Mike said after peering around the side. The station personnel made it four cars from them before turning and heading back in, and he was glad not to have to run. The way he felt, he was certain his grandmother would've caught him before he got ten feet.

"See anything else?" he asked, watching Mike study the area covertly.

"You look like shit." Mike wiped his nose on his sleeve, but Byron closed his eyes and tried to ease the tension out of his shoulders.

"I feel even worse than that, but ain't shit I can do about it. Can you see any kind of sign as to where we are?" The sky overhead was completely gray, tinged with dark clouds that forecast more fucking rain.

"The sign on the station says Poplarville," Mike said, glancing around one more time. They tried to find a more comfortable spot now that they were stopped and wouldn't fall off if they moved. "Think those guys working the station are going to see us when we go by? This thing's going to be moving slow."

"We gotta chance it," he said, trying his best to stifle the coughing fit he wanted to have. "It's cold as hell out here, so they'll probably just stay inside once we start rolling again."

The train whistle blew again, and he finally gave in to the cough deep in his chest when they started moving and kept his eyes to the left to see if the station crew would be a problem. There was one guy on the platform, but his face was hidden behind a newspaper.

"Man, I'm hungry," Mike said loud to be heard over the wind.

He nodded, thinking of where exactly Poplarville was, but he couldn't place it aside from it being in Mississippi. His stomach rumbled as if acknowledging what Mike had said, but they'd starve before they got off this train. He just knew they were headed west and New Orleans would be their final destination.

"Just one more day and we'll be there," he yelled back. "Maybe not even that long."

"I wonder what happened to Daddy."

"The crazy fucker is someone else's problem now." He was glad to be rid of him, but he was curious too about where Big Byron had gone. "He dumped us. It's not like he's ever given a rat's ass about us, so don't be stupid and feel guilty."

They were quiet after that as they watched the landscape go by in a blur. Wherever they were headed, they were going at top speed, and he hoped they ended up where he most wanted to be. If he put his need to see Desi aside, there was still plenty to do in the city. He thought about the garage his father had owned until he lost it to the bail bondsman. If no one had purchased it, there was a chance he could pick up a car to get out of town once he was done.

It was strange that he'd dreamed of the place he'd shared with Desi so often in prison since he'd seldom spent time there, not wanting to deal with her. There'd been plenty of women who'd wanted his attention, and he'd found comfort and welcome in their beds. That was a stark difference to what was waiting for him at home. His marriage might've been a farce, but he'd thought, with time, Desi would come to love him for all he'd tried to do for her.

The life lesson he'd learned was that no woman would love you if they were already in love with someone else. He'd thought the answer to that'd be having a kid to give her something else to think about instead of her past, but that hadn't happened either. His life should've been so different than this—he should be teaching his sons how to play football, and his daughters how to be respectful. All he had now was a record and a target on his back and none of it was his fault.

The day he'd discovered why Desi had never gotten pregnant was the day he knew that it would end with him killing her for her conniving nature. He'd wanted children because that's what real men did. They married, worked, and had families. After years of no luck, he'd started to believe there was something wrong with him. It'd killed him to even think that, and if it was true, his father would have one more thing to bitch about.

When the real reason came to light, it was the beginning of the end that led to the night he'd come so close to bashing her head in with his bat. Had he been able to finish what he'd started, he'd have hoed miles of fields at Angola and been glad to do it for the rest of his miserable life.

"Fuck," he said softly, knowing Mike would never hear him. The chance to give a child all the things he'd never had was one of the reasons he'd gotten married, but like in all things, it was one more thing fate stole from him. He closed his eyes and allowed himself to remember.

Their last anniversary had started with his father piling on the grunt work until he'd wanted to bash his head in with a wrench. He'd decided on flowers and a bottle of wine on the way home in an attempt at romance to hopefully get Desi's head out of the clouds for once, and he'd heard the shower running when he got home.

At least he'd thought she was in the shower, but when he opened the door, she was putting a pill in her mouth, and he recognized the wheel it'd come out of and what that meant. Aside from their last night together when he'd been so close in ending it, he never remembered being that angry. She'd stolen something precious from him, and it was one more thing he hated her for. One more thing that wasn't his fault, and Desi would have to pay for the insult.

The train jerked hard, slamming him from the memory and back into the cold. He'd disappeared for three months after that, afraid that Rachel really would call the cops on him. Desi would never press charges, she knew better, but Rachel was another story.

The other reason he'd left was to give Desi time to recover, so they could start over with a new set of rules. That night he'd finally come back to explain she was no longer allowed to make any decisions for herself, he'd broken her leg and tried to kill her. None of it was his fault, though. All he'd told her was she had two months to get pregnant, or he was going to make good on the threat he'd made to Rachel and dump her somewhere she'd never be found. It shocked the hell out of him, but she'd refused.

It was amazing she still showed backbone after the last beating, but she had. "I'm not bringing a child into this," Desi had said. "It's not fair."

Fair was having a wife who loved him, respected him, and strove to make him happy. Nothing was fair, and it was her job to make it right. It was a job she'd refused over and over, and he hated her for it. The only good thing was it wasn't too late. He'd put his past in the ground, and then he'd find someone who loved him, and he'd finally get that family he wanted. "Then I'll be happy," he said as they juddered over a river.

It was his turn to get all those things. God and fate owed him that.

CHAPTER FIFTEEN

Rachel found a parking place a block from the Ruby Slipper downtown and checked herself in the rearview mirror before she buttoned her coat and got out. This wasn't a date, but she hated running into clients looking like she had no idea what to do with her hair. Ever since moving in with Harry and Desi, she'd let her hair go back to the natural auburn color she'd gotten from Clyde. Desi and their mother were the blondes in the family.

She was early, but she wanted to be done in time to pick Butch up and take him to his favorite place for ice cream. At the wedding he'd told her more than once how much he missed her and how she shouldn't listen to his mother about staying away. She'd smiled, thinking he was much more perceptive than Serena.

"Good morning," Shelby said as she exited her car. "Thanks for saying yes."

The great suit was gone, but Shelby was even more attractive in jeans, a cable-knit sweater, and a peacoat. Her boots were stylish and gave Shelby the height advantage by about four inches. Shelby was the type of woman who'd capture her attention not just because of her good looks but because of the confidence that was easy to read. There was an instant spark, and she tried to find a mental fire extinguisher to douse it.

"I appreciate that you're willing to do this. My sister and I just got our mother and her wife back, and I don't want anything getting in the way of that." Her shoulder pressed against Shelby's arm as they stood in the crowded entrance waiting to be seated. The place was popular and loud, but she could hear Shelby when she spoke to the hostess.

"Shouldn't be too long." Shelby pointed to the chairs along the wall. "I've been researching everything you said your mom and her wife said since we met for drinks. It all sounds like something in a movie, but when you consider the players, I totally see it happening."

"Can we wait until we get a table?" She wanted more privacy and to be able to give Shelby her complete attention. "How long have you worked for the Bureau?"

"Seven years altogether, six here in the city. Everyone has an idea of what it means to be in the FBI, but my job isn't as glamorous as the movies make it out to be. I spend lots of time in cramped spots, so this is nice. It's good to make new friends." Shelby smiled at her, and she couldn't help but return it.

"I promise not to be too nosy," she said. "Can you tell me what you do without having to kill me?"

"Not in detail, no, but I can answer the questions you probably have when it comes to your mom and late father." They were led to a table along the left wall, and her smile widened when she glanced over her shoulder at Shelby, who had pressed her hand to the small of Rachel's back. It was intimate, or it seemed intimate. It's how you wanted to be treated by someone who was interested in you. Maybe she should've invited Serena so she could take notes, and the mental fire extinguisher was failing miserably.

"Is that a move they taught you at the academy?" She nodded when the waitress held up a carafe of coffee.

"Sorry, I should know better than to touch without asking, and I should ask if there's more reasons than manners to keep my hands to myself." Shelby smiled as she flattened both hands on the table, her coffee cup between them. "Serena didn't mention anything, but I should've guessed by how insistent she was that I help you. Are you two together?"

"I'm not a fan of social media, but let's check the *It's complicated* box on that one." She poured creamer in her coffee and slid the porcelain cow toward Shelby. "It's nice not having to think for a little while and have things be uncomplicated. This last week has been like an emotional pummeling, and I'm ready for it to stop."

"You're like a Hallmark and a Lifetime movie all rolled into one," Shelby said and winked. The comment broke through whatever tension was there, and Rachel laughed. "Escaped convicts and a mother you thought was dead really don't happen to many people that close together."

"My sister was married to the escaped convict, so I'm guessing they'll catch him sooner than later. My mother was a huge surprise, but in a good way." She combed her hair behind her ear, surprised Shelby wanted to hear about her past. "At first I didn't think I could forgive her, but both the escaped convict and her absence from our lives can only be blamed on my father."

"Abuse isn't something I understand. Why someone feels the need to do that to someone they supposedly love is a foreign concept to me personally, but intellectually I know it happens more often than people think." Shelby moved slowly as if to give Rachel the chance to pull away if that's what she wanted before she took her hand. "With a little digging, I found your father in the official record. He did work for Bracato but, like I said, wasn't high up in the ranks. He wasn't much more than a fixer who didn't fix much alone. I can't prove it, but it was probably the guys he worked with who went and harassed your moms."

"Where are those guys now?" She had no idea how organized crime worked or why it was called organized crime. Were they that good and precise in their actions that the word *organized* had to be added?

"The agents assigned to Bracato have been reassigned to other units, so they've followed these guys to other syndicates, but for the most part they're all petty criminals—the ones who are still alive, that is. There's nothing I found that would lead me to believe you or your family are in danger." Shelby let go of her hand when their waitress came back and took their order.

She was at ease with Shelby and appreciated that Shelby had done the legwork to dismiss her worries. "We should be safe from them at least. Don't you think?"

"The guys your father worked with are mostly dead, and the ones left aren't looking to harass anyone. They're older, and most of them are out of the game. The ones still involved are with some young guns who use them the same way Bracato did."

"Thank you for doing all this. It seems like you understand what I'm going through." She could see Shelby's outer beauty, but there seemed to be something else in her expression she couldn't figure out.

"My parents were both killed by someone like your father. The grunts were following orders, and to them the murders were to gain leverage, but it devastated me." Shelby's pain was easy to hear in the way she told this story.

"I'm so sorry. That must've been an awful thing to go through."

"It was, and to add to that horrible situation, I ended up blaming someone who didn't do it. I was so angry, and the buildup of my anger made me put aside everything I believe because I didn't care. All I could think of was the litany of sins that person had committed, and I wanted to make them pay." Shelby shrugged but it appeared to be more to release tension.

"I doubt anyone would have blamed you. It sucks when bad things happen to the best people. My sister is the kindest person I know, and she went through hell. The difference is she was able to walk away and find something better." She reached for Shelby's hands and squeezed her fingers. "What happened to you, that's not easy to forget, much less get over."

"It was hard and even more difficult to wrap my head around, but this is the kind of world your father thrived in. He didn't pay for any of it while he was alive, but that's all done now."

"My father was a vindictive sperm donor," Rachel said, "and it pisses me off that I'll never get to confront him for everything he did. It's a hell of a thing we've both lived through, but I'd like to think all the bad is behind us." She liked the softer side of the agent. Listening to her, giving her this kind of attention didn't seem contrived. If there was something Desi had taught her in the last year it was that talking to someone about all the things you simply had to accept because they couldn't be changed helped. Shelby, unlike Serena lately, had taken the time to do just that, and it made her want to be here. "You're right. I've made a friend and that's always a good thing."

"There's only one thing left to worry about, and I talked my boss into helping the locals out. Byron, Mike, and Byron Simoneaux, Sr. all sound like they deserved to be locked up. That they haven't been found worries me, so we'll be keeping up with that."

"Do you know Sept Savoie and Roger Landry? They're the NOPD detectives put in charge of the case." Their breakfast arrived, and she took a minute to butter the ginormous biscuit that had come with hers.

"Sept got put on this?" Shelby poured enough syrup on her pancakes to put half the city into diabetic shock.

Rachel told her the story of Monica and Jude Rose's experience with the Simoneaux brothers, and it made Shelby laugh. "Byron might be good at hide and go seek, but he's your below average pig when it comes to smarts."

"Sounds like it, and Sept is someone I've dealt with before. I'll give her a call so we're all on the same page."

They ate and talked about themselves, things nothing to do with their jobs. Shelby was funny, and they lingered long enough that Rachel was late for Butch. She made it up to him with a sundae big enough to share and a walk through the park to feed the ducks since it wasn't freezing. That was something Harry had gotten Butch into, and he still loved it. Dinner with Serena was pleasant, but she didn't look happy when Rachel kissed them both good night as soon as the dishes were done.

"You can stay," Serena said outside the door.

"I don't want to mislead you, so I was up front about wanting to go slow. Promises are easy to make, babe—it's the living up to them that's a problem sometimes. I like you, a lot actually, but I'm not going to let you hurt me." She kissed Serena's chin and smiled.

"You're never going to forgive me, are you?" Serena sounded defeated. "I screwed up for a couple of weeks, and that's it. No second chances."

"That you can say that means we might have farther to go than I thought. Once the excitement of what we found lost a little polish, you pulled back on me. It might've been reflex, but that's what you did. That was months ago, not a couple of weeks. I've been the one pursuing you, calling when you don't, and trying to make plans when you forget. That you can't see that is disappointing." She put her hand up when Serena stepped closer. "I want us to work so I'm willing to try, but you aren't a victim. Stop acting like one."

"I'm not acting like anything." Serena sounded aggravated and petulant. "I'm all in, and I don't appreciate you thinking for me or announcing how I'm feeling. My job is demanding at times, and I told you that up front."

"You're right. I'll go, and you can celebrate your pity party all by yourself," she said, not holding back.

"You're telling me I'm the only one who's done anything wrong?"

"No, I can admit when I have. My mistake up to now was letting you slide. Unlike you, my job is something I enjoy, but it's not as important as yours. You love what you do, and it's something I admire about you, but you don't know how to turn it off." She bounced her fist off her hip, not liking that she seemed to be angry all the time. "I'm not going to be with someone who only thinks about me when it's convenient."

"I've never treated your job like it doesn't matter. If we're being honest about what bothers us, then I'm tired of you acting like everything I do is wrong." Serena ran her hand through her hair and blew out a long breath. "I do love my job, and it's important to me and the people I try to help. It's not a nine-to-five kind of thing, so you either accept that or you don't."

"Good night, and don't call me until you're ready to hear what I'm saying. Up to now all you're doing is trying to lawyer your way into getting me to admit I'm full of crap." She walked to her car, wanting to be anywhere but here.

What the hell happened to them was something she couldn't figure out, but right now she didn't want to waste time on it. Maybe this wasn't worth fighting for because it wasn't her happily ever after.

❖

Desi tried to hold her breath and release it slowly like she'd learned in Lamaze. Despite being laid up for the last two weeks, the Braxton-Hicks contractions came and went and were starting to get on her nerves. Tony was coming over in an hour to talk about their plans, and to take her mind off her misery. She'd loved being pregnant, but she was ready for it to be over.

Right now, she was enjoying the solitude since Rachel had left for work when Harry had left for an early surgery, so she was left in the house with just Mona, her parents, and her in-laws. She loved them all, but the hovering was something she wasn't used to. The other reason she didn't want to bother anyone was that she wasn't about to go back to the hospital. One more false alarm, and they were going to label her a crazy person.

"How about some tea and an omelet?" Rosa asked. Her mother-in-law was still in her nightgown but managed to look put together as she came in, since Harry had left their door open. "What's wrong?"

"Another round of practice." She exhaled and clutched her stomach, amazed at how rock hard it was. "I swear this kid better slide out in less than an hour."

"This is Harry's child, so don't count on it. The Basantes family knows a good thing when they see it, and this kid is comfortable where he is. It's going to take plenty of pushing and cajoling to get him to leave that warm cocoon."

Rosa made her laugh because that was probably true. "Another week or so. And hopefully you and my mother are right and my brain will forget the actual childbirth so we can do this again as soon as possible. Our siblings are too important to us, so I don't want our baby to be an only child."

"Two more if you hurry, but I'll be happy with however many grandchildren you give me." Rosa sat on the bed and held her hand. "Speaking of, where'd my child disappear to?"

"She's scheduled to be in surgery until noon. The hip replacement she started this morning should be done or close to it, then she's overseeing a couple of knee replacements." She relaxed as the pain left her body, and she hoped she was done with that for the day. "She said she wanted to resign her position at the medical school as soon as this semester is over." It was a conversation she and Harry hadn't finished, so she hoped Harry didn't mind her sharing with her mother.

"Good," Rosa said, squeezing her fingers. "Don't pout, mi hija." It wasn't often Rosa called her *daughter*, and it made her smile. "Francisco taught for a while, and when he saw his children were growing up and doing a million things at once without him, he concentrated on his private practice." It was as if Rosa had conjured Francisco up when he walked through the open door. "He still worked too much, but he was home more."

"In the end we were all much happier," Francisco said, "and the medical school knows to call if they have a case that needs a consult. You and Harry have waited for what you have now for a very long time." Francisco took a seat next to Rosa. "Enjoy it and know she's not going to be resentful of you for giving that up."

"Are you sure?" That had been the one thing she'd worried about. Harry had this life she and Rachel had crashed, and she didn't want all these sweeping changes to hem Harry into a corner she would hate her for.

"Harry's a lot like her father, so I'm sure. Spending time with you and this baby will be her priority until the day she's laid to rest, years from now. All you need to do is support her in her choices, *her* choices, and as far as her career is concerned, she's made those all on her own." Rosa leaned in and kissed her forehead. "She loves you, and it's the main reason she wants to be home more."

"Thank you," she said, wiping her face of the few tears that had fallen. "I love you both and I appreciate you forgiving me."

"Forgiveness for something you had no role in isn't necessary. I'm only glad it was Harry who was waiting that day you arrived in the emergency room. It was the end of that hard life, and if I know my child, those hard days will never come again." Rosa spoke with conviction, and she appreciated the emotion on her behalf. "Now, how about breakfast?"

"That sounds great. Let me run to the bathroom, and I'll meet you guys downstairs." She moved to the side of the bed and took Francisco's hand to get on her feet.

"You two stay here and I'll be back with a tray. I'd rather you didn't attempt the stairs if you don't have to," Rosa said as she stood as well.

"Good morning, everyone," Tony said, arriving way early. He was dressed impeccably with dark slacks and a beautiful pink sweater. "Honey, you look ready to pop."

She closed her eyes at the observation and grimaced. "I think I am."

"Come on, don't look so pained, you're pregnant but still beautiful." He walked in when Francisco looked down and put his arm around Desi. "What?"

"I'm not talking about what you said, I meant I think I'm literally ready to go. My water broke." She glanced down at the puddle on the floor and had an urge for Harry to materialize. It wasn't panic, but it was still early. "Rosa, can you call Harry?"

"Let's not panic," Francisco said, sounding panicked. "We've got hours to go still."

"If Harry misses one minute of this because of you, she'll kill you, old man," Rosa said, flanking her other side. "Let's get you cleaned up and changed—we do have time for that. Mi amor, you call Harry." Francisco left to get his phone. "Tony, you gather everything we'll need and call Kenneth in case he's got to swing by the surgical suites. Tell him to pull her out by the ears if necessary. This baby is early, and she's already having contractions."

"All the bags are in the coat closet downstairs," she said, gripping Rosa's hand as another contraction started. "Do you think something's wrong?" From everyone's expression she'd voiced what was on their minds.

"I think this is Harry Basantes's baby, and if they're anything like her, they're going to be impatient. Get used to it, girlfriend. That might save you the headaches you got coming your way."

Rosa assured her she had time to change and left her with Mona so she could do the same. Her mother and Bobbie were waiting when she stepped out of the bathroom, and it was strangely comforting to have this menagerie of people crowded around her. It was a reminder that she was no longer on her own with only Rachel on her side. Oh God, Rachel.

"Did someone call Rachel?"

Tony held up his phone and nodded. "She's going to meet us at the hospital."

"And Harry is on her way." Francisco held up his phone and laughed. "Let's hope she doesn't get a handful of tickets on the way."

Another contraction hit, and she moaned into it as she did the stupid breathing that was only aggravating her. There was no way this was going to curb the pain or make her forget what she was getting ready to do. Francisco drove them with Rosa at his side and her mothers in the back holding her hands.

"Don't be afraid to scream," her mom said. "I found it more helpful than anything."

"Don't be afraid to curse either," Bobbie said smiling. "Your mom got really creative when Rachel was born and, strangely, blamed me for the labor." That made both June and Bobbie laugh. "So remember that Harry can take it, and it really will make you feel better."

"I'll have to remember that." She tensed when another one hit, and she saw Rosa timing the duration.

"Twelve minutes since the last one, and thirty-two seconds long." Rosa's proclamation made the vehicle jerk a bit when Francisco stepped on the gas. "Keep breathing and we'll be there in a minute."

Francisco stopped at the emergency entrance and promised to be in as soon as he parked. He was also waiting for Harry so she could go right in, but he waved to Rachel when he saw her drive up appearing ready to abandon her car. "Go in and I'll be right behind you with Harry."

"Oh my God," Desi said as she bent over the side of the bed, the contraction preventing her from getting in it. "This is something else."

"You can admit it hurts like a bitch," Rachel said. The room in the emergency department was big enough for all the women crowded into it, but barely. "Why aren't we going up to the birthing room I know you were promised?"

"The nurse can't find the orders," Rosa said. "I gave her another two minutes before I call everyone I know on staff."

"Thank you," Desi said as she took Rachel's hand and lay down.

"We found the paperwork," the woman said. A transporter followed her in, and they seemed in a hurry to move her. "I think it'd be better and faster in a wheelchair."

"Your ideas might need some review, so move," Harry said as she sidestepped the nurse and reached for her hand. "Couldn't wait, huh?"

"You know me," she said, pulling Harry down and kissing her. "Always in a rush with not an ounce of—" She had to stop and groan. The contractions seemed to be getting longer and more intense, but it could also have been that the pain was starting to bend her mind. "Holy hell, this hurts."

Harry leaned over and read the guy's name tag. "Jorge, it's time to go. Desi, close your eyes and concentrate on a happy memory. I don't want you getting motion sickness on top of all this."

They rolled through the halls as fast as Harry and Jorge could manage to the patient elevators and it reminded her of the night Harry had to move her here for her safety. A year had been all it took to complete the total transformation of her life, and her only wish now was to be a good mother. She wanted her child to be happy and to have a home they always wanted to come back to. The one person who'd make all that possible was Harry.

"We're a little early, but there's nothing to worry about. Now kiss the pregnant lady and get out." Ellie didn't have a problem sending everyone except Harry to the waiting room. "Let's see where we are, and we all might have time to take a nap. Enjoy the sleep while you can. If this kid is as hyper as Harry and Sam, your life will never be the same, and since he's a week early, that only proves my point." Ellie glanced up at Harry. "This kid is going to resemble a certain surgeon I know."

The birthing suite looked like a nice hotel room, and she closed her eyes as Ellie examined her. "What's the verdict?"

"You're going to have a baby." Ellie took her gloves off and rolled to the trash to toss them.

"And you're hilarious," Harry said.

"These last sets of contractions must've been going on for a while, my friend. We're probably about five hours out, so try to get some sleep and try to keep the visitors to a minimum if they start sneaking back in." Ellie stood at the side of the bed and pointed her finger at them. "Sam is here—there must be something in the water because we have four patients in labor. If I'm called away, she'll be here, but I promise one of us will deliver this baby."

"Thanks, Ellie, and go ahead and deliver that visitor news yourself. Whenever I say it, no one believes me." Harry's scrubs were wrinkled and there were a few specks of blood along her waist. "It's like I'm not doctory enough."

"Honey, go and talk to the family with Ellie, and change into clean scrubs." She kissed Harry before she left and held her hand up when Rachel came in. "Hey, sorry to cut your day short."

"As if," Rachel said, taking her hand and kissing her forehead. "Is everything okay?"

"We're a little early, but Ellie blames it on Harry, so I think it's safe to think it's not a problem if she's joking around."

"Just promise me you'll be okay." Rachel hugged her and held on.

"She's going to be fine, and if Desi is okay with it, why don't you stay," Harry said. She was in fresh scrubs but appeared ready for a nap. "Like I say all the time, you two come as a pair, and this is something we should all share."

"Thanks, Harry, but this time," Rachel said, kissing Desi's forehead one more time, "I think my nephew needs to start this life with the two people who will love him the best, and I should know. You two have loved me like no one else, and there are no words to say how grateful I am."

Harry put her arms around her and kissed her cheek. "That was deep."

"You're such an ass sometimes," Rachel said, shoving Harry off her, but Harry held on.

"If we're being sappy, then I should say you two have been the brightest parts of my life. You taught me how to love, and I want a life's worth of lessons." Harry hugged Rachel once more and turned her to face Desi.

"You'll be the first to...son of a bitch," she said as another contraction started. These damn things felt like she was going to explode from the pressure.

"Breathe," Harry said.

Desi reached out and pinched Harry's lips to the point she flinched. "Anyone who offers that advice is in real danger of getting banned from this room. Since I really want you here, zip it." She moaned and fell back when the contraction was done. The breathing did help when she wasn't in terrible pain. "Sorry, honey. I promise I love you and it's the pain talking. You can't hold it against me."

Rachel laughed and waved as she opened the door. "Try not to kill her. You're going to need her to take some of those late-night feedings and diaper changes."

"I'm really sorry," she said to Harry when she came and lay down next to her.

"Until we leave this room, don't be afraid to let me have it." Harry put her hand over her middle and rubbed small circles. "Think of it this way—I'm the one who put that kid in there. Might've been a little more clinical than the way most people do it, but it was still all me."

"I do remember that, so no matter what I say, I love you." She turned her head to kiss Harry but screamed when the next contraction was particularly strong. "Fuck." It was out of character for her to curse, but maybe Bobbie was on to something. It did make her feel better, and she smiled when Harry smiled.

"Wow," Harry said, chuckling.

"Kiss me," she said and Harry did. "I love you, and I can't wait to be a mom with you. You know that, right?" Harry nodded. "Think we can talk Tony into having the next one for us?"

"I do know that, and I love you. As for Tony, with his pain threshold, I don't see it, honey." Harry didn't move when Rachel came back with June. "Are you ready to be a grandmother?"

"I pinch myself every morning to make sure I'm not locked up somewhere and this is where my breakdown led me. We're not going to stay long," June said, placing her hand on Desi's chest. "I just wanted you to know I love you. Being a mother is one of the best gifts in the world, and you're going to be a good one."

"Thanks, Mama. I'm so glad you'll be here for this. We deserve all the happiness we have coming." She cried a little when her mom kissed the top of her head, bringing back some vague memories.

"Amen to that, and I'll come get you two if this takes longer than we think," Harry said.

"Start praying it doesn't take longer than we think," she said, winking at Harry. "If not you're in big trouble."

If her life was a thousand-piece puzzle, a majority of the pieces had clicked into place as she stared at the door her mothers had just walked out of. The remaining bits would bring the picture of being a parent with Harry, being married, and being happy into focus. Even if this wasn't the most comfortable thing she'd ever done, she was going to enjoy every minute of it.

Chapter Sixteen

F our hours later Harry moved off the bed so Ellie could examine Desi. The contractions were picking up speed, but through it all Desi refused any drugs, preferring to scream instead. When she wasn't doing that or cursing like she had an advanced degree in it, she was apologizing. The pain was starting to hurt Harry just from watching, and she was about to start convincing Desi to take something to take the edge off.

"Let's take a look," Ellie said. She appeared exhausted from everything going on in the unit but smiled when she sat and rubbed Desi's feet before helping her get into position. "Okay, you're totally effaced and ready to push. This baby is ready to meet you, Moms."

"You ready, sweetheart?" She kissed Desi and held her hand.

"No turning back now." Desi had a strong grip on her. "I need you with me." It was a strange time to panic about that.

"I'm not going anywhere." She lowered her head and kissed Desi's knuckles.

"Okay, Desi," Ellie said, rolling into place. "Time to rock and roll."

The bed faced the bank of windows that had one of the best views of the city, and it was one of the reasons Harry had wanted this room. "Could you open the blinds?" She thought the view would help Desi focus on something other than the pain. "Don't worry, we're high enough that no one can see in."

"Can I push? I'm not really asking, so I'm going to start pushing." Desi gritted her teeth and sat up slightly to make good on her declaration.

"Okay, stop." Ellie glanced at Harry and nodded her head in Desi's direction. It was something they'd talked about when they'd run into each other in the hospital cafeteria, and she'd mentioned how much it had helped her when she'd gone into labor.

Harry climbed behind Desi and put her arms around her until she was able to hold her hands. "Let's bring the baby home." She pressed her lips to the side of Desi's head and tried to comfort Desi as she shivered.

Desi screamed so loud Harry flinched. "Damn, this hurts."

They started the process, and Desi used her as a backrest to gain leverage whenever she tensed to push. After another hour she could see how tired Desi was getting, and she glanced at Ellie for a clue as she wiped Desi's forehead.

"I can see the head." Ellie nodded and Harry could tell she was smiling despite the mask. Desi took some deep breaths as Sam walked in, masked and gloved.

"Basantes, are you slacking? Let's get this done." Sam grabbed another stool and sat next to Ellie. "A couple more pushes and you're done."

Desi pushed when Ellie told her to and put what little energy she had left into it. Harry peered into the mirror above them and saw the baby's head was out. One more push was all they needed. "We are almost there, sweetheart, look." She pointed over Desi's shoulder.

"I'm so tired." Desi sounded exhausted, but she hadn't let go of Harry the entire time. Harry was sure her souvenir from all this would be two bruises on her forearms in the shape of Desi's hands, but she wasn't moving from this spot. "I don't think I can."

"One more, I promise," she said, making eye contact with Ellie.

"She's right, Desi. One more, but let's make it a good one." Ellie's voice was soothing but held a hint of challenge. Desi nodded as she leaned back against her and reached for her hands. "Okay, let's go."

Desi tensed her entire body as she let out a scream, and then she was crying when she relaxed and fell against Harry. It was strange to Harry that it all seemed to happen both in a rush and in slow motion as she watched Sam work. The baby started crying as Desi sobbed, and then she joined her when Sam placed the newborn on Desi's chest.

"Harry and Desi, meet your son," Sam said, and Desi's hands came up to hold him in place.

The first thing Harry noticed was the full head of hair and how long he was. He was two weeks early, but maybe that was a good thing. If he'd gone to term, she didn't know if Desi would've been able to deliver him naturally. The little guy was screaming and shivering, but to Harry he was the most beautiful thing in the world, and she placed her hand over Desi's on his back.

"I need to steal him for a second, but I promise I'll bring him right back," one of the nurses said. She didn't leave the room as they completed all the routine procedures of weighing and measuring.

"We have a son, honey." She kissed Desi's cheek before moving to make Desi more comfortable.

"He looks like you, love." Desi's eyes never left the baby as she wiped her face. "He's perfect."

"We're almost done, Desi," Ellie said. The rest went much quicker, and Desi closed her eyes once she was cleaned up. "You managed no stitches, so you'll have a quicker recovery. Trust me, that's a good thing."

"I'm sorry for screaming at everyone." Desi tightened her fingers around Harry's hand.

"Remind me to show you the video of Ellie. She found new and inventive ways to use the f word, so no apologies necessary." Sam made Desi laugh, and it seem to break through Desi's guilt.

"Hey," Harry said into her phone, "see if you can sneak back in here without a crowd." She hung up and accepted the baby from the nurse. It was hard to let go but she handed him to Desi as Rachel stuck her head in the door. "Come meet your nephew."

"I can't believe it. Are you okay?" Rachel came in and kissed her sister before concentrating her attention on the baby. "He's beautiful."

"I'm tired but happy," Desi said, accepting the baby back. She ran her fingers along the baby's hand, already removing the pale green cap the staff had put on him.

Harry chuckled at the sight. Now that his hair was clean and dry it was sticking up in all directions. He was the cutest kid ever born as far as she was concerned. "Happy doesn't begin to cover it."

"What about a name, honey?"

"You did all that hard work, so you pick. I know we narrowed it down, but can we skip Harry?"

"Even though that's my favorite, I'll let you win that one." Desi glanced down and placed her hand on his chest. "Welcome to the world, Nicolas Harry Basantes." She pronounced his first name with a perfect Spanish accent. "I'm your mommy and I love you."

Harry had lived through so many different experiences in her life. She'd found love, had experienced crippling heartache, and earned professional triumphs. This one moment, though, narrowed down to the most perfect thing she'd ever seen. Seeing her wife with their son would be forever etched on her heart.

"We both do."

❖

The rest of the family waited outside until Desi had fed Nico for the first time. It was Harry's nickname for him, and Desi had fallen in love with it, so Rachel was convinced it'd stick. She'd enjoyed watching the new parents navigate their new reality as Desi held him against her naked chest as a way of bonding with him and patted his diapered little backside as he slept. It was all he was wearing, and he appeared happy with his world.

Rachel laughed when Nico went from a sleepy future baby model to near hysterical a few hours later when he woke up wet and hungry. It was a preview of things to come when she helped Harry change him as Desi waited for Harry to get her nursing pillow. As he latched on and quieted again, she anticipated they were all in for a lot of sleepless nights since Nico cried loud enough to wake the neighborhood.

She'd watched her sister as she held him to her breast and ran her finger along his cheek to encourage him to stay awake when he started to lag and his eyes grew droopy again. She seemed to be in heaven, and Rachel noticed Harry at Desi's back, holding them both. Harry seemed besotted with their new son, and she couldn't blame her. It was amazing how quickly you could fall in love with someone.

It was hard not to be just a bit jealous. The two most important people in her life now had someone who'd replace her spot in their lives. Granted, her jealously was unjustified because that's not who Desi and Harry were, but watching them made her chest tighten in fear of being left out and left behind.

"Dios mío," Rosa said when she stood at the side of the bed and gazed at Nico. Harry had combed his hair down, but it curled at the top like some sort of rooster comb, making him even cuter. "It's like looking at a newborn Harry."

Desi handed him over, and Rosa's smile appeared painful it was so big.

"He's beautiful, girls," Francisco said. He stood behind Rosa and smiled, puffed up with grandfatherly pride.

"What's his name?" Rosa pressed his little hand to her cheek before handing him to his mother.

"Nicolas Harry Basantes," Desi said, smiling up at her mother-in-law. "We wanted him to carry the name of the people who've been important to your family as well as a little of Harry."

"*Our* family, mi hija," Rosa said.

"Nicolas was both Rosa's and Francisco's fathers' name," Rachel explained to her mother and Bobbie. "If Nico gets the doctor bug, he'll be the fifth generation to do that."

"Congratulations, Grandma," Desi said to her mother and winked up at Bobbie. "I hate that we were separated for so long, but I'm so glad you came back in time for this."

"It's like a dream, and he's beautiful," her mom said, wiping at her face. Nico seemed content as he puckered his lips a bit but kept his eyes closed. "He does really look like you, Harry."

"Let's hope he doesn't act like her," Mona said, making them all laugh. "You both did good. He's gorgeous."

"I was a perfect baby," Harry teased back, "but I'm hoping the next one will be a blonde."

"Give Desi the chance to recover from this one," Rosa said. "Are you doing okay, Desi?"

"I'm sore, but I'm so happy that I don't mind."

"I'm here to help if you don't mind us staying." Their mother spoke but never took her eyes off the baby. "The next couple of weeks will be tough."

"You and Bobbie aren't going anywhere. We're lucky you're here, and it'll help that we'll also have a pediatrician in-house. Mama, we weren't kidding when we said how happy we are you're here and back in our lives." Desi pointed between Rachel and herself. "I want Nico to know all his grandparents, and by some miracle he'll have five, including Mona. Having my mom help me get back on my feet is the best I could hope for." Desi accepted her embrace when June handed Bobbie the baby after kissing his hand.

"Good. We're not going anywhere then," their mom said. "We have so much to catch up on, and I'm so happy you're both so open to that."

Bobbie smiled, and June took her hand as well as Desi's, "You and Bobbie will have to think about what you want Nico to call you."

They saw Desi try to stifle a yawn and nodded to each other.

"How about we all come back tomorrow and help you pack up? You're leaving tomorrow, right?" June asked.

"Ellie wants us to spend the night, but we'll be out of here tomorrow," Harry said. "And you can have Rachel drive you guys over in the morning. The baby seat is already set up in the Yukon, so take mine home, Rach."

"We'll go so you can get some rest," Francisco said. "Call if you need something. We're all ready for duty."

Everyone kissed Desi good-bye after Mona got to hold the baby. Rachel stayed to help Harry change Nico again and dress him in a onesie. Desi fed him one more time, and she was glad they wanted to stay and share in the experience. Desi had longed for years to be a mother but not with Byron. Now, along with Harry and the rest of their growing family, they'd be the best thing in Nico's life.

Rachel accepted the baby to burp him as Harry helped Desi with her pajamas. It was hard to hand him back to Harry, but she was ready to get some sleep. Harry took Nico and inhaled deeply through her nose over his head.

"I'm going to head home, but I'll be back first thing with the moms to help pack up for home." She moved closer to Desi and kissed her cheek. Desi was sleeping and she didn't want to wake her. "Congratulations, Dad," Rachel said to Harry as she smiled. "I'm not sure how you pulled it off, but that kid does look just like you. He's the cutest."

"I'm positive that he's got a lot of your sister in there, and hopefully he'll inherit her temperament." Harry moved to the recliner.

"Desi is going to love raising him, but I doubt that he'll be just like her. That's another hero in the making once he follows your lead because he's going to adore you."

"I'm no hero," Harry protested as she always did.

She shook her head as she combed Harry's hair back. "You'll never get Desi or me to agree with you on that. You've been our hero and protector from the day you met us." She leaned down and kissed Nico's forehead and Harry's cheek. "He's beautiful, and he already commands a room like you do." Harry laughed at her teasing. "Take care of her and call if you need anything. Enjoy your first night as a parent."

"Text me when you get home so I don't worry."

"You know the best part of Nicolas looking just like you?" She touched the baby's back as she smiled at Harry.

"What?" Harry's expression as always was open and earnest. Desi really was lucky.

"Every time she sees his face"—she pointed to her sister—"she's going to see the one person she loves most in this world reflected back at her. That's what she's wanted since the day you two talked about having a family. Thank you for loving her."

"You're poetic when you set your mind to it." Harry kissed the back of her hand and smiled up at her. "Thank you, and you know I'll always take care of you both. That'll be true even when you fly off and have a family of your own."

She nodded before leaving but stopped short in the hallway, surprised to see Serena in the waiting room, sitting alone in one corner. Her eyes were closed, and her head was resting on the wall behind her with her hands on her stomach. Rachel watched her to see if the peaceful expression on her face was from sleep or contemplation. Serena startled when she sat next to her.

"Hey, what are you doing?" It was dark outside and it reminded her she hadn't eaten since breakfast, and she was starved.

"Mona called me, but don't get mad at her. I think she likes being here for all these births to get all the kids off to a good start. She was here the night Butch was born." Serena smiled as if reminiscing. "I know I couldn't make it to Desi's show, but this felt like something unforgiveable to miss even if I was stuck out here. I also want to show you I can learn from my mistakes."

"Thank you, and I'll let them know you dropped by. Butch will be happy. It's a boy." She reached over and ran her thumb under Serena's eyes and the dark smudges put there by exhaustion. "Nicolas Harry Basantes."

"They must be thrilled." Serena leaned in to her touch. "Does he look like Harry? If he does, I'm sure Desi is happy."

"Exactly like Harry, and you're right, it thrills Desi to no end." She couldn't help but move closer and kiss Serena. It wasn't about passion or anything aside from connecting with her. To have a person who wanted the same from her cracked the barrier she'd erected to protect her heart. She brought her hands up and put them in Serena's hair.

"I'm happy for them, and for you. You're going to be the best aunt."

"I'm looking forward to that, and I'm also starving." She kissed Serena again.

"I'd love to take you out. Butch is with my parents, so we can go if you're ready." Serena stood and held her hand out to her.

"How about I pick something up and I meet you at your house? I don't feel like sitting in a restaurant right now." She held Serena's hand as they walked out, and Serena led her to Harry's vehicle after Rachel mentioned that's what she was driving home.

"Let's go to my place, and I'll order from that Thai restaurant you like. I don't want you out alone until the Simoneaux family is in custody." Serena kissed her hand and closed the door.

That Serena was this concerned warmed her, and she texted Harry before taking off. She wasn't in a hurry, and she laughed at Harry's response to be good and not take any shit. It was good to have someone aside from Desi who knew her this well and loved her this much. She sent Harry the kissy face emoji and pulled out.

The traffic was heavier than she expected, so Serena had changed by the time she got there and looked relaxed in jeans and a Tulane sweatshirt. The way Serena gazed at her as she dropped her shoes by the door made her warm, and she didn't resist when she pulled her forward.

"You feel so good," Serena said as she kissed the side of her neck. "I've missed you. I've missed us."

"Well—" The doorbell stopped her from saying anything.

"I ordered from the car, so hold that thought." Serena opened the door and paid for their dinner. "Do you want to eat?"

"Not right this minute," she said, wanting Serena close. It was a mixed signal, she realized that, but right this second she didn't care.

Serena didn't need any other clue and put the bag down on the kitchen island and backed her to the edge. Their kissing went from comforting to hot in an instant, and Rachel welcomed the heat. The need Serena was able to create made her smile against her lips as she thought about the aggravation she'd felt only the day before.

"I am hungry, though," she said as Serena started to unbutton her shirt.

"I think I can take care of that," Serena said, taking her hand and walking her to the bedroom. They took their time undressing each other, and she lay down when Serena had her completely naked and got on top when they were on the bed.

Serena pushed herself up enough to be able to skim her hands between Rachel's breasts, then over her belly to the top of her sex. She enjoyed watching as much as the feel of Serena's hands. It was like every cell in her body was alive and electrified by what Serena was doing to her, and it only added to the elation of the day. She lifted her hips as a hint for Serena to get going.

"Uh…" She couldn't help the groan when Serena dragged her fingers through her sex to her clit. "I don't want to wait." She wasn't a fan of begging, but she'd do it if it got her what she wanted.

"You don't have to." Serena kissed her again before moving down where Rachel most wanted her. "God, you taste good." Serena's flat tongue made her want to snap her legs closed to keep her from moving, but Serena held them in place.

"I can't wait." She bent her knees and held Serena's head in place with both hands. "Shit." She was loud as her hips came off the bed when Serena entered her fast and hard. "Like that—don't stop."

Serena sucked her in and didn't let up as she moved with her. She loved sex, but this was more than that. The way Serena touched her was hot, but there was also tenderness in the way she did it. It felt like love and caring, and that was why she'd been so angry when Serena stopped trying. The job and everything else that wasn't her had made Serena forget they both needed to be present to make the relationship work.

"Like…fuck, don't stop. I'm almost there…Don't stop." She shut her eyes and stilled as she came way faster than she wanted to. "I think I needed that," she said and laughed when she was finally able to breathe. Serena moved back over her but kept most of her weight off by pressing her hands to the mattress.

"You're beautiful all the time, but that's especially true when you really let go." Serena moved to lie next to her after kissing her and put her arm around her middle.

"You say things to me no one ever has." She moved to face Serena, holding her arm in place.

Serena smiled as she moved her fingers over her spine. "I say things to you I've never said to anyone."

"I don't think that's true." She tapped Serena's nose with the tip of her index finger, smiling to take the sting out of it.

"You should think of it this way." Serena lifted up again wanting to reach her lips then the side of her neck. "I could've said that to get you naked and let me touch you, but—"

"I made it way easier than that." She laughed, glad to put all the heavy feelings aside for the moment. "You were lucky." She tweaked Serena's nipple before smoothing her hand over it. "Today was a good one to celebrate."

"You can believe me. I'm not that untrustworthy," Serena said, sounding wistful. "Do you think I can come over for a visit tomorrow and bring Butch?" The phone rang before she could answer. "Hello."

Serena sat up and put her feet on the floor. She held the receiver and didn't say anything for a few long minutes. "Are you sure?"

She pressed to Serena's back and waited. "What?" she whispered.

"Give me twenty minutes and I'll meet you over there." Serena ended the call and sighed. "I'm so sorry, but I have to go."

"What? Tell me," she said again. Whatever it was and whoever had called seemed to upset Serena into silence. "Wait, it's about Byron and his family, isn't it?"

"Honey, I have to go."

"No, tell me." She needed to know and was angry Serena was keeping something important from her. Her anger grew, not only at Serena but at the asshole who'd already robbed them of so much joy. And her gut told her she was right. "Tell me," she said loudly.

"When the Simoneaux family went on trial, the attorneys representing them sold off their assets to pay for their defense." Serena spoke slowly as if the conversation was full of landmines, and she didn't want to step on any.

"Just spit it out."

"I just found out a couple of NOPD patrol officers bought the house where Big Byron and his late wife lived. They were fixing it up." Serena stopped and took a breath.

"It's okay to just say it. I'm not going to fall apart on you." She sat next to Serena so she could see her face.

"They were home tonight when someone broke in and shot them both. The woman is fine, but her husband is dead. Before she was shot, his wife was able to call it in, and they found Byron Simoneaux, Sr. was the shooter."

"Fuck." The word exploded out of her, and she wanted to go out and hunt them herself if only to put them out of everyone's misery. "What happened to him?"

"He wouldn't surrender and was waving the gun he'd acquired, so he was shot on sight. He's dead." Serena delivered the news with little emotion. "My boss wants me over there before this turns into a media circus, but I'm sure we're too late for that. A police officer killed in his own home by some asshole who escaped Angola is going to cost a lot of people their jobs if the mayor has anything to do with it."

"I'm going with you."

Serena shook her head and put her hand on her shoulder. "I wish you could, but not this time, honey."

"Why today of all days?" She didn't want to mar the memory of

Nico's birth with something like this. After not hearing anything for a couple of weeks, she thought maybe these guys had gone somewhere away from them. That had been a foolish pipe dream. "Can I tell Harry and Desi?"

"Why don't you give them the night. We can go together tomorrow and let them know. Right now, eat something and get some sleep. I'll be back as soon as I can."

She watched Serena get dressed, and it was like what little energy she had left drained right out of her. Then she thought of her mother, and everyone else in the house. The house Byron had broken into once before, even with the guards outside, and she sat up and searched for her clothes.

"Where are you going?" Serena said, back in her jeans and sweatshirt.

"I have to go home. I can't leave them alone without warning them. But I don't want to call this late and freak them out. Late night phone calls are never good." She started getting dressed, and Serena held her. "Let me go."

"Let me take care of what I need to," Serena said, "and I'll come back for you. I don't think you should be out there alone."

That was a reasonable thing to say. The problem was that Byron and his family weren't reasonable. They were all animals who smashed everything and everyone in their lives and found true pleasure in it. "Go and call me when you're done, but I can't let this happen to my family. I can't sit here and just worry. And you know if their father is here, then so are Byron and Mike."

"I know that, but it's not going to do any good for you to get hurt." Serena tried to pull her closer, but she was desperate to go. She placed a stiff arm on Serena's shoulder and shook her head.

"Thank you, and I hear what you're saying, but I know what's going to happen and so should you. Byron's a lot like his father. Who do you think Byron is going to look for first?" She stared into Serena's eyes and waited for her to see it her way. "He wants to punish Desi, and I'm sure he wants to devastate Harry."

"Let me call an officer to follow you home." Serena stepped away and reached for her phone.

"Go to work and I'll be fine. Trust me, I'd love to run into Byron… with my car." Her joke made Serena smile. "I'll be okay, I promise." She held Serena's hand again as they made their way out to the car. "Call me when you're done."

"How about if I come over?"

"Sure, just call first, so Francisco doesn't take you out if you come in unannounced." She stared at Serena before she got going. It took effort not to turn toward the hospital and tell Harry and her sister what had happened. Serena was right, though. They deserved peace for the night at least. That they'd never have peace until the problem was as dead as Big Byron was something that worried her. "Damn you, Byron."

If his story ended like his father's, she'd have no problem with that. He'd never change, and at times she wondered how such an evil man was able to thrive when his existence meant pain for so many others. No matter what his plans were, she wasn't going to back down.

"If I have to, I'll kill you myself, consequences be damned." She slammed the car door and headed into the darkness.

Chapter Seventeen

T he next morning Desi spit her toothpaste into the sink and laughed at the one-sided conversation Harry was having with Nico. Their son was happy with his slice of the world at the moment, since she'd fed him, and Harry had cleaned him up. She laughed harder when she saw him in a set of navy blue scrubs that had been a gift from Francisco. They were the same color Harry was partial to, and they were adorable on the sleeping little boy.

"Is he ready to do rounds?" She was sore but felt much lighter as she walked slowly toward them.

"Right after pottery classes he'll head into surgery." Harry held Nico against her shoulder and Desi's eyes glassed over. "What's wrong? Are you in pain?"

"No, I just can't believe all this is real. That you still love me is something that still catches me by surprise sometimes." She wiped her face and smiled in an effort not to freak Harry out. "I'm so happy it's hard to contain, and my hormones are crazy at the moment, so ignore me. These are happy tears, believe me."

"Life wasn't fair to us, and we lost so many years together, but we're going to be okay. We deserve to be happy—you deserve all this and more." Harry took her hand and led her to the sofa.

"You are the best thing that I've ever been gifted, and you have to admit we make beautiful babies." Nico's hair was standing on end again, and he was the most beautiful thing she'd ever seen.

Harry nodded as she put her free arm around her. "I didn't want to brag but—"

The newscaster on the television facing the bed was talking, and Desi raised her hand, stopping Harry from saying anything else. It was the street name that made her pay attention to the story. She lifted her other hand to her mouth when the camera panned in on the house. Police tape fluttered behind the reporter, and the chyron under the man talking spelled out the gist of why he was there. *One officer dead and one in critical condition.*

"What?" Harry asked. She put the baby down and moved back to put her arms around her.

The house on the screen was miles from their home, but how far she'd come to escape from there was like a trip to Mars. There was no forgetting, though. Not that hellhole—not Big Byron—not his sons. It twisted her stomach with shame and resentment.

"Listen," she said, having to force the word out. She turned up the volume.

"Police are reporting the death of one of the escaped convicts after he refused to put his weapon down, instead aiming it at the officers who responded to the call." The reporter pointed to the house. *"No one is sure how Byron Simoneaux, Sr. was able to make his way to the city, much less how he was able to break in and kill one of the new owners. NOPD has released the name of Officer Dwaine Jones as the officer killed, and his wife Gloria is still in intensive care. There's no news on his sons, who escaped with him. Back to you, Randi, and we'll report back once there is more information available."* The screen cut back to the studio.

"This can't be happening again." All they should be worrying about was their son's next feeding, when he needed to be changed, and when he needed to be held and loved. It was like Byron and his family couldn't stand the thought of her happiness and wanted to smash it like a baseball bat to the head.

"He's dead." Harry tightened her hold and kissed her temple. "Concentrate on that."

"Honey, if Big Byron is here, you know what that means." Maybe Rosa was right. They should leave until Byron and his brother were back where they belonged. "That poor man lost his life because of me."

"Don't say that." Harry's voice was firm. "That old bastard came home for God knows what, but it had nothing to do with you. None of this is on you."

"Listen to her, sis," Rachel said from the door. There were dark circles under her eyes. "And, Harry, don't curse in front of the baby."

"They're never going to stop, and there's no incentive for them to." Desi closed her eyes taking comfort in Harry's warmth. "There's one simple truth we all need to accept. Once they're caught, they're going back to jail for years, but I know Byron. Before that reality of life in prison, he's going to make it worth his while by destroying everything we have."

"He can try." Harry framed her face with her hands and looked into her eyes before kissing her. "You, Nico, and Rachel are my priority, and I'm not going to let anything happen to you."

"Serena called this morning and said there was no sign of Byron or Mike," Rachel said. "The woman who bought the house survived and was able to give a brief statement before surgery. It sounds like Big Byron kept screaming about his wife cheating on him, and he thought the female officer was her. How he got into the house is a mystery, but he shot both her and her husband with the officer's gun."

"Both of you promise you'll be careful," Desi said. "They might not have been found, but you know they're both coming back here. Byron is like his father. No matter the consequences, he'll come back for all three of us." It wasn't often she thought of their father, but all this started with him, and she damned him for it.

She remembered his face the day Clyde insisted on walking her down the short aisle of the neighborhood church they'd never attended. He'd been almost gleeful when he forced her hand into Byron's. When he leaned toward her as he gave her away, it was for no loving kiss, but to remind her of Rachel and what would happen to her if she tried to get back to Harry. How someone could inflict so much misery on everyone around him and take so much pleasure in it was something she found incomprehensible.

"The guards are back, and I'm sure the police are working on this," Harry said. "All we have to do is enjoy Nico for the next few weeks while I'm off work. There's also a house full of people who want to protect you because they love you." Harry, as always, was her rock, but there was no missing the worry lines around her eyes.

"She's right about that too," Rachel said.

Everyone froze when someone knocked. They all exhaled when the door opened to Sept with a younger man with jet hair and a purple tie. "From everyone's expression, I take it you've heard the news. I apologize for not coming sooner, but what happened has the mayor and every other official person who thinks they're important in a full-blown conniption. I've been threatened to get this solved by so many people my ass hurts. Judge Jude Rose is at the top of that list."

"Uncle Jude has as much reason as us to worry about these guys. I'm sure what happened at his house is still on his mind." Harry held up her finger. "And before you take the blame for that, that wasn't your fault either," she said to Desi.

"This time around, Judge Rose's tirade was all about Desi and you. He was screaming he's a great-uncle now, so get this done, or I'll spend the rest of my career writing parking tickets."

"There hasn't been much news. Will the other officer make it?" Harry beat Desi to the question.

"She's stable, and the doctors report she's going to be fine. Turns out the news got it wrong. The other officer wasn't her husband, just her partner and roommate. When I say partner, I mean her work partner. Dwaine was her roommate." Sept glanced at the guy with her. "This is *my* partner, Nathan Blackman. We're officially moving from a consultant role to taking over your case because of what happened last night. Finding these guys is a priority, so the major case team will be focused on getting that done. The FBI has also taken an interest in this case for some reason, and this time around, I'll be happy to accept whatever they want to throw at this."

"Please apologize to the officer. This happened to her because of me." Desi was tired of crying, but she couldn't stop.

"Listen to me."

Sept's hand was warm like Harry's, and she tried smiling at her, but her lips were trembling too much to pull it off.

"From what Gloria said, Byron Sr. had some serious mental health issues. He kept screaming his late wife's name before he pulled the trigger. That makes Byron Simoneaux, Sr. guilty of what happened—it had nothing at all to do with you. I know you'll have a hard time not thinking that, but you need to look at it like I do. Because his actions resulted in his death, there'll be no need for his apology. In my book, and Gloria's, that's justice. The asshole who broke into her house and killed her friend got what he deserved, and she's more than okay with that."

"What we need is any information about where you think the Simoneaux brothers might go," Nathan said. "Anyone they'd contact."

"I never really understood my ex-husband, but if he's come back here, it's to hurt me and to get the money he stashed in our house that he thinks no one knows about."

"How far can you get on six hundred bucks?" Rachel asked. "If he comes for it, I left a note letting him know I donated it to Oz in the Quarter to fix their ice machine." Oz welcomed everyone, but it was a gay bar in the French Quarter and the last place Byron or anyone in his family would be caught dead in.

"You took it?" Desi asked. She finally found something to laugh about, thinking of Rachel doing just that. "Of course you did, and it's amazing it was that much. His father never paid him much, and most of the extra went into Byron's fun. That he managed to save six hundred dollars is a miracle."

"I've got a unit sitting on your old house," Sept said. "It'll make our job that much easier if he really is that stupid."

"Thank you." The dump she'd shared with Byron and Rachel was another place that was sold off to pay for the Simoneaux defense, but her attorney, Jerry, had fought for her half even after she said she didn't really want it. It wasn't much, but she'd given it to Harry to invest for their children's education. It was the only thing she could think of to make something good out of something horrible.

"You all need to be vigilant until we find these guys," Sept went on. "We're working on getting leads, so we can see if they know anything about the brothers."

"We've also stepped up patrols around your house," Nathan said.

"Enough about that." Sept glanced at Harry and pointed to the bassinet. "Let's see this gorgeous new baby I heard the nurses talking about. That must mean he looks like you, Desi."

"Believe me, he's definitely Harry's baby." She smiled when the baby kicked his feet up and let out a mewl. "Pick him up before he starts crying, honey."

Sept laughed at her when Harry moved quickly.

"Meet our son," Harry said. The pride in Harry's voice was hard to miss, and she wanted nothing more than to enjoy their son.

Byron might be headed right for them, but Desi had faith that everything would be okay. She and Harry had paid enough in pain and misery, so she refused to believe someone as petty and small as Byron would drive them apart again.

"Nicolas Basantes," she said as Sept accepted their boy from Harry. "See, there's no denying who he belongs to." Nico's hair was dark like Harry's, and he was also long for a newborn.

"Congratulations, and stop worrying. We have you covered." Sept stayed a bit longer before she and Nathan were called back to work.

"We'll be fine," she said as she brought Nico to her breast. She said the words out loud, willing them to be true.

❖

For the first time in two weeks, Byron opened his eyes without wanting to put a dagger through both of them. The train ride into the city had made his cold or whatever the hell he had that much worse, and Mike had practically had to carry him to an abandoned building close the train station. After a few days he was able to walk to the abandoned public housing development close to the train yard. Mike had kicked in a door to one of the apartments in the middle of the corridor and eased him onto a mattress left behind.

The place was cold and disgusting, but it was the best they could do until he was stronger. Not being able to go to a doctor was the pits, but Mike had managed to shoplift some medicine from a pharmacy a few miles away. That had helped a little with his headache and congestion, though his chest felt like his lungs were packed with wet sand. His rage-fueled drive to see Desi had drained out of him since all he wanted to do all day was sleep.

"Here." Mike handed him a container of half-eaten fried chicken, and he couldn't believe he'd gotten to the point of eating out of dumpsters to survive. "It's the best of what was out there today."

"I'm tired of this shit," he said and started coughing. Any little thing sent him into a coughing fit, and the exercise made his entire body hurt. "We need to start thinking about moving closer to either the garage or to Basantes's house."

"Either place will be the quickest way to get caught." Mike ate his serving of the cold chicken and shook his head as if he was more disgusted with him than the food. "You can barely stay awake for more than twenty minutes, and I'm not going to go in there and hurt them for you. For all we know Daddy has been caught and told them everything you have planned. There's no way in hell you're getting anywhere near anyone you want to take your revenge on."

"Look, we need to get out of this cold before this shit kills me. I'm shocked you haven't gotten sick yet." He tried to keep his voice even, so he wouldn't start coughing again. "All I want is to survive all this crap, and the more time that goes by, the more they'll relax. Just remember that no one knows where we are."

He needed to get out of this dump. All they'd found were some old blankets that smelled like a few things had died on them, and they were stiff from what appeared to be mold, but it was better than trying to sleep in the frigid temperatures. He had to man up and get out of here before everything caught up with him. Adding a humiliating death so close to his goal would be one more sad pathetic thing.

"I only go out at night, and there aren't a lot of cars to pick from in this area, so we're going to have to walk if you want to go anywhere. Getting back to the garage is going to take forever if you can't walk much, so let me think about it." Mike put the Styrofoam container down and closed his eyes.

"How about going out again tonight, and I'll come with you?" He wiped the sweat from his forehead. Despite the cold snap, his fever made him hot and clammy to the point of craving a shower. The sour body odor coming off him in waves was starting to add to his nausea and disgust. "We can scope the places close by, or the train station, and see what we find."

"It's better than sitting in here, I guess. Get some sleep and I'll wake you."

New Orleans never really completely slept, but it was quiet when Mike shook him and helped him to his feet. He took his blanket with him and followed Mike down the sidewalk until they were able to make it through the fence at the train yard. The place itself didn't have a parking lot, but Mike had told him the federal building and hotel next door had plenty of cars.

By the time they made it to the buildings he was gasping and trying not to stand out by coughing hard enough to expel a bucket of phlegm. "I know this is going to sound crazy, but the federal building will be our best bet."

"How do you figure?" Mike stared at him as if he had a tattoo on his forehead that spelled his mental disorder in detail.

"It's the last place they'd think someone would hit to steal a car, and it's not like we can keep it longer than tonight. If there's cameras out here, everyone and their brother are going to be looking for us." There was a sedan close to the exit with no alarm and old enough to not be flashy. "This one," he said, trying the door.

It took a rock to the driver's side window to get into it, and they paused to see if anyone would come running. Mike took care of the wiring when the noise raised no alarms, and they drove to the garage first. He wasn't stupid enough to think the cops weren't sitting on it, so he had Mike park a few blocks away and get as close a look as he could manage.

"It's completely empty, and part of the garage is gone. I think they're getting ready to build something else, and the cars have been cleared out." Mike was breathing hard when he got back.

"Man, if Pop saw that, he'd take somebody's head off. That place has been in his family for sixty years." He closed his eyes again, trying to center himself, but nothing was working. His cold was better in some ways, but it was like it had gone deep into his chest and was slowly draining the life out of him. "Did you see any cops?"

"There's a few cars parked across the street, and if they're cops, they're in unmarked cars. You want to drive somewhere while we have the chance?" Mike started the engine again and put it in drive. "It's not too late to change your mind."

"You have some kind of stupid streak running through you. We ain't leaving until I finish—" He started coughing again, and he had to open the door and throw up. Mike took that as an invitation to start driving.

"Fucker, you think *I'm* stupid?" Mike laughed and it sounded like more of an insult than him cursing at him. "You're never going to change, and it's never going to matter how many times you lose. You want to run to your death, then I'll drop you off and you can do it by yourself."

He stared out the window and realized Mike was headed uptown. If his brother decided to abandon him now, he'd never make it. "I know we've never been tight, and you think I'm a dumbass, but what Desi did…" He had to stop and think about how best to put it. "It was embarrassing. All those guys we've been locked up with pegged me as the weak one because my wife…*my wife*…ran off with some woman. They did things to me I ain't ever going to forget because I couldn't keep a woman satisfied."

"They did things to both of us because it's prison. No one in there would've known what had happened to you if you'd kept your mouth shut. The problem is, you're obsessed and won't face the truth. We've been in prison having a shitty time of it for a year, but Desi's served sixteen years with you, and it was an even shittier time." Mike didn't raise his voice, and his flat delivery made Byron want to hit him. "So you do what you want, but this is what I'm doing. I'm going to look for Daddy because he's our father, but I'm not going to forget growing up under his roof."

"Be careful, brother. Coming up with your own ideas now might drive the old man to kill you," he said and laughed. It was short lived because of the coughing.

"You think I'm some fag because I never chased women or went drinking with you. The way I've tried to live my life is to forget all those parts of me because I'm not going to turn into Daddy. There's no way in hell I'm going to exist by having to beat some woman every night because my peas are cold or because she forgot to shine my shoes." Mike glanced at him, and he could see the contempt in his eyes. "I read and try to forget that I sat in my room while he slowly killed Mama and I didn't do anything to stop it."

"That wasn't our place." The excuse was weak, but Mike was right. He couldn't understand the intoxicating power of getting your way no matter what you had to do to get it.

"She was our mother, and he killed her. He can act crazy now, but that's the truth. You want to do the same thing, and I'm not going to have nothing to do with it."

The streets were starting to look familiar. He'd have never been able to afford any of the places they were driving by, and it irritated him that Desi now called this area home. It was like she'd sold herself into some deviant lifestyle for the money and all it could buy, and not because she was in love with Basantes. Maybe he'd give her one more chance. Her choice would be loving and accepting her place in his life, or death.

"Don't drive past the front."

Mike seemed glad to turn off and drive along the high brick wall around the property at the back. The houses along the street at the back of the property were nice but not as big. All of them were well-maintained, with cars parked in front except for one at the end of the block. "Look," he said, pointing to the front door when Mike stopped at the corner.

"What?"

There were four newspapers on the small front porch, and there were no lights on in the house. "I don't think anyone's home." The only problem would be an alarm system. "Pull over."

"That place is probably wired for the police to come running if we break in there." But Mike did as he asked.

"Just go and check it out. The panel has to be close to the door, or the owner would set it off every single time they went in. If it's something easy, it'll get us a warm bed for the night, if nothing else."

"Stay in the car. I don't need your dumb ass trying something stupid while I'm gone."

He wanted to bitch Mike out, but the headache was starting to build again, and the fever was getting worse. This had to be something worse than a cold because he'd never felt this bad. It was like something evil had crawled inside him and there wasn't shit he could do about it.

"Come on," Mike said, shaking him awake. "One of the back windows was unlocked, and there was a note on the counter for the maid. These guys are out of town for the next two weeks, and the house will be empty."

He could barely hear what Mike was saying, and he groaned when he lifted him out of the car and put his arm around him to hold him up. It took effort to put one foot in front of the other, but he did his best to help Mike as they went through the side gate to the yard. Mike left him on the couch and told him to sleep it off while he dumped the car.

Sleep came quickly and his dreams landed him on the football field calling a play. Those were the only good memories he had of his whole life. At least he had that. There was nothing else.

CHAPTER EIGHTEEN

Harry changed Nico and watched Desi pick at the sandwich Mona had brought her. It seemed the love affair with chicken salad was over. Once the row of buttons was done on the onesie from hell, she picked the baby up and headed to the bed.

"I don't want to nag, but you have to eat, love. This little guy will drain you if you don't." They were alone for a bit since Rachel had taken everyone to lunch. The report of what Byron had done led to a slew of opinions from everyone in the family as to what should happen next. Rachel saved her the trouble of throwing everyone out of Desi's room by ushering them down to the cafeteria.

"I'm sorry, but I'm really not hungry. All I want to do is go home and concentrate on anything but my fear." Desi took a deep breath and shook her head. "It's hard to explain what it's like spending day after day being terrified, and even harder to describe what it's like when it's a given that there's nothing left to be afraid of. The relief of being with you is something so foreign to me sometimes, and I have to convince myself it's true."

"It kills me that you experienced any of that." The past was a son of a bitch that couldn't be changed. There was no magic wand that'd erase all of Desi's nightmares, so she did her best to always be in the present, showing Desi how she felt about her.

"I didn't say that to make you feel guilty, honey. You're the reason I was able to let that go. You're the one person aside from my sister who loves me and would never do anything to hurt me. Now that my moms and your parents are here, we've only added to that list of people looking out for us." She leaned against Harry when she put the baby down. "I'm just tired of being afraid. I want us to go home and enjoy our family. You're right that there are enough people working to keep us safe. I want to let Sept and the police handle Byron so we can forget about all of it."

"Sounds like I won't have to twist your arm to get out of here then," Ellie said from the door. "Harry keeps bragging about how she's a doctor, so I guess we'll have to take her word for it and entrust you to her care."

Desi laughed hard enough to snort. "That's true, but we all know Mona and Rosa rule the roost, so we'll be fine."

"Just remember to take it easy and let Harry do all the work." Ellie took Desi's hand and kissed her cheek. "We'll see you both next week for your first checkup, but call if you need anything."

"Thank Sam for us," Desi said.

"I'll do that, but you take care of yourself. One more thing, and I know this will be impossible, but try not to dwell. Trust me, the baby will pick up on that." Ellie spoke softly and Desi nodded. "You'll lose enough sleep as it is, so don't compound that."

"Thanks, Ellie, and if you have rounds, I'll take care of the discharge paperwork." Harry took her place next to Desi and put her arm around her shoulders. "Where's Sam?"

"Nico should have plenty of friends who share his birthday week, so she's napping. We have another eight patients in early labor, which means it'll be a long night." Ellie bent over the bassinet. "How about we make a house call next week? It'll be nicer, and you won't have to worry about getting dressed. Make sure you have coffee ready, Harry, and we can make it a visit to introduce our daughter to this beautiful boy."

"Thanks, Ellie. I'm sure Desi would love to stay home."

"I doubt Mona or Rosa will let us take the baby out in the cold weather, so thank you," Desi said, winking when the family returned from lunch. They both noticed Serena walking in last. That she wasn't anywhere near Rachel made Desi stare.

"Good news," Desi said softly. "We're going home."

Harry stepped out with Ellie, leaving the family to celebrate their early release. She stood by the nurses' station as Ellie finished Desi's discharge instructions. One of the nurses leaned over the countertop and smiled as she wagged her fingers in Harry's direction.

"It's good to see you, Dr. Harry." The woman seemed overfriendly, and Harry was trying to place her. "Are you lost?"

"Cathy, put this in Desi Basantes's file, and you can congratulate

Dr. Basantes on the birth of her son." Ellie's voice held some warning, and Harry tried to keep her expression flat. "That's really all you have to talk about."

At the beginning of her career she'd made the mistake of dating some of the hospital personnel, and her father had given her a long lecture when he heard some of the gossip. Most hospitals were bastions of gossip, and *womanizer* wasn't a title she wanted hung around her neck.

"That's wonderful," Cathy said with no enthusiasm. "We could have lunch maybe and talk about it. I'm always available to you."

Harry had to laugh as the woman reached for her hand. "Do I know you?" She delivered the words in a cold tone. It was never her intent to be cruel, but this woman was too much.

"We worked together on the fifth floor, and we never got the chance to go out." Cathy flexed her flat hand into a fist when Harry stepped back from her. "I'm just happy to see you. Gives me the chance to collect on dinner."

"My wife just had a baby. That means dinner or anything else will never happen. I'll meet you back in there, Ellie." She turned and headed back to Desi but stepped into the bathroom in the hallway at the last second to calm down.

The door stayed unlocked as she bent over the sink to splash cold water on her face. Women like Cathy drove her insane. It wasn't the aggression that bothered her, she liked strong independent women, but dismissing the most important relationship in her life was disgusting. She shut the water off and let the water drip with her eyes closed when she felt something pressed into her lower back.

"Look," she said emphatically, thinking it was Cathy again, but she stopped short when she looked in the mirror. The tall burly man standing behind her made her stand still. He either had a knife or a gun where it'd do significant damage. She hated that this guy was able to get this close to her family. "Mr. Lagrie, what can I do for you?"

His eyes widened when she called him by name, but his weapon didn't move. "How d'you know me?"

"I know everything about the people who were with Byron Simoneaux and his family when he escaped. If you're here to hurt my family, you're going to have to kill me to get to them."

He laughed and shook his head, making him appear less menacing. Whatever was pressed to her back eased away. "That fool talked plenty about you, and it made me curious. If you ask me, he needs killing. The problem is, I ain't no killer."

"Not what the police said." It probably wasn't the wise thing to say, but the disappearance of the weapon made her honest.

"Guess they didn't tell you the whole story." He took a step away from her and moved to put something in his jacket pocket. "I did kill some asshole, and I'd do it again if they gave me a do-over. The bastard I killed put my sister in a wheelchair, and she's lived in pain every day since."

"Serena Ladding from the DA's office told me your story. You weren't wrong, in my opinion." She sat back against the sink and waited to see what this was about. "You took care of an abuser, so I wouldn't have convicted you had I been on your jury. My problem is you helped two abusers escape and a third person—an officer—is dead."

"I saw a chance and I took it, and I wasn't going to kill the people who followed me. If I get caught, I'm going back forever, and I will with no bitching if you help me." He told her the story of his sister and the man who broke her back. After a few surgeries, she was left in pain, with no use of her legs. Her attacker had bragged about it, and Tyrell had beat him to death.

"My wife, Desi, lived in that same hell, and Byron came close to killing her." She stared at Tyrell and knew in her heart she wouldn't hesitate to keep Desi safe no matter the consequences. "Knowing he's out there waiting to try again makes me insane."

"I got my boys looking for them. You aren't going to believe me, but I left him way away from the city and told him to keep his ass moving away from here. How his daddy managed to get back, I don't know, but no one seen Byron or Mike. But I needed to see you, and I wasn't about to drive them to your doorstep."

"What can I do for you?" She had to get back to Desi.

"Why you ain't calling for help?" He cocked his head to the side. "I told you I'm no killer, but I'm doing a lot of years for just that."

"Like you, I'm curious, and I'm not used to being held at gunpoint. I'd think me calling out might make you want to shoot me."

He laughed again and took another step back. "I don't intend to kill you, Doc. I want you to take my sister on as a patient. She got some crap insurance, so don't expect a lot of money, but she deserves a chance."

"A call would've gotten you that. Why take the chance of coming here?"

"I wanted you to see I love my sister. She's the only reason I didn't end up running the streets selling nickel bags. I was on my way to becoming a plumber before all this shit went down. The cops will tell you I ended up where I belong, and they might be right. Before I go back, all I want is to repay her for all she did for me. You see her, and I'll protect you and yours until them bastards get caught again."

Harry offered him her hand. "Have her call my office and make an appointment. I give you my word she'll get my best, and I'll give you ten minutes to get out of here." She handed him her card, and he acted as if it was a treasure, putting it in his breast pocket reverently.

"Thanks, Doc, and me and my gang will watch over you and your girl until those assholes are found." He shook her hand and left.

She stepped out and was surprised there was no sign of him. For a big guy he was fast, and the only people around appeared to belong there. She had to lean against the wall and take a breath. That had been like nothing she'd ever experienced, but she couldn't help liking the big man with the guarded but honest-looking eyes. She understood every one of his motivations. And yet, a complete stranger had not only gotten into the hospital, but damn near Desi's room. It wasn't safe.

"You okay?" Sam Casey asked when she walked up and placed her hand on her shoulder.

Harry took her time straightening up and asked Sam for her phone. Sept yelled for what seemed like five minutes straight and told her she and her partner would meet them at the house for a formal statement.

All she shared was that Tyrell had come to see her. His sister she kept to herself since she'd given him her word, and she was going to honor that. She wasn't going to be another person in Tyrell's life to write him off. That might be a mistake, but she had to go with her gut.

"That didn't go well," Sam said.

"That'll be calm compared to when I tell Desi."

❖

Desi closed her eyes and concentrated on the feel of Nico lying on her chest instead of on the conversation she'd had with Harry about the visit from Tyrell. She'd just finished feeding him, and he'd fallen instantly asleep when he finished. It was still early in the afternoon, so she was planning on joining him for a nap. The house was quiet, so it was easy to make out Harry running up the stairs, probably taking them two at a time.

They'd been home for five days, and Harry had a hard time putting Nico down, not that she was any better at not wanting to hold him. That meant Harry had woken him more than once, and Desi had finally exiled her from the bedroom and told her to go run on the treadmill when she'd picked him up after he'd only been asleep fifteen minutes. An overexcited Harry was hard to keep still, and Desi wanted Nico on some kind of schedule. The door opened and closed quietly, and Harry was in the bathroom before she opened her eyes again.

"She's learning," she whispered to the baby. The shower came on and she glanced at the door when it opened again after a soft knock.

"Hey, sweet girl. Want me to put him down?" Mona didn't wait for an answer as she picked Nico up and held him before placing him in the bassinet next to her side of the bed.

"He just finished eating, so he should be out for the next couple of hours. If only we could give Harry a glass of milk and get the same results, we'd be set." They laughed. She was finally over being upset about Tyrell's visit and the fact that Harry hadn't called for help. That the escaped convict had gotten that close made her shiver. Had it been Byron, God only knew how it would've ended.

"That troublemaker will rile up this kid for years to come, so get used to it," Mona said. "Hell, if she wasn't a cutie, though, and made one who looks just like her. I figure they're all so easy on the eyes so we don't run them out of town when they aggravate us." Mona was gazing down at the baby with a huge smile. There was no doubt she'd be as protective of Nico as she'd been with Harry for years.

"He's certainly big, and he's got an even bigger appetite. I'm sure the aggravation might come later, but I'm enjoying this phase for as long as it'll last." She smiled and it hit her how happy she was. "Seeing him is all my wishes coming true in one little person because he's such a part of my favorite person."

"He does look like a carbon copy of her, God help us." Mona sat in the chair next to the bassinet and placed her hand on the edge. "I have to say, though, you picked a really good genetic pool to dip into. You mix in your good heart and pretty face, and this is one special little boy."

"I remember the first day I realized there was nothing I wanted more in my life than Harry." She smiled and closed her eyes for a moment. "We were starting our senior year, and I was meeting her for a ride home, and she was leaning against her locker reading a book. It was strange, but it was like I'd never really noticed her until that one second."

"Got your attention, did she?" Mona laughed again.

"Definitely," she said, fanning herself. "She'd grown into all that height, and she'd bulked up because of all the sports. If she'd asked me right then to have her baby, I would've." She pressed her hands to her face to cool the blush she knew was there when Mona winked at her. "Being together where I would be free to look at her is something I never thought I'd have again. I keep telling her it's hard to believe this is real."

"You've waited a long time to be here, sweet girl, and I hope you have years to enjoy it. You certainly had to pay enough to get here. The truth is, you're never going to shake her now." Mona winked again and she felt her face heat. "Now tell me what you want for dinner."

The bathroom door opened, and the steam Harry had built up billowed out. She was in a pair of lounge pants and a sweatshirt, reminding Desi of their high school years. Harry loved to be comfortable, and this was the perfect day for it. The temperatures had dropped significantly by New Orleans standards, and the rain had been falling for most of the day. It was dreary and dark outside, and really all Desi was in the mood for was lying in bed in Harry's arms.

"Come here," she said, holding her hand up to Harry. "I missed you."

"You're the one who sent me downstairs," Harry said, taking her hand anyway.

"Don't you give Desi a hard time about that," Mona said, shaking her finger. "You wake this baby one more time, and I'll put you over my knee. Now tell me what you want to eat, so you can get to proving you can behave."

"Surprise us as long as it's not spicy." Harry glanced toward the bassinet and smiled. "And I'm going to spend my time kissing my wife."

Mona pointed at her again before closing the door behind her. Harry leaned back against the pillows and opened her arms. The thunder had started outside, and it made Desi shiver. She'd never loved bad weather except when she went through it with Harry. Even as children Harry had held her and made her feel safe.

The phone buzzing on Harry's side of the bed wasn't what she was expecting, and Harry seemed happy to ignore it. "Go ahead," Desi said. "Like I tell you all the time, they'll only keep calling."

"Basantes," Harry said softly. "I'm not on call, and I'm on leave for the next couple of weeks. Give Burrow a call. She's the attending until I get back." She listened some more and sighed. "It's going to take me a minute, so call her and have her meet me there."

"What?" she asked when Harry tapped the phone against her chin.

"This is why I need to resign the medical school job and just keep my private practice. Sometimes you'd swear they need an instruction manual." Harry pressed her hand to the side of her face and looked at her as if she was trying to memorize her. "I have to go in for a couple of hours, so go ahead and eat without me."

"You have to go out in this?" The room lit up with lightning and the thunder boomed.

"I promise I'll keep dry, but this'll give me the chance to warn the rest of the staff what calling me will cost them if they try it again." Harry kissed her and stepped into the closet to change. "I'll call you when I'm done and I'm on my way back."

"Be careful and I love you."

"Love you too." Harry kissed her one more time before taking off.

Desi stayed upstairs until Nico woke her with a small cry, which stopped when she picked him up. She changed him and handed him to her mother when she joined her in the bathroom. "Want me to carry him down, or do you want to feed him up here?"

"Let's go downstairs," she said, tying off her robe. Harry's parents were at the hotel with the grandchildren for the night since Miguel and his wife wanted to visit some old friends for dinner. "That way we can all sit together while I feed him."

She was still sore, but she was starting to feel better. Moving around seemed to help, so while taking the stairs wasn't pleasant, she managed them a couple times a day. Now she wanted to spend some time with her moms, Rachel, and Mona, especially since Harry was gone. While Harry had been her fantasy in all the years they'd been apart, a night like this was equally surprising. The laughter and love that flowed through the room made her want to memorize every second.

"Then she told me she wanted tiger stripes in green and yellow. She was pretty cool for a grandmother of ten," Rachel said, making them all laugh.

Desi opened her robe and unbuttoned her pajama shirt to get Nico situated. He'd gone from arm to arm when they'd made it into the kitchen, but now there was only one thing that was going to satisfy him. "Come on, handsome," she cooed to him. "You need to stay awake so you won't be up in an hour." She loved the way he seemed to concentrate with his hand on the top of her breast like he was holding her in place.

"Yes," Rachel teased, "your daddy needs to sleep before she connects the wrong bones together. God, this kid looks just like Harry."

The rain seemed to intensify even more, and Desi held Nico tighter.

"She'll be okay, so lose the frown, sweetie."

Desi glanced outside, worried about Harry as she watched the branches of the oak trees whip in the wind. "He does, and daddy? Seriously."

Rachel opened her mouth to say something else but stopped and walked to the window and stared out into the darkness of the yard. The sun had set less than an hour ago, so Desi doubted she'd be able to make out much with the rain falling.

"What?" She moved Nico to her shoulder to burp him and patted his back. "Is there a cat or something?"

"No," Rachel said slowly. She turned and smiled at them, but it seemed forced. "Ever get that creepy feeling?"

"I certainly do. Do you see anything?" June asked.

"No." Rachel came and sat next to Desi. "Sorry, it must be the weather making me so morose." Rachel's gaze stayed on the window, staring out into the yard as Desi continued to feed Nico.

"The roast I put in is ready to come out of the oven, and Harry told me not to wait on her, so let's eat," Mona said.

The electricity went out right as Mona finished speaking, and they heard a huge crash. It was loud enough to startle Nico into letting her nipple go, and he began whimpering. "What the heck was that?" She got Nico to start eating again, but the house seemed to shake from the wind outside.

"That didn't sound good at all. Let me go take a look," Bobbie said as she grabbed her coat from the hook close to the back door. "Stay here and don't get close to the windows just in case."

It took Bobbie fifteen minutes to walk around the house with Rachel following her progress through the windows. Their mom went upstairs and got a blanket for Nico, even though Desi doubted the house would get cold before the power came back on. Bobbie finally made it back inside after shaking herself and the umbrella off under the portico that was still missing Harry's car.

"Did you see anything?" Rachel asked.

"A giant oak branch crashed through the roof. It cracked off the tree closest to the sunroom," Bobbie said, rubbing the tops of her arms. "The hole is pretty big, so there's water streaming into the attic, which means we need to get you girls and the baby out of here."

"Let me call Harry," she said, handing Nico to Rachel. She called and explained what happened, and Harry told her to stay put and she'd give her a call back. It didn't take long for Harry's secretary to make arrangements even though it was after-hours. "There's a crew headed over here to deal with the roof, and Irma made us some reservations at the Piquant, so pack for the night, I guess. That's all we can do right now," she said to everyone.

It seemed like some kind of omen of things to come, but she put it aside, deciding to worry about the baby and her family instead. If there was a huge hole in their roof, it wouldn't be an overnight fix, which would be inconvenient with the baby. Harry sounded calm, so she'd do her best to follow her lead.

"I'll take care of getting you, Harry, and Nico ready, so stay down here," Rachel said. "And please, stop worrying. It's only material things."

It was like her sister could read her thoughts as easily as if she had a bubble over her head.

Bobbie and Rachel took care of packing and taking a look at the attic. As Bobbie had feared, the water was pouring in, but there was no sense in panicking about it. She heard doors slamming outside and a knock on the door right after.

"Are you Desi?" a young guy asked, glancing at everyone behind her. "I'm Chester. Harry called and told me to get my butt over here. My guys did a lot of the reno on this place, so we know the layout."

"Wow, you got here fast," Rachel said.

"When Harry tells you to move your ass, you move your ass." He laughed and shrugged. "Sorry for the language, but you've all met Harry. She's someone you want to make happy, so we didn't block you in. Mona can tell you my guys are solid, so don't worry about them in the house. For tonight all we're planning is to put a tarp up and get rid of any wet insulation. Once the sun comes up, we'll have a better idea of what we're facing."

"Thank you for coming so quickly, and you have Harry's number if you have any questions." She put her coat on and threw a blanket over the car seat to keep the wind off Nico. When they pulled out of the drive, one car with guards was left behind, and the other followed them to the city.

Irma was waiting in the lobby of the Piquant with everyone's keys and told her Harry would arrive in another hour. The house would be tarped to keep the damage to a minimum, and Harry's message to her was that as long as they were okay, anything was possible.

"I'd listen to her," Irma said. "It's aggravating as hell, but she's usually right."

"Usually?" Rachel asked.

"There have been some questionable shirt purchases in her past, but the big things don't rattle her too much. Your rooms are side by side, so keep her company until Harry gets back," Irma said to Rachel.

"Don't worry, I won't let her out of my sight." Rachel sat with her and they watched Nico sleep in the playpen they'd set up for him.

"Icy," Harry said when she came in twenty minutes later. "You two okay?"

"We're good and I'm going to bed," Rachel said, kissing them both.

Desi watched as Harry got ready for bed, then checked on Nico one more time before getting in beside her. It'd been a strange day, and she was glad it was finally over. Harry had a way of making even the worst of days manageable.

"I wish we could make love," she whispered into Harry's chest. Ellie had given them instructions, and she'd warned Harry to keep her hands to herself.

"Hopefully time won't drag to a crawl and it'll be sooner than we think, but I know what you mean." Harry held her and kissed her temple. "Are you sure you're okay?"

"It's been an interesting day," was all she could think to say.

"I promise to listen if there's something on your mind."

"I…" She lengthened the word not knowing exactly how to finish. What had happened that night was an act of God, but it was like the story of her life. "The damage to the house—"

"Can be fixed, and we'll figure something out until that's done."

"It's not that. What happened is like my life. When I find a safe place, something comes along to take it away from me." She was glad the lights were off as her tears started to fall. "I'm so ready for normal."

"Your place in my life, our lives, isn't something anyone can take away from you." Harry kissed her forehead then her lips. "Think of it this way—now's the time to make changes if there's something you don't like about the house, or we can look for a whole new place and start over."

"I don't want a new house, honey. I love my studio, and I want to raise Nicolas and his siblings there." She wiped her tears with the sheet and smiled up at Harry when she lifted onto an elbow.

"Then leave it to Chester, and don't be afraid to let him know what you want."

"How about Bryon? I can't believe there hasn't been any news."

"All you have to concentrate on is that, like his father, Byron and his brother will eventually get caught. For all we know, they're miles from here, so worrying about it isn't something you should waste your time on." Harry gently caressed her jaw before kissing her again. "There's nothing except death that'll keep me from protecting you."

"Don't even joke about that, and I'm trying my best not to make us both crazy. So we agree to fix the house?"

"We'll start in the morning." Harry kissed her before moving so she could hold her.

"Thank you for loving me."

"That's easy to do, and I've had plenty of practice."

"That you have, honey, and I'll take your advice and concentrate on getting us home." The words were easy to say, but she knew there was nothing short of seeing Byron either in a cell or dead that was going to stop her from worrying. "I love you."

❖

Byron woke when the house got unusually quiet during a break in the storm. It was dark, and he had to smile at how much better he felt. After two days of rest, hot showers, eating everything in the pantry, and taking the antibiotics they'd found in the medicine cabinet, his head was finally starting to clear. He was still weak, but moving around didn't exhaust him as much as it used to.

He sat up and rubbed his face, feeling the stubble of his beard that was starting to fill out. It might help keep them from getting recognized. They'd watched the news, and they were still a priority for the media as well as the police, but they'd reported no new leads. The bastards knew how to lie well, so he didn't believe a word.

The rain sounded like a monsoon, so he was glad to be inside and warm, and the lights going out gave him an idea. They'd been monitoring the house, and aside from Rachel leaving every so often, no one else left. The rent-a-cops were back, but they only drove along the back of the house and didn't have anyone posted. He didn't understand the lack of activity, which led him to fantasize about Basantes being sick and dying.

He got up and put on the black jacket he'd found in the closet by the door, moving quietly so he didn't wake Mike. The last thing he needed was him whining. The rain was freezing when it hit his face, and while this was probably a horrible idea, he was too close to the end not to man up and get it done. There wasn't much happening when he walked down the sidewalk trying to see over the brick fence.

It was the neighbor's fence that made him smile. It was like a ladder where it butted up to the Basantes place, and he let go of his fear and took his chance. On a night like this no one would expect him to come in and take back what was his by law. He dropped into the yard and waited, almost expecting someone to come and tackle him to the ground and put a bullet in his head.

The area was still blanketed in darkness, but the house was lit up, and he could hear the hum of generators. It was easy to see the damage the storm had caused. He sat under the eaves of the pool house and watched as the workmen unfurled a tarp and nailed it in place. The tree branch was cut into smaller pieces and thrown into the yard, and by two in the morning they were done and the area got quiet again. One of the security cars parked across the open gate up front since the electricity wasn't back on yet, and the weather kept them from getting out.

Byron stayed in the shadows and walked until he was back at the windows Basantes had thrown him through the year before. When he'd lain in his bunk in Angola, waiting to fall asleep, he couldn't stop touching the scar on the side of his face. That, and his fingers were never really the same after Basantes broke them as easily as if she'd been snapping small twigs.

There was no way he was falling victim to the same dumbass moves as before. The lights might've been out, but the alarm was still working because of the battery backup, so he needed another way in. He tried the back door, and it was unlocked, so he swung it open and ran back to his hiding spot. After what seemed like an hour nothing had happened, so he went back and stepped in, closing the door behind him.

It was strange to have the run of the house, and he squinted into all the rooms upstairs, noticing that they all seemed lived-in. He figured Rachel had made herself as at home here as Desi had, but he stopped and stared into the room next to the one at the end of the hall. The baby bed, changing table, and bookshelf full of children's books made him close his eyes. If someone had shot him in the gut, it wouldn't have hurt as much as this.

He went back down, needing to get out of this place, and stopped at the refrigerator. There were ultrasound pictures with Desi's name on them, and at the center was a picture of Basantes holding a baby with dark hair. He punched the appliance hard enough to dent the door, then walked out. If he'd been humiliated before, this was a whole new level.

"Where the hell have you been?" Mike asked when he got back.

He stared at his brother and wondered if he should've learned to adopt Mike's philosophy of life. Mike had sacrificed a life that might have included a wife and children to stop passing down the fucked-up way they'd been raised. "She fucking had a kid with that bitch. That's all I ever wanted."

"I'm out of here then. There's no way I'm helping you hurt anyone if there's a kid involved." Mike ran his hand through his hair and paced.

"Shut up and listen. I don't want to hurt anyone. All I want is what's rightfully mine. That kid belongs to me, and once I have it, we're out of here. The moment we're safe, you can fuck off or stay." He clenched his hands into fists and exhaled until he felt his lungs burn. "I don't really give a shit."

"You know what your problem is?" Mike gave him that pitying gaze he'd perfected.

"I'm sure you're going to tell me."

"No one's questioning your manhood, but you live your life like you have to prove it to yourself and the whole fucking world. Going after a woman who doesn't want you doesn't just make you an asshole, it shows the world you got no learning curve." Mike threw his jacket on and left.

The sun was starting to rise, and Byron sat in the kitchen with the bottle of bourbon he'd found in the pantry. His only smart play was to walk away, like Mike told him to. Leaving would make Desi have to look over her shoulder for the rest of her life, but this he couldn't let go. His wife…his fucking wife had given Basantes the one thing she'd refused him from the first day. It had nothing to do with a baby, nothing at all.

Desi had given that bitch herself. It was something she'd never given him a glimpse of no matter how he'd treated her or how much pain he'd inflicted. Basantes owned Desi, and he was going to make her suffer by taking Desi away permanently.

CHAPTER NINETEEN

G ood morning, love," Harry said as Desi kissed the side of her neck. The rain was still falling, and the hotel was quiet as if everyone was content to sleep in because of the solid bank of dark clouds dumping water on the entire city. They'd worn pajamas the night before in case they had to run out for some reason, considering the craziness happening in their lives lately.

"Did you sedate the baby?" Desi teased. Their last feeding and changing had been at two in the morning, and Nico had dropped right off.

"It's only five, and I guess he stayed up long enough to get his fill, so he's still sleeping off his milk stupor." Harry rolled on top of her, being careful to keep most of her weight off. "That gives me time to properly thank my wife for our beautiful boy, for this amazing life, and for loving me."

Harry kissed her like she hadn't since giving birth. It was proof she'd have a hard time holding out for another two months. They'd both wanted to have children, but they'd also been apart so long that it was nice reconnecting as often as they could manage. Harry's enthusiasm to touch her hadn't diminished, and it was almost like when they were teenagers and she'd adored being the center of all that attention.

"You're making me crazy." Ellie told her that her sex drive might diminish while she was healing and breastfeeding, but that wasn't her problem. "You're making me want things we can't do right now."

"You have to remember two things," Harry said as she started lifting her nightgown up, touching as she went.

"What's that?" She started on the buttons of Harry's top and yanked it off when she was done.

"I'm a doctor, so tell me where it hurts," Harry said, before kissing her again. She opened her mouth to Harry's tongue and moaned when Harry covered her breast with her hand. "And you don't have to take Ellie quite so seriously."

"What…oh God…what does that mean?" She pressed herself more firmly against Harry. There was something about Harry that always made her crave the feel of her skin on hers. It hadn't dissipated from the first time they were together. "Honey," she said. She didn't know if she had the willpower to stop.

"It means you should let me take care of you." Harry kissed the side of her neck before moving down to swipe her tongue over an erect nipple. The sensation was like an electric pulse through her breast down to her sex.

"I'm not sure." It was the last thing she wanted to say, but childbirth hadn't exactly done sexy things to her body.

Harry kept moving down, kissing her abdomen before spreading her legs. "Let me see if you miss me."

"Are you sure? It's only been a week." She didn't want to give in and end up turning Harry off.

"Trust me," Harry said. She lowered her head and placed her tongue flat on Desi's clit and hummed. "Tell me to stop if you want."

"Please, Harry." She didn't mean to sound like she was in pain or desperate, but that's how it came out.

Harry stopped and raised her head. "Did I hurt you?"

"No." She wiped her eyes. The damn tears sneaked up on her when she least wanted them. Hormones were a bitch.

"Are you okay? Do you want me to stop?" Harry moved up and held her, kissing the side of her head, more for comfort than anything sexual.

"That felt good. I'm sorry. I'm all over the place." She turned, pressing the fronts of their bodies together. "I didn't mean for you to stop. Unless you're grossed—"

"Don't finish that," Harry said, putting her finger against her lips. "I had a beautiful sexy wife before Nico, and I still have a beautiful sexy wife. Right now, I'd like to show her how true that is, and what a lucky bastard I am she's mine."

"Touch me," she said, meaning it. Harry went back down and put her tongue where she'd had it a moment ago. It didn't take much time before she was rattling apart. She gripped Harry's hair, not wanting her to move. Harry's tongue was all she used to touch her, but it was like magic that drove her to an orgasm that made her open her legs wider and buck her hips. "Oh my God."

They'd made love plenty of times since they'd gotten back together, but right at that moment, it felt like the first time. She couldn't get enough, and Harry was flicking her tongue against her hard clit, making her want to scream, so she bit the pillow instead. The end came quick, and she slammed her legs together, trapping Harry between them as she rode out the last of her pleasure.

She uncovered her face and took some deep breaths as Harry reappeared from under the covers and kissed her. All those clichéd things she'd ever read about tasting yourself on your lover's lips were true. It was erotic, and knowing Harry still found her attractive boosted her self-confidence.

"I hope you don't share this kind of treatment with anyone else, Dr. Basantes. I'm also glad our son is a heavy sleeper."

Harry laughed as she held her. "You, my love, are—" Harry's phone rang, which startled the baby awake. "Dammit." The room went from peaceful to chaos in a second when Nico started crying, and Harry appeared ready to flush her phone. "Basantes."

Desi got up to deal with Nico, hoping Harry didn't have to go anywhere. The baby waved his arms when she laid him on the bed and started unbuttoning his pajamas. He appeared as aggravated with the world as Harry did, and she cooed to him as she tried not to gag at the odor coming from his diaper.

"If he left a number, tell him not to come with her. I'll see her in an hour. Make sure she's the only patient today, and go ahead and print that letter I sent you last week." Harry came up behind her and held her finger up for Nico to hold as she finished cleaning him up.

"What's going on?" She leaned back against Harry when they moved back to the bed so she could feed Nico. Breastfeeding had so far been special, but she loved sharing this time with Harry as she held both her and the baby as he nursed, holding Harry's finger.

"Tyrell's sister is coming in for her first consult today. Sounds like she took a bad fall from her wheelchair, which intensified the pain she's in." Harry sighed before pressing her lips to Desi's temple. "I'm sorry, and I'll be as quick as I can. Once I get back, we can leave this guy with his grandmothers while we go and take a look at the house."

"What are we going to do if we can't live there while it's being repaired? That's going to be a lot of noise for the baby." The baby hummed against her chest when she started to burp him, and it made her chuckle. "This kid is so you."

"We'll figure it out, and me and my buddy are going to spend a lifetime adoring his mommy. Let me go take a shower." Harry looked disappointed as she headed to the bathroom, and more so when she came out dressed and ready to go. "Love you both." Harry kissed the baby's forehead before kissing her on the lips. "Have fun, and I'll be back soon."

"You didn't rupture anything, did you?" Rachel came in after Harry unlocked the adjoining room's door.

"Stop making fun of me and tell me what's going on with you. We haven't exactly had a moment alone in days." She handed the baby over and pointed to the bathroom. "Come keep me company."

"There's nothing new to report. My life still isn't in the bliss realm yours is." Rachel paced with Nico in her arms before deciding on the seat in front of the vanity. "I've done all I can when it comes to Serena, but she's decided to ghost me again, and I'm tired of it. We had a really great night together, and then, *bam*. She's gone again. It's a good thing I didn't fall for the line of bull she was promising me, because it was all a lie. *I love you and I promise to make you a priority*," Rachel said, trying to sound like Serena.

Desi was as surprised as her sister when it came to Harry's old friend. She'd hoped Serena had finally come to realize what a great opportunity she had in Rachel, not only for her own happiness, but for her son's. Butch adored Rachel, and he needed two stable people in his life who'd love him unconditionally. Up to now that role had been filled by Harry, but they had their own family now, and Harry was wrapped up in Nico. Butch wouldn't understand why Harry wouldn't be the center of his world any longer.

"I'm not sure what that's about," Desi said, enjoying the hot water on her back. "Has she called at all?"

"No, and I'm done being the one who initiates all the contact. I'm starting to feel like an inconvenience she has to fit into the life she really wants." Rachel walked out but came back without the baby.

She accepted a towel from Rachel. "Her little boy is missing out as much as you are when it comes to Serena's attention." She put on the robe behind the door that Harry had used and put her arms around her sister. "When it comes to her, though, I can't help but think it's not completely done."

"The upside there is that Serena's parents love Butch and do spend a lot of time with him. I'll see him as much as she allows, and I need you to support me on this. No more telling me to try, if I'm done." Rachel took the brush and blow dryer from her to fix her hair. "I deserve better than Serena Ladding, but hell if it doesn't hurt."

"You do, and that person will come along. It just takes patience." They both heard the knock as soon as the room was quiet again. "Please see who that is. If they wake Nico, they're going out the window."

She didn't recognize the woman standing in the hall, but Rachel waved her in. "Desi, this is Special Agent Shelby Phillips. Shelby, this is my sister, Desi Basantes." Rachel seemed familiar with Shelby, and Shelby seemed interested in more than whatever business she was there for, if the look she gave Rachel was any indication.

"It's nice to meet you, and I'm sorry about all this stuff happening to you." Shelby offered her hand but hardly took her eyes off Rachel. "I stopped by the house this morning, and the contractor told me where I could find you. Hopefully that's okay. I did mention not to share that with anyone else unless they had a badge."

"What can we do for you, Special Agent Phillips?" she asked. She was naked under the robe, and it was making her uncomfortable. "Actually, would you mind if I got dressed before we talk?"

"Take your time," Shelby said, moving to the sofa with Rachel.

Desi arched her brow and glanced at her sister. There was a story here, and she wanted to know what it was. She went into the bedroom, glad to see the baby was still sleeping, and then decided to let Harry know what was going on. "Hey, honey." Thankfully Harry had answered her phone. "Has your patient gotten there yet?"

"Still waiting. Are you okay?" Harry sounded like she was walking somewhere.

"I'm fine, and I have an FBI agent in our outer room." She could hear the soft conversation Rachel and Shelby were engaged in. "Can you call me when you're done?"

"Why is there an FBI agent in our room?" Harry's voice was serious, and it meant she was about to cancel what she had going on. "Desi?"

"Baby, please don't get upset. Rachel clearly knows who she is and trusts her." She slipped on her jeans and sweater before putting on her boots.

"Do you need me to come back?"

"I want you to help your patient. If there's a problem, I'll call you." She heard some rustling from the playpen and saw Nico was up and lying quietly but moving his feet. "Someone is up and looks like he misses you since he's doing that full body stretch you like doing when you wake up."

"Tell him to take care of his mama," Harry said, "and I love you both. I'll see you in a bit."

She picked the baby up and pressed her lips to the top of his head. Whatever Shelby wanted, she doubted it was only about seeing Rachel, and she wanted a moment to ground herself in what was most important to her. Nico did a full-body shiver, and she smiled at how cute he was. "We're going to be okay, handsome." All she had to do was believe it.

Rachel glanced down to where her thigh was pressed up against Shelby's, and it felt oddly comforting. She hadn't seen the one person she wanted that from since the day Big Byron had killed a police officer. Rachel had called and texted Serena, but it wasn't the same as laying eyes on her, and it was like going right back to square one. Shelby had called. She seemed interested in how she was doing, and that had fueled how upset she was with Serena.

This time, though, she'd made a promise to herself to not be the one who reached out. It wasn't that she wanted to punish Serena, but to prove her point that she'd finally had enough. She'd never thought of herself as high maintenance, neither her or Desi were, but this was ridiculous.

"Want to tell me about it?" Shelby placed her hand on her knee and waited. It was like she didn't want to influence what she was going to say.

"You're very observant," she said, running her finger along Shelby's knuckles.

"It's almost like I'm in the FBI or something." Shelby gave her a little lopsided grin. "You don't have to tell me, but it might make you feel better." They looked at each other for a tension-laden moment until the door opening finally broke the spell. "Mrs. Basantes, I'm really sorry for bothering you this morning."

"If you have some news for us, you can drop by whenever you like." Desi sat with Nico resting back against her chest as he hung on to her fingers. She glanced quickly at Shelby's hand resting on Rachel's knee.

"I'm sure Rachel told you that our office took an interest in your case because of the people involved, and we might have a lead." Shelby took out her notebook and flipped a couple of pages. "The NOPD and our office have concentrated on your home because of the threat Byron Simoneaux posed to your family."

"I'm sure he's dying to see me again, to repay what I did to him," Desi said. "The house would seem like the logical place he'd go even if that would be a crazy move."

"No one ever accused your ex of high intelligence, honey," Rachel said.

"The majority of criminals aren't, so Byron isn't an anomaly," Shelby said.

"Did you find something?" Rachel asked, gripping Shelby's hand. "Tell us."

"I know you hired security." Shelby didn't move away from her, but she didn't cross the lines of professionalism. "They've been pretty good at patrolling the property, but one of your neighbors sent us this." Shelby's phone was queued to a video. "This house is in the block behind you, down that street, and the people who live there were in Honduras on business."

Desi placed the baby on his blanket and sat on Shelby's other side as she started the video. Desi gasped as Byron and Mike appeared on the video, sitting in the kitchen like they owned the place. Byron had a patchy beard, as if he had some bald spots on his face, and he was only picking at his food. He mostly spent the time coughing while Mike didn't look any different than when he went to jail. He was neat, clean, and his face was smooth.

"Unfortunately, this is the first of a few days of video, and we alerted the police early this morning along with our tactical team, but they were gone when we got there. From the last of the coverage, we assume the brothers got into an argument and Mike Simoneaux left. Byron left an hour later, and they haven't been back." Shelby placed her phone on her lap and completely covered Desi's hand with hers. "Sept was the lead on the raid and is in the house trying to find any evidence of where they might've gone."

"She knew about this?" Desi sounded tired of being kept in the dark.

"She and the police department found out two hours before we moved in. There was no way we were going to wake you up until we were done, and we placed a team around your house in case that's where they ran. As I mentioned, that's how I found out you were here."

"Now what?" she asked. She put her free arm around Desi, not liking how tense she was.

"I know you won't believe me, but even if we didn't catch them, we have more information than we did before." Shelby sounded reasonable, but this situation was screwed up.

"What? That he's that much closer to killing me, Harry, and our baby?" Desi stood and picked Nico up.

"We know he's in the city, and he's fixated on you." Shelby held her hand but her attention was on her sister. "Have you ever heard of Cain Casey?"

"We grew up in New Orleans, so yes," Desi answered.

"Our team and a few others before us have watched the Casey family, trying to find something on them to lock them up. Every generation seems to have that one leader that makes them all elusive."

Desi kissed the top of Nico's head. "If you're trying to make me feel better, you're only confusing me."

Shelby chuckled. "What I'm saying is Cain is smart, driven, and charmingly diabolical. She's free to live her life because she's all those things. That in no way describes your ex-husband." Both she and Desi laughed. "When it comes to Byron Simoneaux, he's one-dimensional. He wants revenge, and he wants you and to hurt those around you. Eventually he'll come to us."

"He never has been able to help himself," Rachel said.

"There's no way the police and FBI are going to invest that kind of time and manpower in protecting me and my family, Agent Phillips, so please don't lie to me." Desi's humor was gone, but Rachel couldn't blame her.

"The police will have no choice, and the FBI is all-in. Believe me, Judge Rose carries a very long stick and casts a very long shadow. He wants this case resolved as quickly as possible." Shelby glanced at Rachel before standing and moving toward Desi. "I give you my word that I'll do everything I can to keep you and yours safe, and I came here today to let you know there's always going to be someone watching."

"That includes my sister, parents, and Harry's family?"

"We're almost at the goal line, and no one is dropping the ball." Shelby placed her hand on Nico's back, and Desi's expression relaxed.

Desi's cell rang in the other room, so she excused herself to get it. Rachel placed her hand on the cushion next to her and Shelby sat back down. "Thank you. I have a feeling Judge Rose wasn't the only one advocating on our behalf."

"I did bully my boss a little, but in full disclosure, Serena fought for this too." Shelby slowly lifted her hand and pressed it to her cheek. "Tell me if I'm out of line here."

"If you're asking if there's something between me and Serena, I'd be lying if I said yes or no. Like I told you before, it's complicated to the point I don't even know the answer." She leaned into Shelby's touch, wanting what her sister had even if it was for a moment. She was coming to see having someone you could lean on was a gift. Her problem was she couldn't forget Serena.

"I've known her for a while, and she never struck me as stupid." Shelby held her when she started to cry, much to her embarrassment. She held her until she stopped. "Do you want me to go?"

"No, but I know you're working, so I won't keep you." She rested her head on Shelby's shoulder and sighed against her neck.

"Let me go work out the logistics with the police." Shelby pressed her lips to her forehead in a friendly sort of way. "Once I'm done, how about I come back and treat you to dinner downstairs? We can talk about that thousand-pound boulder you've got on your back."

"I'd love that," she said, cocking her head back to look Shelby in the eye. "Thank you."

"No need to thank me. I want to break up that big rock so you can use the gravel to pave the way to your future."

Rachel smiled. "Very poetic, G-woman."

"Don't tell anyone—it'll ruin my street cred." Shelby took her hand once again before going, and she was sorry to see her go.

"Is there something you forgot to mention?" Desi asked when she joined her again. "Like the fact the FBI is interested in you and not in a legal sort of way. And that was Sept, by the way. They didn't find anything in the house that's going to help them."

"She's just a friend interested in helping us." That was the only explanation she wanted to give at the moment, and someone knocking on the door saved her from the squirming Desi would put her through. There'd be time enough for that later once she understood what the hell was going on.

CHAPTER TWENTY

Jesus, could one more thing happen to you guys," Tony said when he came in with a woman Desi didn't know. "Kenneth called me after he talked to Harry."

"A tree limb isn't someone out to get us," Desi said, kissing Tony's cheek. "Who's your friend?" The woman's suit had to be designer, and it fit her like it was especially made for her incredible body. Her face could win a beauty contest.

"We'll get to that, but the contractor called me, and we have to run by and make some decisions. Chester thinks the roof alone is going to take three weeks. It might be a good time to think about redoing the bathrooms and some of the other things I left undone so Harry's wife could decide." Tony waved her to the table on the other side of the room while Rachel took care of Nico.

"That'll take weeks, weeks I don't want to spend here." The hotel room was nice, but not long-term for Nico and Harry.

"This is where Harry's old friend comes into play," Tony said, crooking his finger at the model with a day planner. "Desi, meet Darla Vandercamp."

"It's great to finally meet you." Darla held her hand out, and Desi had the words *Harry's old friend* rolling around in her head. That probably meant Harry dated this woman who was perfect in every way, which in no way described her or her body at the moment. She barely touched the woman's hand.

Tony held up his index finger at Darla before taking Desi by the hand and pulling her into the bedroom. "What the hell was that?"

"She dated Harry, didn't she?" There was no sense in hiding her jealousy. Tony had a way of getting it out of her, and she wasn't in the mood for a long conversation about it.

"Darla was interested in dating Harry but settled for selling her the house you live in now. They had one lunch with me to sign the papers, and that was it. Harry called her this morning because she's the only real estate person she knows. I highly doubt she's interested in dating Harry now since she got married six months ago." Tony's lecture was thankfully short, but he kept his hands on his hips the whole time, which meant he wasn't pleased. "Kenneth and I went, and it was a lovely ceremony."

"What's she doing here?" She wasn't ready to let go of the pettiness yet.

"Girl, get a lasso around those hormones and get your ass out there. I'm not really sure why she's here since all Harry told me was to pick her up. The longer we're in here working through your nonexistent issues, the longer we won't know." Tony pointed to the door with one hand, the other on his hip.

"Sorry," she said, and this time she offered Darla her hand.

"Don't worry, and you have a beautiful baby. I'm sure my partner will want to know how you managed to make a miniature version of *your* partner. We're going to start trying soon." Darla acted like Desi hadn't been such a bitch moments before. "And I'm sure you want to know why I'm here."

"Thank you and I really am sorry. Tony blames the hormones, but that's no excuse. What can we do for you?" She waited for Darla to sit before taking the chair across from her.

"Can we bundle up the baby and go out for a bit?" Darla's smile was as perfect as the rest of her.

"Sure, but where are we going? Harry should be back in an hour or so." She saw Rachel already getting Nico ready, so she went to get her purse and coat.

"Harry mentioned she'll meet us if she's done." Darla put her coat back on and ushered everyone to the elevator. Two agents joined them and their guards, and it was odd that they were dressed almost identically.

Their first stop was a condo not far from the house. Granted, it was about one-fourth of the space they had, but it still had three bedrooms and a couple of baths. The second condo they looked at had three bedrooms with three baths. They were nice, but Desi had no idea why they were there. The last thing she wanted was to downsize this much.

"A house remodel isn't a good place for a baby, and the landlord here is willing to lease by the month until the house is done. It's the best

I could find," Darla explained as she walked behind her as she looked at the three bedroom with two baths again. "I thought you, Harry, the baby, and Rachel in here, and the parents and Mona in the other one since it has a bathroom for each room."

"A move is going to be a pain, but this place would work." She would miss the house, but it was a good compromise for the short-term.

"It comes with twenty-four-hour concierge and grocery service. I'll also take care of getting these places furnished and your stuff in storage," Darla said, taking some paperwork out of her planner. "If it's a yes, then sign both of these and we'll get started."

"Thank you. This is one less thing I have to worry about." She accepted the keys and handed them to Rachel when she handed over the baby.

"One more stop and we'll be done."

Darla sat in the front seat with Tony as they drove to wherever else they were going. Desi smiled when she saw Harry's face pop up on her phone. "Hey, honey. Are you done?"

"I had to send her for some tests since her records are a mess. What did you think about the apartments?" Harry sounded relaxed, which meant she hadn't run into any problems, and she wasn't worried about anything.

"I signed the lease, so I hope that's okay with you." It just occurred to her that she should've checked with Harry.

"I'm fine as long as you're okay with it, so stop rethinking it. You didn't do anything wrong by making the decision all on your own. That's what I want you to do, and when it comes to more than just a temporary home."

"She said we had one more stop," she said, glancing at a sleeping Nico. "Are you going to give me a hint?"

"It's not a surprise if I tell you, darlin'. Have fun, and I'll see you at the hotel later." Harry spoke to someone else but kept her phone close by. "Let me wrap this up so I can have dinner with you guys. Love you."

Darla pointed the turns Tony had to make until they were in the French Quarter, coming to a stop on Royal Street. It was one of her favorite places with all the galleries and antique stores. They'd shopped along the street for a few pieces they'd agreed on for the house, and they'd enjoyed all the art galleries.

Tony parked in the alley Darla showed him, and they got out into a drizzle. She walked under the copper canopy of the building holding

Nico as Rachel held an umbrella over all three of them. The building they were standing in front of was empty, and it appeared to need some work, but it was right in the center of the street's art district.

"Oh my God," Tony said, holding his hands over his mouth. "Look at the sign."

The small carved wooden sign hanging from the frame of the overhang had *Basantes & Reynolds Gallery* carved into it. She accepted the keys Darla handed her and traded her the baby. Even though the space appeared worn, the key turned easily in the door, and she stepped inside.

"She told me to start searching a while ago, and this is the one she thought you'd love. There were a couple I thought would work better, but Harry had a good feeling about this one." Darla bounced Nico in her arms and pointed to the only furnishing in the cavernous room. The counter at the front held a book and an envelope. "Harry told me it shouldn't take you long to figure out why she had a good feeling about this one."

In a glance Desi noticed the exposed brick walls, wide-planked wooden floor, and the cast iron columns. Once her gaze landed on the back corner, she couldn't look away, and Rachel held her hand when she seemed to notice it as well.

"Was that always there?" she asked Darla.

"It was a Persian rug store until five years ago, and it's been empty ever since, but the owner said that was there from when he purchased the building over twenty years ago."

The swing bolted into the rafters of the space could've been the twin to the one she and Harry fell in love on. They still sat on it when the weather was nice since Harry had purchased it from the new owners of the house she'd grown up in. She moved closer to it, squeezing Rachel's hand, and saw another envelope on the seat. Only this one had her name on it in Harry's messy handwriting.

She sat with her sister and set the swing in motion as she held the envelope, wanting to remember the moment.

"Go ahead and open it," Rachel said.

My Love,
 It needs a bit of work, but I saw this place and I thought it was perfect for the big dreams you have. Know that I'll do whatever I can to make all those dreams come true, but how

you do that is up to you. Start here with this clean slate, and
make it something you can be as proud of as I am of you.

  It'll make me happy to watch you fly and show the
world the strong woman you are while you make this place a
success with Tony at your side. Renovate this space and make
it a reflection of who you are, and I promise not only will it
be a success, but beautiful too. The swing, I thought, was a
good reminder of where we started and how far we've come
from the kids who knew exactly who their perfect match was.
The only thing to remember is to have fun, and know that no
matter what you try in life, I'll be right there to support you.

  I love you with all I am, and I can't wait to see how far
you go.

She folded the letter and placed it back in the envelope as she let
her tears fall. Rachel hugged her, and someone stepped up to hand her
a tissue. It was a surprise to see the guy from the night before, Chester,
holding a clipboard.

"She had to find the dustiest place in the city, but the demo should
be easy," Chester said.

"Are you done with the roof?"

"He'll be doing that along with this place, so don't let him slack
any," Harry said from the door. Desi thrust the envelope into Rachel's
chest and ran to Harry, throwing her arms around her. "Do you like it?"
Harry asked after their first kiss.

"I love it, and you. Thank you for all this." She put her arms
around Harry's neck and tried to find the right words to convey how
grateful she was, but Harry put her finger over her lips.

"You deserve nothing but good things in your life, and if you
really like it, then sign the papers and the keys really will belong to
you." The envelope in the front had the sale contract inside, and the
book was her new checkbook with the first check already filled out and
awaiting her signature.

Harry took the baby so she, Rachel, and Tony could do the walk-
through with Chester and decide on what needed to be done. Harry
showed them the door in the back that led to a smaller space next door
that was actually part of the building they were buying.

"Is this warehouse space or something?" Desi asked, but there was
a door and glass storefront that faced Royal.

"I was thinking about how much you and Rachel love spending time together. I thought with a few sinks and chairs this would make a wonderful salon." That was all her sister needed to hear before she jumped on Harry's back. "I think my job here is done." Harry spun around as Rachel laughed.

Desi's world was in that room, and her heart almost hurt with the joy and beauty of it. She should be used to Harry's compassion and understanding, but she was good at delivering dreams Desi had never thought would come true.

❖

They celebrated that night, and both Harry and Desi kissed Rachel's cheek when she left to have a drink with Shelby. The FBI agent seemed nice, and Harry couldn't help but think her old friend Serena was making the biggest mistake of her life. Perhaps Serena was happy with the life she had now, which was fine, but she needed to set that straight with Rachel.

"What are you thinking so hard about?" Desi lifted Nico to her shoulder after getting him ready for bed and paced to get him to sleep.

"Your sister, actually. She deserves to be happy, but what do we know about Agent Phillips?"

Desi put Nico down and moved to her arms. "I love that you're this protective of her, and she'll be fine. Rachel learned plenty from you growing up, and she's got no issue with getting her point across." She took Harry's hand and led her to the bed. "Tell me about your appointment today."

"Tyrell's sister has been in a lot of pain for a long time, so I'm glad he got her to my office. I ran some new tests and scheduled her for surgery in the morning. The guys who brought her told me Tyrell was close by and saw the security around me, so he stayed back." Harry laid her back and held her. "Maybe the Simoneaux brothers will give up when they know they can't get close to us."

"That's wishful thinking, honey, but I'm glad you're going to help her. What's her name?"

"Diana, and she's really sweet. It's hard to hide that kind of pain, but she does a good job of not complaining. The guys at the university promised to keep her name under wraps. I think that'll keep her off anyone's radar and might allow Tyrell to visit her once the surgery is finished." Harry leaned over and kissed her.

"You're a good person, my love, and I wanted to thank you for everything you did today. A couple more nights here and we can move to the apartment." She lifted up and touched Harry's face. "That gallery space, though," she said, sighing. "There are no words to tell you how much I appreciate that."

"I belong to you, Desi, always have, and I did what I could to find you a place where you can show the world what I already know. You're a beautiful soul who creates beautiful things, and you can take me and Nico along for the ride."

They talked until Harry couldn't stop yawning, so they went to sleep. Nico woke up three hours later, and Harry loved holding Desi as she fed him. He slept until it was time for her to leave, and she fed him a bottle before she had to go. It allowed Desi to get some sleep, and she envied her as she drove to University. She'd scheduled Diana as the first case of the day. Her phone buzzed as she changed into a set of scrubs, and she smiled when she saw Desi's name.

"Hey, love. Everything okay?"

"Thanks for letting me sleep, and I was wondering how long you're going to be today?"

"This one might take a while, but I'll have one of the nurses call and give you an update if you want." She headed out to meet with Diana before she was brought down for surgery. Being alone for something like this wasn't easy, and she wanted to see Diana, more to relax her than for anything medical. "The only family she has is Tyrell, and he can't just come and sit with her."

"I thought I'd get started on moving us today, but I need to stop by the house. I want you there before we make any big changes." Desi sounded sleepy, but Harry heard Nico as well. "If you want, we can just fix the roof and whatever needs repairing inside and keep everything the way it is."

"Love, the way the house is now, is all Tony, and we both know it still needs some remodeling. It's time to make it our place, and this is a good time to do it. The apartment isn't the house, but we'll be okay."

"That's true, but I still want you there." Desi had come far, but there was still a little of that scared woman she'd encountered the year before. "It should be our place."

"I'll be there, I promise." She got into the elevator and pressed Diana's floor. "I love you, and I'll try my best to make it after lunch."

"Take your time, honey, and I'll say a prayer for Diana."

She'd loved Desi all her life, even when she was living through the heartbreak of losing her, but there were times when she fell all over again. That she was married to this caring, vibrant, and perfect soul squeezed everything in her chest.

"Good morning," she said softly. Diana's room was dark, and she appeared apprehensive. "You haven't known me long, but I promise to help you."

"I'm sorry my brother got you to do this the way he did." Diana reminded her of Desi a little—she'd been beaten down by life but was still kind. "He's been in that awful place because of me," Diana said, wiping her face of tears. "That's no excuse, though."

"Listen, you're going to be okay." She picked up the phone in the room and dialed. "And I can prove it to you."

Diana's face changed when she listened to Tyrell say what he had to. Harry held up the porters until she was done. "Thank you, Doc."

"You're welcome, and all I want you to concentrate on is an easy recovery."

She gave the staff the go-ahead and left to prepare. The surgery took hours. She took her time reversing both the damage from the initial injury, and what had been exacerbated by scar tissue. She sat with Diana in recovery for a bit and had her moved back to a private room when she was stable.

It wasn't her smartest move, but she opened the door to Tyrell and left him with his sister. Granted, he was wanted for his escape, but at that moment all she could see was a concerned brother who loved his sister. He'd put his life on the line to help the one person in the world he loved, and that was something she could understand.

"Thank you," he said, taking her hand. "There's nothing I can do to repay you."

"Stay out of trouble, and start thinking about how you end all this." She checked Diana one more time and adjusted her medication. "You can't run forever, and she's going to need to know you're okay."

"Don't worry, I got what I wanted, so I'll do the right thing."

"I'm going to trust you," she said.

"I'm not going to mess you up, Doc. All I wanted was to help my sister. Even if I never get out, I'll do the time now that I know she's being taken care of." Tyrell shook her hand again before taking a seat next to the bed. "I won't stay long, and I haven't reneged on my promise. My boys are keeping an eye out for your girl."

If that was true, then Tyrell's guys were nothing but shadows. She'd never seen anyone other than the security they'd hired, but somehow, she knew Tyrell was telling the truth. "I'll be back tonight to check on her." She dialed Desi and had to smile at the excitement in her voice. "I'm headed home."

"I'll be waiting."

That was all that mattered. It was corny as hell, and it made her sappy, but having Desi always waiting for her was all she needed in life.

Harry made it back and drove Desi, Tony, and Rachel to the house. Rachel smiled as she watched Harry walk around outside looking at the damage, which was now uncovered as a crew repaired the rafters. Desi watched Harry as well through the window as they talked remodel as well as repair with Chester.

There was a knock at the door, and Rachel waved Desi off to get it. The fun of the afternoon ended when she opened the front door and found Serena talking to Harry. When they came inside, she watched the smile fade from Desi's face, and she knew the change in mood was on her behalf.

"I think Harry's right," Desi said as she took her hand.

"About what?" Rachel stared at Serena, trying to put her emotions in order.

"Don't take any shit from her or anyone, and we love you."

Serena stared at her as if she was dissecting what was in her head. The last time they'd seen each other, they'd made love and then, as usual, Serena disappeared to do whatever else she thought was important. This time there was no excuse Rachel was willing to accept.

"Hey," Serena said, coming to a stop in front of her. When she leaned in to kiss her, Rachel placed her hand in the middle of her chest, stopping her cold. "I know you're mad."

"I'm not mad—I'm pissed." She turned and started up the stairs. If they were doing this, she didn't want to do it in front of Harry and Desi. Once Serena was in her room, she slammed the door. She halfway expected the room to be in shambles or the roof to collapse from the noise, but the only damage that was visible was a water stain on the ceiling.

"Give me a minute to explain." Serena tried to touch her, and she moved away from her with her hands up. "Come on, Rachel, just let me talk to you."

"You've had days to talk to me. Days to see me, and days for you to leave Butch with me. But hey, that's not in you, is it? Well, now I'm not interested in whatever bull you have to say. Do you remember any of the promises you made? You bought flowers, dinner, and expected me to fall in line. Your problem, honey, is that I'm not an idiot."

"First off, I had no idea where you were. When did all this happen?" Serena pointed up.

"You had no idea where I was? That's rich. This happened last night, and all it would've taken was a call, but let me guess. Your phone is broken or was eaten by your nonexistent dog?"

"I was working on something for us, Rachel. That's it. There's nothing nefarious to it. Once we knew Byron Simoneaux, Sr. was found, I pushed the NOPD and the FBI to start more surveillance around you and your family to catch Byron and Mike. That's my only priority." Serena pulled the hair at the sides of her head and seemed frustrated. "If their father died here, it's only a matter of time before they show up."

"I know that already, and they've been close." She sat on the window seat and crossed her arms over her chest. It was quickly becoming her spot to listen to Serena's explanations of bullshit. The sight of her, though, made her hurt from how much she missed her. "And you still could have called or texted. But you didn't. Again."

"What's that supposed to mean? Did you see those assholes and you didn't call me?" Serena came close to levitating off the ground she seemed so excited.

"Shelby was working but found the time to stop by and show us a video one of the neighbors sent them. *She* came by here, saw what happened, and found us at the Piquant." She didn't raise her voice because she was tired. All this was like being stuck in a loop, and she didn't know how else to say it was broken and Serena needed to try harder. Serena needed to do that before it was too late. "She found us because it was important to our safety. It's what I thought you'd do, but you've been radio silent. Again."

"I introduce you and she's coming by to see you?" Serena actually sounded jealous, which was the right response, but right now all Rachel wanted was to throw her out of the house for it. The act of giving a damn was way late. "What the hell?"

"That's rich, baby. You disappear whenever you want, and now you want to act like the jealous girlfriend. This has nothing to do with you, and in case you forgot what it's about, some assholes are out there waiting to hurt us. Shelby and her people understand that, and she came to warn us. She also wanted to reassure us. Now, if you're done, then it's time to go. I need to get back to my sister and family." She stood and walked by Serena, not caring if she followed.

"Rachel, please. I love you and I still have something to say."

She stopped at the top of the stairs, but she needed to calm down before they talked about anything else so she went down. When she made it to the kitchen, Desi and Tony were in a deep discussion with Chester while Harry stood off to the side holding the baby. That's who she headed toward and leaned against once she was close enough. She wanted to cry when Harry put her arm around her and kissed her forehead. That her sister had this kind of consistent comfort in her life made her happy, but also lonely. Someone like Harry was hard to find.

"It's going to be okay, squirt," Harry said, using her old nickname. "I promise, and I'd get over there before they decorate your room with a princess theme."

"Harry, what the hell happened to your refrigerator?" Chester asked, getting them all to look in that direction.

Aside from the dent there was something missing. Desi stared at the appliance, trying to figure out what it was, and it finally hit her. The picture of Harry holding Nico right after his birth was gone. Where it had been there was now only a fist-sized dent. The only conclusion as to who would've done it made her sick and made her want to run out of the house.

"Oh my God," she said, holding the counter. Her distress made Harry rush to her side, Rachel right with her. "He was here. He was here in our house."

"Okay," Harry said. "Take a breath, baby." There was a scream from the second floor, followed by a thumping down the stairs. "Rachel, get your sister out of here and take Nico."

"You're not fucking going anywhere." Byron stood in the doorway of the kitchen with a nickel-plated revolver, and it was aimed right at Rachel and the baby. "You fucking had a baby," he screamed. The emotion made his hand waver, and she could see how white the finger on the trigger was.

Harry stepped in front of Rachel and seemed unafraid of the lunatic Desi had been married to. "Rachel, go," Harry said with authority.

"She's not fucking going anywhere," Byron screamed. "That baby belongs to me." For a moment he used the gun to point at his chest. "Me."

Rachel managed to sidle out the door, holding Nico tightly against her.

"The only thing that belongs to you, moron, is your imagination. We've been over this," Harry said as if she was trying to provoke him into shooting her. "You needed your daddy to get you a girl, and it turns out all you were good at was hitting."

"Shut up." Byron seemed to only have one volume—loud and overbearing. "You can't stand that she was married to me. I was fucking her, loving her, and she'd forgotten all about you."

"Byron, please." She tried to get his attention on her. If he killed her, Harry and Nico could still have a life.

"Why couldn't you love me?" His volume finally came down, but the gun stayed aimed at Harry.

"Because she was already in love, you idiot. I've loved her since we were children. She's the one person in the world who is my match. There was no room for you or anyone else," Harry said, moving to stand in front of Desi now that Rachel had run out. "What you had was some screwed-up thing cooked up by Clyde and your daddy. Now they're both dead, so do the right thing and walk out of here. Where you go, and what you do, I don't give a damn about, but leave my family alone."

Byron's eyes narrowed. "My daddy's not dead, bitch."

The news was clearly a surprise, and a wave of what appeared to be pain crossed his face. Just as quickly, though, his emotional response to Harry's words passed, and his hatred once again took hold of him.

Desi knew that tone so well. He used it when he hit her, when he berated her for being cold and stupid, and when he touched her because he supposedly loved her. The cold tone was a reminder that he really had no idea what love was. His father had taught him that normal human emotion was a weakness no man had, and in the end, he'd raised another monster. A monster she'd feared until this moment. If she couldn't stand up to him now, she never would.

"Your father went home and was killed after he shot an innocent man," she said, pressing her hand on Harry's back before she stood beside her. "You keep blaming me, Harry, Rachel, and the world for what happened to you, but you tried to kill me. You tried to kill Harry, and for what? To try to win me back?" She could see the rage build until there was only one outlet. "I was never yours no matter what you did. I'm hers and will always be hers. And yes, I had her baby, and he won't be the last."

Her mind slowed at what happened next, but in reality, it happened in a flash. Byron pulled the trigger as she pulled Harry behind her again. The squelch of a bullet hitting flesh made bile rise in her throat, and she heard Harry howl. Someone moved behind Byron, and the gun wavered for a split second. Harry grabbed her, trying to move her out of the way. There were a few more shots, and her vision went black.

She'd known all her life that real love came with sacrifice. It was something she'd done to keep her sister and lover safe when Clyde had demanded it of her. That choice hadn't been easy—letting Harry go was the hardest thing she'd done in her life. It'd allowed her love to be free to live, to be happy, and to thrive. What she hadn't considered was she'd have to keep on sacrificing, but it had been an easy choice. The truth that she'd faced him and taken the worst he had to dish out wasn't as important as keeping Harry safe.

The hand pressed to the side of her neck was as familiar to her as her own reflection, and she cried at the cruelty of the trick her mind conjured up.

"Open your eyes for me, love. Are you okay?"

"Harry?" The image of her spouse was blurry from her tears, but Harry was alive and touching her.

"Of course, now tell me if you're hurt."

Harry was alive and running her hands over her in a medical way, making her realize she was sweating despite the cold because of the open door. Harry was blocking her view of the rest of the kitchen by standing right in front of her. "What's wrong?" The stinging in her leg made her wince.

"It's over." Harry led her outside, limping the whole way before collapsing onto the bench in the back garden. Her jeans were dark on one leg, but nothing like the stains Harry had on hers, and Desi was the one to moan when she realized it was blood. "Shh, it's over."

She had no idea of anything except that Harry was hurt. And when it came to Byron, would this truly ever be over? She placed her hand on Harry's forehead and tried to concentrate on Harry's blue eyes. They were alive, and that truth slowed the hammering in her chest, but Harry was still bleeding, and she couldn't lose her. She couldn't.

CHAPTER TWENTY-ONE

Harry concentrated with her eyes closed as she swam up through the inky darkness. Wherever she was, it was quiet but familiar. The sound of medical equipment along with the smell of disinfectant were part of her being. She forced her eyes open and twitched her lips with some effort into what she hoped was a slight smile at the sight of Desi feeding Nico.

"There she is," Rachel said softly. "When you nap, you really nap."

"That's because she's a slacker—always has been," Sept said. She'd entered the hospital room without knocking and stood by her bed, not looking pleased with her. "You're also an ass for worrying your wife and family like that."

"What the hell happened?" She had trouble forming the words her mouth was so dry, and the heavy sensation in her limbs meant there were drugs involved.

"Wait," Desi said. She buttoned her blouse and handed Rachel the baby to burp before coming to sit beside her. "Are you okay?"

"Did you shoot me with a tranquilizer gun or something?" Her joke made Desi snort.

"I think Fred from anesthesia did that without a gun. You got yourself shot, which is something we'll talk about later. Right now, Sept promised to recap for us, but I made her wait for you." Desi took her hand and lifted it to kiss her knuckles.

"We think, but can't be sure, that Byron spent the night in your house. He got in the night you all left because of the storm damage, but he figured you'd have to come back." Sept referred to her notes. "The missing picture you pointed out to us, Desi, makes me think he was hoping to get you alone, and if you had Nico with you, all the better. He stole the gun from the house he and Mike broke into."

"Did you find Mike?" Harry asked. It tasted like heaven when Desi held a straw to her lips so she could take a sip of water.

"He's at University in the CCU unit. His brother shot him in the chest when he charged him, but Mike prevented you both from getting more seriously injured. The shot went through the fleshy part of Desi's leg before it hit your leg and broke the bone, but your wounds will be much easier to recover from than the injuries he sustained. Thanks to Desi slowing the bullet down, you're still here to be a pain in everyone's ass. And you two have matching bandages." Sept rested her fist on the bed and shook her head. "In another surprising development, the other patient at University is Tyrell Lagrie. They were both in that house, how, I don't know, but they worked as a team to save you and your family."

"Is he okay?"

"One of the bullets grazed his head, and he took one in the shoulder, but he'll be fine. What I'd like to know is what you did to make these guys so loyal to you?"

"If Tyrell is stable, have him moved to Diana Landry's room. She's his sister, and it'll give them some time together before you send him back to jail, a place he wouldn't be if he'd had a decent lawyer." She felt Desi's hand tighten in hers.

"That's probably true, but out of my wheelhouse. All I know is the distraction they provided gave the FBI guys enough of a window to get off their own shot." Sept hesitated long enough to allow Desi to lie next to her, as if needing the comfort. "Byron is dead. He would've shot you again once he took care of Mike and Tyrell, so they shot him to neutralize the threat."

"I'd never celebrate the death of anyone, but now it's truly over. He never would've stopped," she said, and Desi nodded against her side. Something occurred to her then. "Is Serena okay? All this started when we heard the noise and then something falling down the stairs, I think."

"She's in surgery," Rachel said. "She tried stopping Byron, so he hit her and pushed her down the stairs. He broke her ankle, arm, and wrist. She's going to be upset it's not you in there putting her back together."

"How about you?" She'd ordered Rachel to run with their son, wanting them both away from danger. Her only regret was not being able to give Desi the same chance.

"Stop," Desi said. "I know what you're thinking. I was never going to leave you there alone."

"And to answer your question, I'm fine. I'll be better once Serena is out and we can finish our talk. I think it'll go much better since she can't run away and will have no choice but to listen to everything I have to say." Rachel kissed Harry's cheek then glanced at her phone when it chirped. "She's in recovery."

"Hand me the phone, love." She made a call downstairs and gave Rachel the name of the nurse who would let her into recovery, to sit with Serena until she was moved to a room.

"We'll need statements from both of you," Sept said, "but not today. Desi gave me the address of the apartment you're staying in, so I'll call first. Take care of yourself and try your best to not be a crabby patient." Sept pointed at her and kissed Desi's cheek. "Call me if she gives you any trouble, and I'll let you borrow my handcuffs."

"I'm so sorry this happened to you," Desi said when they were alone.

"I'd do it again if it means we're finally free of the past." She lifted her arm and held Desi against her. "We can't ever forget, but everyone who ever added to our hell is buried. Clyde, Big Byron, and Byron are gone, and their ghosts won't ever haunt us." Harry kissed the side of her head, pulling her closer when Desi started crying. "Besides, now everyone knows what I've known all this time."

"What?" Desi took some deep breaths.

"You're a hero who's the most selfless soul I've ever known."

"I love you, and I will forever."

"Then I'm still a lucky bastard." Her voice cracked at the end of her statement, as she thought of how much she'd almost lost. That Desi had been hurt but still managed to save her was something she was sure her wife hadn't thought about. Desi's first thoughts were always for those she loved, and she really was lucky to be the center of that love. It was going to be her goal to make sure Desi knew how much she was loved, and that there wasn't anything waiting in the shadows ready to hurt them.

They were all finally free.

❖

Rachel felt the hitch in Serena's breathing. She'd woken up in recovery, but the nurse had told her not to have any serious conversations since Serena would most likely not remember a word. They were now in the room next to Harry's, and Serena appeared more battered than she had before as the bruises set in.

"Rach," Serena said with her eyes closed. "I'm so sorry."

"Don't try to talk yet." She held up the straw, having learned from Harry.

"I have to." Serena's eyes opened and she appeared miserable. "I fucked up, but I'm not losing you until you hear me out. You think me saying you scare me is a cop-out, but I was serious. You're not like anyone I've ever been with, and letting you all the way in scares me because I'd break if you left."

"Why would I leave if I love you?" She was a woman, but other women in general confused the hell out of her. "I *do* love you."

"What about Shelby?"

"She's my friend, you idiot, but she's not you. The one woman I'm interested in that way has done a great job of running in the opposite direction, so tell me   are you done running?" She'd really thought they didn't have a chance. She thought she'd have to bury these feelings until she heard Serena had gotten hurt trying to protect them. What they had was worth fighting for. "You can't keep doing that when things are hard. Are you going to treat me right?"

"Look, I've done everything wrong from the beginning, and I've been a fool. I was there to talk to you about my job."

If she wasn't in love, she'd have poured the pitcher of cold water over Serena's head and walked out. "Are you seriously going to bring up your job now instead of answering my question?"

"Come closer, and just listen." Serena held up her good hand. "I talked to the DA and gave him my resignation. I'm joining Dad's firm, and he promised I could still concentrate on domestic violence cases if I tried a few corporate cases too. Working for the city was fulfilling, but the private gig will give me a more stable life and better hours."

"Oh no. You do this, and you're going to resent me forever. Why can't you keep doing what you do but blend in a little moderation?" A life with Serena was something she'd fought up to now. It was plain that getting Serena to learn to discuss big decisions with her was either going to be an impossibility or a lifelong process. But sometimes there was no accounting who you fell in love with, and for all of Serena's faults, she was kind, funny, sexy, and had that indefinable something that made Rachel's knees weak. As much as it would have been nice to feel that for Shelby, it hadn't been there. It was Serena she wanted.

"First, I love you and I'm not capable of hating you. Second, I don't want to keep missing things in *our* son's life. Butch is starting school, which means sports, plays, and other events. He shouldn't look up and only see me when I'm available, and you when I allow you to get close to us before I run again." Serena tugged her closer. "I'm changing things in my life so we can make this work. No more running—I love you."

"I love you too." She hesitated and she hated that little bit of doubt. "But you've told me this before, and then I've gone days and days without hearing from you. How is this time different? I love you and I want to believe you, but…"

"I'm not asking you to believe me. Belief will come with time, when you see how committed I am day after day until we have a lifetime behind us. Trust me, I'm so sorry for how I treated you. I'm also sorry for acting like a jealous idiot. The thought of you with anyone else made me nuts." Serena sighed so Rachel kissed the side of her neck. "I also got pushed down the stairs before I got to ask you something."

"What?" She looked Serena in the eye and waited. "If it's to move in with you, we need a new bed."

"What? Why?"

"I keep thinking of all the women you brought home, so I want a fresh start."

Serena laughed and shook her head. "You're the only woman I've ever brought home, and into Butch's life, aside from Harry. Uncle Harry and Aunt Desi have their place, and your place is with me in our new house, on our new bed."

She'd scream if Serena had bought a house without her. "What new house?"

"The one we're going to pick out together," Serena said, kissing her hand. "I had this all planned, but there's no dropping to one knee anytime soon."

The words made Rachel hold her breath.

"Rachel Thompson, you've turned my world upside down in the best possible ways. Despite my dumb ass, you love me, and you love our son."

"I do, and I agree on the dumb ass comment."

Serena laughed again. "Marry me, and I promise to always love you the way you deserve."

"Yes." They kissed until Rach's mother walked in with a worried-looking little boy. "Hey, buddy."

Butch hesitated before letting her hand go and launching himself across the room. "Hey, Grandma said I could sign my name on your cast, Mom."

"Did Grandma bring a pen?" Serena asked.

"Sorry to interrupt, but he couldn't wait anymore." Her mother opened the door wider for Bobbie. "Are you both doing okay? What happened today was hard, but we're both here for you."

"Thanks, Mom, and thanks for picking Butch up. I'm sure Serena's parents will appreciate you keeping him tonight so they can come visit." She held Butch steady as he signed Serena's leg cast. "And you, little man, you're coming home with me."

"Yes," Butch said making a fist in the air.

"Will you be okay with Grandma until I get home?" She chuckled when Butch put his arms around her and squeezed. He put all he could into his hugs, and she loved him for it. The hug she received from her parents proved she and Desi had another place in the world where they belonged. Once they were alone again, she looked at Serena before kissing her.

"I love you, and I'm never going to get tired of saying that." Serena held on to her as best she could and kissed her again. "Thank you for giving me another chance."

"Are you sure about the job?" Running the domestic violence crime unit for the district attorney's office had been part of who Serena was for so long. "You don't have to quit."

"I want you and our family more than I need a job. We'll have some bumps we'll have to work through, but my job isn't going to be one of them. My dad made the new position sound pretty good, and there's plenty of stuff we need to do, so we'll need the time."

"The most important thing was surviving, and we've done that. You and Harry might be beat up, but we'll be fine." She kissed Serena again, long and slow. "And I love you. Never think otherwise."

"Then you'll both be fine," Serena's dad said when he walked in with her mother.

"You're right, Dad, we will be."

Rachel put her head down on Serena's chest after she'd spoken and believed everything she'd said. There was no more second-guessing.

CHAPTER TWENTY-TWO

Harry was still in a cast a month after the shooting, which was driving her crazy. The end of her career with LSU Medical School had come sooner than she'd planned, but Desi was glad she'd hardly complained at all. Desi watched her navigate around on crutches as she moved to the sunroom to sit with Nico and her parents. Her mother and Bobbie had been in town for the duration, and she'd loved sitting and talking to them both.

The house still needed lots of work, and she was enjoying the process with Tony at her side. They took some time off to help Rachel and Serena pick a new house and decorate it. Harry's parents had gone home for the week but were due back today. She guessed they'd have houseguests forever, but that's how she wanted it.

"Do you promise not to move?" She sat next to Harry and combed her hair back.

"We have to leave in an hour, but until then, me and the little guy will be right here looking at birds."

They were scheduled in court for something Harry would've never considered a year ago, but she owed Michael Simoneaux and Tyrell Lagrie more than her life. She wanted to repay that, and the only thing she could think to do was hire a better lawyer than the crappy ones who'd represented them before. Mike was facing a slew of charges stemming from his escape. Tyrell's case would take longer since they were trying to change the outcome of the first trial that'd sent him to prison for years.

"Are you sure you want to take the baby?" Desi didn't seem opposed but wasn't as enthusiastic as she could be.

"We don't have to, but what Tyrell did," she said, glancing down at Nico sprawled on her chest, "allowed Rachel to leave with him and prevented you from being more seriously injured. I want the judge to see our guy and know what was on the line for us."

"I still can't believe Byron is gone. It seems like a good dream. Does that make me a bad person?" Desi still had nightmares about that night, only it was Harry who lay dead on their kitchen floor and not Byron. Those were becoming less frequent and had prompted a lot of talks about selling their house, but she'd been adamant about not giving up anything else because of Byron Simoneaux.

"That's the last thing you are, love. I keep telling you that we can start over somewhere else. All I need is you, Nico, and our family." Harry made everything sound so easy.

"This is our home. We were married here, and in the early summer Rachel will be married here. No ghosts will chase us out, and thank you for not giving up on me and the slew of problems I come with." She kissed Harry before pressing her lips to the top of Nico's head. The baby smacked his lips at her, making them both laugh.

For another hour she walked the house with Chester and Tony, checking on the things they were changing and the things that were already being repaired.

When they arrived at the courthouse, Mike seemed surprised at Harry's statement in support of a lenient sentence. It was Mike's good fortune to have his case heard in Jude's court, and he took Harry's words into consideration.

"Thank you," Mike said as they started to lead him away. The bailiff told them to take their time before they transported him back to the parish jail. Her ex-brother-in-law was still recovering from the bullet wounds Byron hadn't hesitated to give him. "And I haven't really had a chance before now to say I'm sorry."

"You don't have to apologize," Desi said, meaning it. He'd never been part of her nightmare.

"Not for that. All those years, I should've done something. You deserved better than my brother and father, and if I'd done something, maybe my mother would still be alive." His eyes filled with tears, and he appeared truly ashamed. "I was such a coward, but I couldn't let him hurt your baby."

Nico was awake in her arms looking more like Harry every day. "We all did the best we could, Mike, and I appreciate what you did. The past is best left to die, so don't dwell on it. Think about what you'll do with the rest of your life once you get out of here." They'd never be friends, but she wished him well. Now that his family was dead, maybe he'd have a chance to make a life he could be happy about. "We all deserve to be happy with our second chances."

"Thank you, Desi, and you too, Dr. Basantes. Even if I have to serve the rest of my stretch and then some, I wouldn't have done this any differently." He walked away, lifting his hand before disappearing out the side door.

She walked slowly to Harry. There was plenty to look forward to, and she was loving having Harry all to herself. Harry glanced at her and gave her the kind of smile that made her knees weak.

"What's on your mind, Dr. Basantes?" She took the front steps slowly so Harry wouldn't trip on the way down.

"Plenty of things, Mrs. Basantes, so strap that handsome guy in and let's take a drive."

The directions Harry gave made her think they were heading back to the house, but she told her to keep driving. They pulled up in front of a nice Acadian style house with gas lanterns in front and black shutters, which contrasted nicely with the white paint. "Friends of yours?" She got the baby out when Harry maneuvered herself onto her feet.

"Sort of, and we're here to offer some advice on things to do in town since they're new residents. The moving van hasn't arrived yet, so maybe you can offer some decorating tips along with paint colors." Harry let her go ahead, and she rang the doorbell when Harry pointed to it.

Her mom opened the door and immediately took the baby. "Hey, how did it go?"

"Okay, thanks. Um, what are you doing here?" She gave Bobbie a hug when she joined her mom, and she and Harry were temporarily forgotten while they made a fuss over Nico.

"I got a new part-time job working with Kenneth and thought the commute from New York would've been killer, so we bought this place. A nice young lady named Darla found it for us." Bobbie took Nico and held him over her head. "We figured if we lived close enough, we could babysit whenever you let Nico come over."

"Really?" she said, hugging her mom.

"A certain handsome surgeon told us you and your sister didn't want us to leave, and she was pretty convincing. Reminds me of the handsome doctor I fell for, once upon a time." Her mom hugged Harry next.

"Isn't this great? We wanted to surprise you," Rachel said when she joined them from the back of the house. "Welcome home, Moms."

Harry balanced herself on one crutch and put her hand on the side of Desi's neck. "It took us a little while to get it right, but I love you, and we deserve to be a big happy family. That goes for Nico too since he'll be lucky enough to have his grandmothers around all the time."

"You're so perfect."

Harry kissed her. "Hardly, but I'd like to think I'm perfect for you."

"Trust me, you are." She kissed Harry longer, with her arms around her neck. "And thank you for talking them into staying."

"I think that had more to do with their kids than anything I had to say, baby. You and Rachel welcoming them into your lives and sharing your children with them is everything they've wanted from the day Clyde drove them off." Harry held her as she leaned on one crutch. "Go ahead and have fun with your moms, and make sure they order a crib for the extra room."

"We did," Bobbie said. She appeared thrilled to be holding Nico. "He's ready to spend the night."

"That's great." Harry didn't let go of her. "This damn thing comes off in a couple of weeks, and my first plan is to chase your daughter through the house until I catch her and drag her to the bedroom."

Desi felt the heat sweep up her face to the point she thought she'd lost the ability to speak. "Harry," she said when she recovered, "get in there. I need a moment." She pointed to the bedroom.

Bobbie laughed when Harry wiggled her eyebrows.

"I'm sorry," Harry said when Desi closed the door. "I was just teasing you."

"So you didn't mean it?" Desi slammed her against the door before standing on her toes to reach her lips.

Harry dropped her crutches and smoothed her hands down Desi's back, stopping at her ass. It didn't take much encouragement for Desi to wrap her legs around her waist, hugging Harry with her entire body. "I don't want your parents to think I'm a total animal, but I can't look at you without wanting you."

"That's okay with me, but try not to shock them into dropping Nicolas next time."

Harry simply held her as she kissed her in a way that reached into her soul. This woman who'd rescued her as a child would spend the rest of her life loving her like no one else was capable of. She'd found her perfect match, and she was never letting go.

"Life is good, isn't it?" she asked Harry pressing their foreheads together.

"It's the best because you're here."

"We finally have it all, my love, and I can't wait to share it with you."

EPILOGUE

Fourteen months later

"What's this one called?" Abe had finished his residency but still loyally attended every opening at Desi's gallery.

Harry stared at her old student and shook her head. "A vase."

"Mama," Nico said from his perch on Harry's shoulders. She lifted him off, and he pointed in Desi's direction.

Chester and his crew had done a great job on the gallery, but not as great a job as Desi had done of making it the place a young artist wanted to exhibit their art. The shelves were lined with Desi's pottery since tonight would be her last show before the new creation she'd been working on arrived. She was sharing the space with Tony's art, and the gallery was filled with friends, family, and eager buyers.

"Don't get cocktail sauce on anything," she warned Abe. Desi and Rachel abruptly headed to the office, so she and Nico followed.

She had to remind herself that she was a doctor, and panicking shouldn't be in her nature, but seeing both sisters standing over twin puddles would've freaked anyone out. Desi appeared sheepish, and Rachel looked like she was getting ready to unleash a string of curses.

"You were right," Desi said. "They were contractions."

"Really? Because I thought it was someone trying to rip me in half. Damn," Rachel said loud enough that Harry was sure the crowd outside heard her.

"Think of all the money we'll save on joint birthday parties," Desi said before grabbing Harry's hand when another contraction hit.

The last year had been memorable, and after all the court dates, nightmares, and general anxiety over that day in their kitchen, they'd decided to live and be happy. Rachel and Serena's wedding had taken place in the exact spot where theirs had, and Rachel's adoption of Butch was finalized a few months after that. What she and Desi couldn't wait for was to add to their family, so they'd gone back to Ellie and Sam, only this time, Serena and Rachel joined them. The sisters had gone through pain, joy, and everything in between together, so this wouldn't be any different.

"Do not make me laugh." Rachel clutched her abdomen, and Serena came in after Harry texted her. "And the first person who tells me to relax and not curse is banned from the delivery room."

The trip to the hospital was organized chaos as every family member gathered to get underfoot. Rachel was put in the room beside Desi's, and between the two of them, the ceiling was singed with swear words.

Eight hours later Harry held their new little girl, who could've been Nico's twin. The delivery had been much smoother than the first, and Desi appeared relaxed and happy. "Congratulations, Moms," Ellie said. She held her arms out for the baby, so Harry went to help Desi onto the recovery bed. "Do we have a name for this little girl?"

"Sydney Desi Basantes," Desi said. "Harry said if Nico got part of her name, then the next one had to have mine if it was a girl. Is she okay?"

"She's perfect, though, the same cannot be said of your sister. If she curses Sam out one more time, my baby's going to develop an eye twitch or something." They all laughed, especially since Serena had offered to get pregnant, but Rachel wanted the experience. "Let me go check on them. Are you up for visitors?"

"Give us an hour, and I'll go out and get the crowd out there," Harry said. Desi had undone her gown and had Sydney lying on her chest. Harry felt her heart fill at the sight of them.

"Harry, come over here." Desi held up her hand and sighed when Harry lay next to them. "I love you."

"I love you more." The baby opened her eyes as well as spread her fingers when Desi spoke. "She's beautiful like her mother." She laid her hand over Desi's and the tears came without warning. "This life you've given me—it's more than my imagination ever conjured up."

"Do you remember the first time you touched me?" Desi wiped Harry's face, leaving her hand against her cheek.

"I can't forget something seared into my brain."

"Do you remember what you said to me when we sneaked back inside?" Desi still had that same smile.

"I told you everything was going to be okay because we were going to get married, have kids, and I'd love you forever." The baby interrupted their reminiscing, so Harry helped Desi sit up and positioned her to nurse.

"The thing about you, Harry Basantes, is you keep your promises. We did get married, we have kids, and you're going to love me forever." Desi glanced down at the baby before she pulled her closer for a kiss.

"Sorry to barge in," one of the nurses said. "Your sister wanted you to know it's a girl, and this whole thing is a bitch." They both laughed, knowing that's exactly what Rachel had said.

"Well, Sydney, you have an instant best friend and bad influence right next door," Harry said, kissing Desi again. "Thank you for loving me, and for making it possible to keep all my promises."

"And just think, my love, there's so much more to come."

About the Author

Ali Vali is the author of the long-running Cain Casey "Devil" series, the newest being *The Devil Incarnate*, and the Genesis Clan "Forces" series, as well as numerous standalone romances including three Lambda Literary Award finalists, *Calling the Dead*, *Love Match*, and *One More Chance*. Ali's latest release is *A Good Chance*, the sequel to *One More Chance*.

Originally from Cuba, Ali has retained much of her family's traditions and language and uses them frequently in her stories. Having her father read her stories and poetry before bed every night as a child infused her with a love of reading, which she carries till today. Ali currently lives outside New Orleans, where she enjoys cheering LSU and trying new restaurants.

Books Available From Bold Strokes Books

A Good Chance by Ali Vali. Harry, Desi, and Desi's sister Rachel are so close to getting everything they've ever wanted, but Desi's ex-husband is coming back to get his revenge and rip apart their chance at happiness. (978-1-63679-023-7)

A Perfect Fifth by Jaycie Morrison. Streetwise pianist Zara Keller and Lady Jillian Stansfield couldn't be more different, yet their connection brings a new awareness of who they are and what they truly want in their lives—including each other. (978-1-63679-132-6)

Catching Feelings by Ana Hartnett Reichardt. Andrea Foster expected to catch a lot of pitches from the Alder Lions' star pitcher, Maya, but she didn't expect to catch feelings. (978-1-63679-227-9)

Defiant Hearts by Lee Lynch. In these stories, you'll find your lovers, friends, and lesbians you wish you knew—maybe even yourself. (978-1-63679-237-8)

Love and Duty by Catherine Young. All Princess Roseli wants is to marry her three lovers, but with war looming, she must instead marry Princess Lucia to establish a military alliance between their planets. (978-1-63679-256-9)

Serendipity by Kris Bryant. Serendipity brings jingle writer Annie Foster and celebrity pop star Bristol Baines together, and their undeniable attraction keeps them close, but will their different paths drive them apart? (978-1-63679-224-8)

The Haunted Heart by Jane Kolven. A ghost, a ring, and a quest to find a missing psychic—it's a spell for love. (978-1-63679-245-3)

The Rules of Forever by Nan Campbell. After reconnecting at their high school reunion, Cara and Lauren agree to embark on a textbook definition friends-with-benefits relationship, but trying to keep it uncomplicated is harder than it seems. (978-1-63679-248-4)

Vision of Virtue by Brey Willows. When virtue and desire come together, be prepared for sparks in this next installment of the Memory's Muses series. (978-1-63679-118-0)

The Artist by Sheri Lewis Wohl. Detective Casey Wilson and reclusive artist Tula Crane are drawn together in a web of passion, intrigue, and art that might just hold the key to stopping a killer. (978-1-63679-150-0)

Cherry on Top by Georgia Beers. A chance meeting leaves Cherry and Ellis longing for a different life, but when Ellis's search for truth crashes into Cherry's insta-filter world, do they have any hope at all of a happily ever after? (978-1-63679-158-6)

Love and Other Rare Birds by Angie Williams. Ornithologist Dr. Jamie Martin and park ranger Rowan Fleming are searching the Alaskan wilderness for a bird thought to be extinct, and they're about to discover opposites really do attract. (978-1-63679-108-1)

Parallel Paradise by Mayapee Chowdhury. When their love affair is put to the test by the homophobia of their family, community, and culture, Bindi and Rimli will need to fight for a chance at love. (978-1-63679-203-3)

Perfectly Matched by Toni Logan. A beautiful Cupid named Hannah, a runaway arrow, and just seventy-two hours to fix a mishap that could be the best mistake she has ever made. (978-1-63679-120-3)

Slow Burn by Missouri Vaun. A wounded wildland firefighter from California and a struggling artist find solace and love in a small southern town. (978-1-63679-098-5)

The Inconvenient Heiress by Jane Walsh. An unlikely heiress and a spinster evade the Marriage Mart only to discover true love together. (978-1-63679-173-9)

The Value of Sylver and Gold by Michelle Larkin. When word gets out that former Boston Homicide Detective Reid Sylver can talk to the dead, the FBI solicits her help on a serial murder case, prompting Reid to assemble forces once again with Detective London Gold. (978-1-63679-093-0)

Wildflower by Cathleen Collins. When a plane crash leaves seven-year-old Lily Andrews stranded in the vast wilderness of Arkansas, will she be able to overcome the odds and make it back to civilization and the one person who holds the key to her future? (978-1-63679-244-6)

CPSIA information can be obtained
at www.ICGtesting.com
Printed in the USA
JSHW020229090123
35924JS00002B/2